Viking Legacy

Book 21 in the Dragon Heart Series

By

Griff Hosker

Published by Sword Books Ltd 2018
Copyright © Griff Hosker First Edition

The author has asserted their moral right under the Copyright, Designs and Patents Act, 1988, to be identified as the author of this work.

All Rights reserved. No part of this publication may be reproduced, copied, stored in a retrieval system, or transmitted, in any form or by any means, without the prior written consent of the copyright holder, nor be otherwise circulated in any form of binding or cover other than that in which it is published and without a similar condition being imposed on the subsequent purchaser.

Cover by Design for Writers

Dedication

To Steve Flynn (USMC) who always has my back!

Contents

Viking Legacy 1
Prologue 4
Chapter 1 7
Chapter 2 19
Chapter 3 32
Chapter 4 50
Chapter 5 65
Chapter 6 77
Chapter 7 88
Chapter 8 98
Chapter 9 109
Chapter 10 122
Chapter 11 135
Chapter 12 148
Chapter 13 160
Chapter 14 170
Chapter 15 184
Chapter 16 195
Epilogue 203
Norse Calendar 205
Glossary 206
Maps and drawings 213
Historical note 214
Other books by Griff Hosker 215

Part One
Gift from the gods

Prologue

I had to use a staff these days to climb the mountain we called Old Olaf. Uhtric had found it for me and I used it when I had to climb Old Olaf. There would have been a time when I could have almost run up it. Yet I knew that I was fitter now than a year ago when I had been passing blood and facing death. The voyage to Miklagård and my stay there had healed me and made me even stronger. When we returned I was strong enough to lead my men and defeat the Mercian King and his Danish mercenaries. We had so much treasure that my men did not know how to spend all that they had. Some of the younger ones had taken to adorning their helmets with gold and silver. The older, wiser warriors did not. And so, as I took the familiar path up the mountain we called Old Olaf I used a staff. I was wrapped in my wolf cloak with Ragnar's Spirit at my waist for there was a thick mist about the mountain. Old Olaf was wreathed in cloud and fog. The path was treacherous and with sheer drops down both sides, it was prudent to use a staff. Even though the sword which was touched by the gods would protect me.

The younger men of my clan had thought my journey unnecessary. They could not understand why I needed to climb the mountain and speak with the land. We would not need to war again. We had coin and weapons. Our borders were safe and secure. If we went to war then it would be for the sheer joy of battle and slaying enemies. As jarl and the oldest man any in the clan knew, then I could enjoy the Land of the Wolf. I could enjoy the reprieve that the Allfather had given me. Ylva, my daughter, Aiden and the few Ulfheonar who remained knew differently. They knew the heart of Dragonheart. They knew that my heart was the heart of the land.

I climbed up the path which led around the blue tarn. Today it was a murky grey but when the sun shone then it was a blue only matched by the pommel stone on my sword or Sámr's eyes. My great-grandson, Sámr, understood why I needed to make the journey. He had fought at my side since he had been little more than a child and he had grown into a young warrior on the cusp of manhood who would one day lead the clan. He knew that the reason for my journey was to ask for forgiveness.

The mist and drizzle clung to my thinning hair and beard like the rime of a winter frost. It made me look even older and greyer than I was. I smiled. I had never been vain. I cared not what I looked like. I was Jarl Dragonheart and I wielded the sword which was touched by the gods. Men took me as they found me. Those who were my friends lived and those who were not usually died. As I climbed the last few paces I saw the sky becoming lighter above me and, as I reached the col just below the peak, I cleared the fog and low clouds. It was strange for the sun shone and all that I could see below me was white and grey cloud. It was as though I had ascended to the place the followers of the White Christ called heaven.

I took off my cloak and laid it on a rock to dry. I placed my staff there too and then I sat on a smaller rock with my sword cradled on my lap. I had been to Viking heaven. When I had had the blackness cut from my body I had been at the door of Valhalla. I had peered in and seen what awaited me. I was not afraid of death. However, a dream I had had, back in my hall at Cyninges-tūn had disturbed me. Ylva had told me that some dreams were just memories dredged from the past and not premonitions of the future. This dream had been just such a one. I remembered peering through Valhalla's doors. I saw, with crystal clear clarity all the warriors who had died with a sword in their hands. I had not seen Haraldr Leifsson, Sweyn Alfsson, Cnut Axe Hand or Galmr Galmrsson. They had all set sail, before I became ill, in the knarr, *'Örlög'*. They had taken the former Greek slave, Atticus to the river where we had mined the blue stone and close to the place we had found the mysterious sword of my ancestor. That sword now hung over the fire in my hall. Atticus had been interested in the river which lay in the heart of the people we called Walhaz.

I took out my ale skin and drank some of the brew. Had I not been ill at the time and hiding the illness from all then I might have sent more men to protect Atticus. I had thought I was dying and there was some hope that my Greek might discover some talisman along the river which would heal me. For some reason, the blue stones seemed to give me comfort. I had wondered if they afforded protection too. I idly stroked the pommel stone. Atticus had taken the knarr with a crew of Haraldr Leifsson, Sweyn Alfsson, Cnut Axe Hand and Galmr Galmrsson. All were good sailors and good warriors. I had thought it enough men. They were the best who were not Ulfheonar. My illness had driven them and their quest from my mind until, when one of our drekar, **'King's Gift'** was sailing up the coast close to the island of the puffins, they had found the wreckage of *'Örlög'*. They knew it was her from the prow which

Bolli Bollison had carved. We had thought them dead but if they were then why were they not in Valhalla? Had they been attacked at sea they would have died fighting. If the storm had taken them then, as they sank beneath the waves for the last time they would have grasped their swords. I had not seen them in Valhalla. We did not know where they were.

Aiden, Kara and Ylva had dreamed but they had seen nothing. That was not their fault. They were all volvas and seers yet their strength lay in the spirits of the dead of our family. My wife Erika, son, Wolf Killer, and grandson, Garth, were the spirits who spoke. They did not know the spirit of Atticus. They were not certain if the men lived or died. They saw them not in the spirit world but they were not certain. They thought there was a fog which prevented them from seeing. Close to my land they were able to see more. I needed the clarity of the mountain to focus my thoughts.

If they were unable to die with their swords in their hands then what had happened to them? I had come to Old Olaf to clear my thoughts and to make a decision. The world was wide and the sea even wider. When you were a Viking and sailed the empty oceans then you were in awe of the vast emptiness that was the sea. Where would we begin to search for them?

I know not how long I sat and stared. I had sat with my back against the larger rock upon which my cloak was drying and I was facing south. Old Olaf had determined my position. My right hand fingered the hilt of my sword. I found myself playing with the blue stone while staring south. I felt a breeze upon my face. It was from the south and then I saw the clouds as they began to part. It was like a wife tearing an old sheet in two to make cleaning cloths. It was as though the clouds were torn. And I saw, to the south, the sea. I saw, in the distance, a trading ship as she headed for Whale Island and in that moment Old Olaf told me what to do. I should take to the sea and follow the trail of my knarr. I should search for their bodies and bury them. Then my dreams would not be haunted by their faces for I would know the truth. The sun shone more brightly. This would be a swift voyage. It would take four days to reach the river, discover the truth, and then sail home. My dreams would not be haunted by those I had abandoned.

Chapter 1

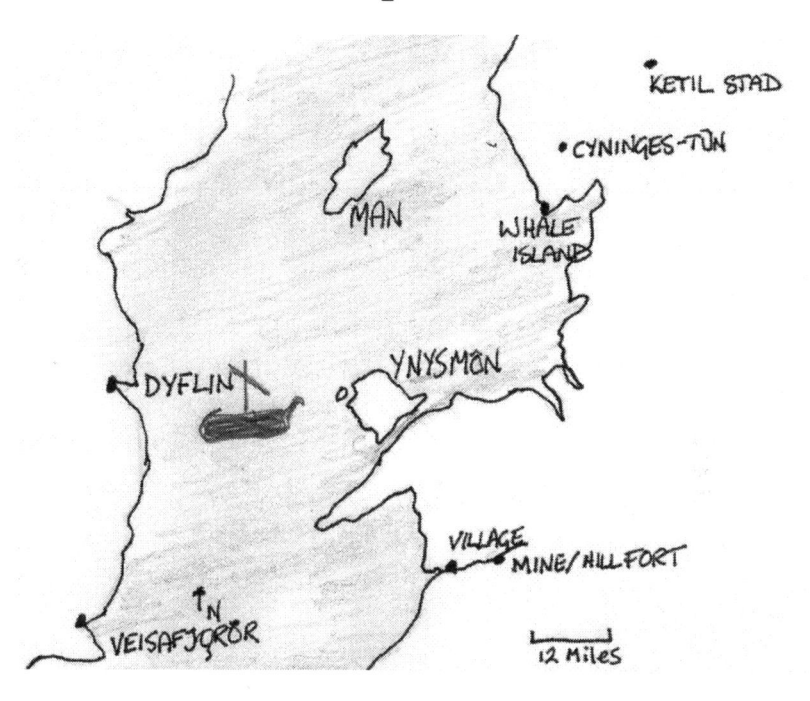

The crew who had asked to accompany me on *'Heart of the Dragon'* were all waiting for me at my grandson's home close to Whale Island where we kept our fleet of ships. Once they had received my request Erik Short Toe and Bolli Bollison had soon prepared my drekar for sea. Gruffyd had asked to come with me as had Ragnar but I knew that both did not really mean it. Ragnar ruled the southern half of my land and he was wrapped up in that. Gruffyd seemed distracted. My son and I were not as close as we should have been. I put that down to his new family. He and Einar Fair face had married women from Om Walum. When I returned I would spend time talking with my son. It was something I had put off too long. The men we sought in the river were my men. My son and grandson had their own warriors and they each had raids to make.

As well as the Ulfheonar I chose leaders such as Ráðgeir Ráðgeirson, Lars Long Nose, and Siggi Eainarson. My great-grandson, Sámr was an easy choice for he had chosen to live in my hall. Where I went so did he. Baldr Saviour of Witches had asked to come but he had been hurt by a horse he had been training just a month earlier and his leg had not healed. He was angry with himself for having been so careless and missing the chance to raid. He had been a slave we had rescued when we had been in the east. His people were horsemen who lived in the flatlands north of Miklagård. Mordaf wished to come too but his mother was loath to let him go to sea. The witch at Syllingar had almost taken his life and she wished him to become a man before he sailed again. I did not blame her but I was disappointed for Mordaf. He saw Sámr, his cousin, having adventures whilst he stayed safely at home. The rest of the crew was made up of the warriors who had yet to take part in a successful raid. These were the ones who had a sword and a shield. They had sealskin boots and a rough cloak. They had a seax and that was all. They were as I had been when I had first sailed with Old Olaf and Prince Butar.

My daughter and her family had dreamed but seen nothing. Something was masking my men from them. They did not know if it was good or it was ill. I thought that this was a bad thing. When they could not see it normally meant a stronger power was at work. The mine lay to the south of Wyddfa. Was that significant? Aiden had made me maps and told me all that he could remember of the river and the mine where we had found the stones. Before I had left Cyninges-tūn I had asked them bluntly, "Have you dreamed my death? Should I make my farewells now?"

Ylva had slipped her arm through mine and squeezed it, "No, Dragonheart. Your thread has yet to be cut but I have woven a spell to keep you safe." She held up a small piece of material. I saw that there was a wolf and a shiny crescent moon.

"What is the meaning of the moon?"

"It is the moon of the east. Atticus is not Norse. You need to find him and I have put him in the spell. If he is alive then you will find him and if not..." she shrugged, "it is *wyrd*."

I had clutched my wolf amulet. I might survive the voyage but my family did not know the fate of my men. It would be up to the Dragonheart.

As I left my grandson's hall and walked towards my ship, with Sámr by my side, I saw the new sail which had been fitted to my drekar. There had been so much treasure from the ransom for the priests of Mercia that we had been able to buy a new canvas and great quantities of the dye we needed. The sail now had a wolf upon it. I confess that I felt tingles down my neck when I had seen it. It made my old drekar come alive. I say old but all the damaged and weakened timbers had been replaced and she had a new steering board. We might fail in our quest but our ship would not let us down. I had made a blót on her deck, close by the steering board the previous night. The blood was still there and it would bring us both luck and the favour of the gods.

Since I had been reborn in Miklagård my view on life had changed. Each day was now a gift from the gods. I found myself smiling more and worrying less about minor inconveniences. When one of the ship's boys dropped one of the pots of pine tar which we would take with us in case a repair was needed while Erik Short Toe ranted and railed and the boy, Sven, quivered I said, "Erik, we have more pine tar. It was fortunate that it fell close to the bow where nothing is stored. It will soak into the deck and make us stronger. This is a good thing."

I saw the relief on Sven Tomasson's face. Erik shook his head, "But the deck will be sticky there for some days."

I shrugged, "Then we avoid it. This is not worth getting upset about. Had it happened at sea when we could not replace it then there might have been a problem."

Haaken One Eye was nearby and he could not help laughing, "Is this the same Dragonheart who would rant and rave if the wind changed direction and slowed our voyage?"

I nodded, "We all change... all save you! You are still the same. A little greyer, a little gaunter but still the same youth who stood back to back with me in Norway all those years ago."

"Aye and now my granddaughter is to be wed then I know my age. How did that happen? Why are we not yet dead?"

"The Norns are saving us for something and I doubt it will be pleasant."

The pot of pine tar had been replaced and Erik shouted, "Prepare to cast off! We had best hurry before Sven the Clumsy drops something else."

I saw Sven's face fall. He had no name as yet and if Erik's stuck then he would have to live with it.

I shouted, "Then cast off but I do not think that Sven the Ship Sealer will ever drop anything else!"

I was Jarl Dragonheart and my word was law. Sven had just been given his Viking name. He looked relieved. Men would, I knew, ask him how he got his name and he would still have to tell them the story but men would not judge him first. If he had been Sven the Clumsy then he would.

Our families had come to wave us off. There were no tears. That was not the way of the Clan of the Wolf. They would all go about their own business and carry on as though we had not gone across the western seas. They knew that it would do no good to brood. If the Norns had spun then we might be away for a year or more. We might never return. When our sail was seen over the horizon then there would be a great celebration and there would be joy unbounded. The life of a Viking was hard and it was dangerous but we had all chosen it.

We had to row against the tide to reach the open sea. We used a simple chant. It would begin to bind the crew together. This was a new crew.

> *The Clan of the Wolf have backs that are broad*
> *All our enemies are put to the sword*
> *When we roar and howl then fear*
> *The Clan of the Wolf have teeth and are near*
> *The Clan of the Wolf have backs that are broad*
> *All our enemies are put to the sword*
> *When we roar and howl then fear*
> *The Clan of the Wolf have teeth and are near*

As soon as we cleared the island Erik put the steering board over and shouted, "In oars! Loose sail!"

The ship's boys were already at the masthead and the half-furled sail dropped to reveal the red dragon. Those who had not seen it cheered and, almost as though it came to life the wind caught us and the sail billowed. It looked as though the wolf was roaring. It was a good sign and a good start to the voyage. We headed west along the coast. The wind was from the north and east. Once we cleared the coast of my land then the wind would be stronger and we would have open water.

I stood at the steering board with Erik as the crew stacked their oars at the mast fish. Olaf Leather Neck cuffed the ones who did it wrong. He believed that a Viking did not make mistakes. His mighty fists were just his way of enforcing that diktat. No one minded for they knew that Olaf was the ultimate warrior. He had never married and spent each day honing his already mighty skills. It was a mixed crew. Many had grown up in the Land of the Wolf and I either knew them or had fought with their fathers. Cnut Cnutson's grandfather had been with me when the gods had struck my sword. Now the youngest of that family sailed with me. Then there were others whom I knew less well. Vikings still drifted towards my land. Some were ones who had left their own clan or been banished. Others had fallen on hard times when others, like Bergil Hafþórrsson, had sought us out. He, his brothers and their families had landed close to the Stad on the Eden. Their tiny ship had succumbed to the rocks just off the shore and they had scrambled ashore. They were a family of three brothers and their wives with two children. Bergil was the head of the family. They had come from the islands off the coast of Strathclyde. The family were not pure Norse. They all had dark hair. From what Bergil told me their ancestors had come from the land of Hibernia. That explained their hair but they were Norse in their ways. Aiden had said that they might have got their hair from their mother. In all likelihood, she had been a slave. Certainly, the name Hafþórr was Norse.

They were all well-built warriors but they had precious little with them. I could see why they had come. Our land offered prosperity and the chance to be warriors. They had arrived when I had been in Miklagård and Aiden and Ylva had deemed them to be worthy to join our clan. That first winter the brothers had gone up the Lang's Dale and killed four wolves. They wore their cloaks. They were not Ulfheonar but that did not prevent them from wearing a wolf skin. Bergil had been in battles when he had fought as a paid sword. Fighting without a helmet was a risk and he had lost the front part of his scalp to a sword. He was lucky not to have lost his head and his life. Their families farmed at Torver which lay at the southern end of the Water. They were hardy people and after the remote island where they had lived then the Land of the Wolf seemed like paradise. I knew that I was lucky to have Bergil, Beorn and Benni.

The presence of the three brothers meant that I had ten experienced warriors. The only ones with mail were the Ulfheonar, Sámr, Ráðgeir Ráðgeirson, Lars Long Nose and Siggi Eainarson. Like all of my veteran warriors, they had good mail and good helmets. They had mail aventails and some had face masks. If we found trouble then they would be their steel which would save us.

Sámr had now seen more than thirteen summers. I had young warriors at the oars who were the same age. He did not wear mail for it would be a waste; he was still growing. He had, instead, a thick leather fighting vest. He wore it over his other clothes. With two belts hanging diagonally across his chest and back he had good protection. He had two swords hanging from the belts. He had had one made and the other he had taken from a Dane he had killed. His helmet was a simple open one. Bagsecg's son, Haldi had made it for him and with the padded hood he wore beneath it he was as well protected as any of the young warriors. He too had a wolf cloak but Sámr wanted to be Ulfheonar. He had killed the wolf on a hunt with his father and my son Gruffydd. I did not think there would be any more Ulfheonar. When the last of us died we would become a memory, a legend. Behind him stood Germund. He was a slave whom we had been given in Miklagård. He was devoted to me and to Sámr. He acted as a bodyguard for my great-grandson. His lamed leg meant he was not as agile as he might have wished but he was a good warrior. Sámr stood with Olaf making sure that the oars were stacked correctly and then he joined me. Germund went to the chest he had carried aboard for Sámr and sat upon it. Germund was a true Viking. He would carve pieces of bone when he was not needed to row or to watch Sámr. I knew that the Allfather had sent him to us.

Sámr loved being at sea and he loved being with me. I felt closer to Sámr than any other in my family. He felt like me. I had never seen my own face when I was young but I liked to think that Sámr looked like me. My son and grandson now had wives and children. They were their chief concern. I liked it this way. He grinned as he came to the steering board to join me, "There are some in the crew who are but a little older than I am!"

"Then as you have made many voyages you can teach them as you were taught when you first sailed."

"Of course." He glanced up at the masthead. He was learning how to steer and navigate. The best way was to watch a master mariner such as Erik. "Captain, how long will it take us to reach the mouth of the river?"

Erik smiled, "Young Sámr, you will learn that a captain is always cautious for if Ran decides to send unexpected winds and seas and delays then a bold captain merely looks foolish. All I will say is that if we have to row it will take the best part of eight days. If we have winds with us then it will be less."

Sámr nodded, "And do we risk the straits?"

Erik looked at me and I shook my head, "There is little need for such a risk. Atticus, Haraldr and the crew have been missing for a year. A delay of a day or so will not change their circumstance. The straits can be dangerous and this crew is not experienced enough."

Sámr then asked quietly and simply, as only the young can, "And will they be alive when we find them?"

I looked up at the mast where sea birds were swooping, hoping to get titbits of food from the crew. Their cries were said to be the cries of the dead who had not made Valhalla. "We seek them so that we shall know. They may well be dead. It has been so long that if they were alive then they would have found a way home but as someone who died and came back to life, I see hope in the most unlikely of places. Let us not judge, Sámr Ship Killer."

He nodded and wandered off to speak with Haaken. He loved to hear Haaken's stories for they were all about me and Haaken never tired of telling them. Sadly, the truth became stretched with each telling of the story. The flash of lightning which had struck my sword now stretched from earth to heaven across the western seas to the edge of the world and down into the bowels where Hel ruled! I pondered my words to Sámr. In truth, I did not know what I would find. I suspected we might find nothing and the journey would be a waste of time. Then I thought again. A voyage with Vikings was never a waste of time. If we found nothing then we would seek that which Atticus had sought, the mine. The stones we found there had power. They were like the jet that was mined at Hwitebi. It was not just their colour which made them attractive it was the protection they afforded those who wore such jewels. Sámr's eyes were the same colour as the stone. They were a blue which seemed to reach inside you and see your heart. Since my great-grandson had been born I had become more interested in the blue stones. One of them was in the old sword which hung on the wall of my hall. They were a link to my past. I had learned that such tenuous links were not to be ignored. They were threads which were like the threads of a Norn's spell.

I leaned over the stern and watched the sea. The gods were being kind for it was as flat as the Water at Cyninges-tūn. The wind was gentle and pushed us along as though we were being rowed. What had the Norns planned for us? This was unusual.

Erik said, quietly, "If they found the knarr's wreckage by the island of the puffins that does not mean they were wrecked at sea. The currents there are strong. They could have landed and not moored properly."

I nodded, "Yet they were good men and I cannot see them making such a mistake. It is idle to speculate. We sail up the river and we look. I am not seeking an ending to this which fits one of Haaken One Eye's sagas. I want to find answers no matter how unpalatable they are."

The crew lay on the deck. Some slept. Haaken was regaling the new members of the crew with his tales. Some men, like Germund, carved. Some played with dice. The Ulfheonar slept. They had seen more voyages than the whole of the crew combined. They were all ultimate warriors. When they were at home then they adored their families. They played with their children and were dutiful to their wives. The exception was Olaf Leather Neck. When he was at home he just worked at being a better warrior. He did not seek death on the battlefield but if it came close then he would embrace it. He had seen most of his shield brothers die. He was ready for death. And me? That fantasy had passed. I was a plaything in the hands of the gods and the Norns.

As the day slipped by and the gods sent the wind more men slept. Haaken's stories dried up and even Sámr left him. A Viking spent most of his life enduring such boredom. When it ended then there would be violence and blood. That was our way. I had died and seen Valhalla. Each day was now a gift from Odin.

When dawn broke I rose early. I had to make water. It was Erik's son Arne who was at the steering board. "All well, Arne?"

"All is well, jarl. The wind has veered a little but we keep the same speed. We passed the calf of Man in the first watch. There was no danger."

I would have been surprised if there had been trouble. Man was our nearest neighbour and the men who lived there were little more than pirates who preyed on the weak. There were far easier victims than our drekar. I knew that one day we would have to take back the island which had once been our home. It was where my mother had died and was now buried. For now, we ignored them. They feared us.

Life aboard the drekar would be dull for those new to going a-Viking. When we had set sail they had expected action from the moment we left the land. It was not so. There would be more empty days watching the grey sea than short sharp battles. The sea was vast and empty. I looked to the east. There was land there but it was below the horizon. It was the land which lay between Mercia and the Land of the Wolf. The ones who farmed that incredibly fertile plain did so at great risk to themselves. My warriors did not patrol as far south as that and any Viking who farmed needed to be able to look after themselves. We did not raid the Mercians save in times of hardship. Then we might take their cattle, sheep and women. Since our battle at the Belisama, the Mercians had withdrawn and our farmers prospered. It would not last. The Mercians, like all

Saxons, resented and hated us. I made water at the prow. I avoided the patch of pine tar which was still a little sticky. The island of Anglesey lay ahead. Some men still called it that even though the Angles who had briefly held it were now long dead. Some memories endure. If my knarr had been attacked there then its wreckage might have floated south. I would visit there if we did not find them at the river.

All day we ploughed through the empty waters. Once it had teemed with ships. When we had been in Miklagård we had heard of ships sailing from that port to Britannia to trade. That had been in the long ago. That had been in the time of the Warlord. It had not been an isolated ship. Sometimes a ship a day left the Blue Sea to sail to the grey waters of Britannia. Other ships had sailed from what was now Frankia. That had changed with the coming of the Saxons. Now the only ships which traded from there were the ships of Hrolf the Horseman. Since I had been reborn I could think of the future and the land I would leave to Sámr, Mordaf and Ulla War Cry. I wanted a future which was as prosperous as in the time of my ancestor. My brush with Valhalla had made me see a world after I was gone and I wished it to be as secure as possible.

When Erik rose and looked at the pennant he checked his charts. He made an adjustment and we headed further west. It increased our speed and gave the island of the men of Gwynedd a wide berth. We ate and we drank ale. This was not a long voyage. We would be able to replenish our supplies once we reached the river. We called it the Blue River because of the stones. I had no doubt that the men who lived there called it something else. When night came we would be halfway to our destination.

Sámr was of an age with many of the ship's boys. His first voyage with me had been as a ship's boy. He was not lazy and he joined them at the masthead when they trimmed the sails or tightened sheets. I knew they liked that and when he led the clan he would have loyal warriors to follow him. Only one or two of the boys would go on to become mariners. Most were like me, they went to sea in a drekar to become warriors.

Haaken One Eye joined me as the sun began to drop towards Hibernia. He looked at me, "You are feeling guilty about Atticus."

I smiled, "You are becoming a galdramenn I think. Of course, I am. Atticus was a gentle soul. Had I not been ill and more attentive I would not have allowed him to go. The copper which we know is in the mines and the blue stones were a lure for him. He had a curious mind."

"You said, 'had'. You think he is dead."

"I think it is likely. The men of the mountains are barbarians. Their language is almost unintelligible. He would be of little use to them. He has skills but they were not the skills that those wild men want."

"And our men?"

"Had we sent a drekar then they would have a chance to be alive but there were too few of them. This voyage, Haaken One Eye, is to scratch an itch. It is to help me sleep at night. I need this door closed. Then I can open the doors to the future. We are getting old and we need to make our land secure." I shrugged, "Besides men chose to come. They want the adventure."

He held up two hands, "I am not complaining, Dragonheart. I was more than ready to ride the waves with you once more. When I write the saga which will come from this I need to know all."

"So that the lies you tell will have a nugget of truth behind them."

He laughed, "The sagas I sing are true. It is the truth as I see it. You lead and I follow. I am able to see more than you, Dragonheart. When my tales are told, many years hence, they will know the worth of Dragonheart, his Ulfheonar and the Clan of the Wolf."

I wondered if that was true or would the songs disappear like the tomb of the Warlord. Would the earth simply swallow it up and remove all traces?

It took another two days to reach the Blue River. We reached it during the night and I was woken by Arne Eriksson. "Jarl, we are here. I have dropped the anchor for I need my father to guide us through the mouth."

"You did right. I will watch with you."

I went to the prow and made water. Then I clambered up to the gunwale and, holding the dragon, peered towards the white-flecked water which marked the mouth of the river. To the north lay Wyddfa and the other mountains which ringed the tomb of Myrddyn. We would never find that tomb again for the gods had buried it beneath a layer of stones and rocks so deep that it would take a lifetime to uncover them. The presence of the tomb of the wizard and one of my ancestors was somehow reassuring. Their spirits would help me. Aiden would have come with me but he was not a warrior. He was now old too and, for some reason not as fit as I was. I found that ironical for he was the healer yet I had better health than he. When the doctor had cut out my badness he had taken away my only weakness. Aiden had aching and painful joints. Kara constantly administered the salve they made. If he had been here then he would have been able to speak with the spirits. As it was I would have to try to speak with them.

The ship was quiet for all but the boys who were on watch were asleep and as we bobbed up and down with reefed sails and a sea anchor, I closed my eyes and listened. The creak of the hull and the ropes gradually faded. I entered the darkness that was my head. A man's head is never truly empty. There are always voices. Kara had told me that. I heard voices. They were the voices of Kara and Ylva. I knew them to be memories. My dead wife's voice came to me. Erika had been a volva and she was always close to me. Then the voice changed and I knew that it was my mother. The words were indistinct at first and then they grew in volume. She kept repeating them until they almost deafened me.

"Seek the princess, seek the princess, seek the princess."

"Peace! I hear you, mother, although I know not who this princess is!"

I must have spoken the words aloud for Sven Ship Sealer said, "Yes Jarl, what do you wish?"

I opened my eyes and smiled at the boy, "It is nothing, Sven. The past is talking to me and when it does that then you must listen." I turned and put my arm around his shoulder, "Come, I am hungry. You and I shall eat before the others awake."

I sat with Sven and we ate pickled fish and the last of the bread. The ale washed it down. Sven's grandfather, Sweyn Olegson, had been one of my warriors. As I recalled he had died on a raid on Aberffraw. That was not far away from where we bobbed on the water.

"And you would be a sailor or a warrior?"

Sven laughed, "As you saw, Jarl Dragonheart, I am too clumsy to be a sailor. I am big." He held out his hands for me to see. "These lumps of fingers are too big to tie knots. My father is a big man as is my mother. I will be a better warrior. I have practised with my father's sword. I have held his shield. I will be a warrior. I will stand behind Sámr Ship Killer." He smiled. "We both have names which are similar. It is *wyrd*, is it not?"

"It is indeed," and I saw the threads and heard the Norns who were spinning. When I had named Sven, I had thought it was to save him from ridicule but now I saw that the Norns had planted that thought in my head. I would not worry about the future for I could do little about it. I would heed my mother's words. I would seek the princess. If we found the remains of Atticus and Haraldr then we would bury them and I would look for a princess but where I would find one in this wild land I did not know.

Chapter 2

When dawn broke we saw that the tide was on the way in and Erik wasted no time in ordering the men to their oars. They were happy to do so for they had had a restful voyage up to that point. Haaken began the chant for we would have a long row up the river. With the ship's boys and Sámr at the prow watching for shoals and rocks we began the voyage up the Blue River. Haaken had a sense of the dramatic and with Wyddfa peering at us from the far north there was only one choice.

> *The wolf snake-crawled from the mountain side*
> *Hiding the spell-wight in cave deep and wide*
> *He swallowed him whole and Warlord too*
> *Returned to pay the price that was due*
> *There they stayed through years of man*
> *Until the day Jarl Dragon Heart began*
> *He climbed up Wyddfa filled with ghosts*
> *With Arturus his son, he loved the most*
> *The mouth was dark, hiding death*
> *Dragon Heart stepped in and held his breath*
> *He lit the torch so strong and bright*
> *The wolf's mouth snarled with red firelight*
> *Fearlessly he walked and found his kin*
> *The Warlord of Rheged buried deep within*
> *Cloaked in mail with sharp bright blade*
> *A thing of beauty by Thor made*
> *And there lay too, his wizard friend,*
> *Myrddyn protecting to the end*
> *With wolf charm blue they left the lair*
> *Then Thor he spoke, he filled the air*
> *The storm it raged, the rain it fell*
> *Then the earth shook from deep Queen Hel*
> *The rocks they crashed, they tumbled down*
> *Burying the wizard and the Rheged crown.*
> *Till world it ends the secret's there*
> *Buried beneath wolf warrior's lair*

Once we entered the mouth of the river then we took half of the crew from the oars. That way we could row for longer. It would be a slower voyage but a steadier one. When the tide began to turn then we might have to take stock. I stood with Erik and peered north. There were isolated farms but nothing that would suggest a princess. I was also looking for signs that my men had been here. We rowed for a long time. At first, the river mouth was almost as wide as my Water at home but then it narrowed and it began to twist.

Sven Ship Sealer shouted, "Smoke to the south!"

As we turned a bend we saw a cluster of huts on the south bank. Even as our dragon prow was seen we saw those who lived there driving their animals south towards the hills. They were fleeing the Vikings. They would have a stronghold there. Erik looked at me and I nodded, "Aye, we will stop here. If our men came up this river they would have had to land."

There was neither wharf nor jetty to the south but there was a beach and fishing boats were drawn up. The men who were not rowing donned helmets and readied their weapons. The people had fled but we would still be cautious. I had my mail on already. To me, it was normal to wear it. I also wore my wolf cloak. I saw that Bergil and his brothers were eager to get ashore and they stood by me at the prow as Erik slid us gently in. The three bothers leapt into the water first and ran up to the village. They were fast. I shouted as I landed in the chilly river, "See if you can catch a villager. Alive would be better than dead!"

Bergil raised his sword in answer and with their shields around their backs they loped off after the villagers.

As the rest of my men landed and Erik began to turn the ship I shouted, "Search the village and look for signs of our men!"

I counted ten huts and that meant ten families. This was not a small village. Our knarr could not have passed without being seen. The villagers might have run from a drekar filled with warriors but a knarr with a handful of men was a different prospect. It was Sámr who found evidence that our men had been there. He had wandered up the river looking for signs and he shouted. I ran to the sound of his voice along with the Ulfheonar. He stood next to two spears with skulls on them. Although birds and time had taken much of their flesh, hair still clung to the remains and even without the eyes, we could see that they were Cnut Axe Hand and Galmr Galmrsson. I clutched my wolf amulet. "I hope you died with your swords in your hands, shield brothers! I will see you in Valhalla."

Rolf Horse Killer and Rollo Thin Skin took down the heads and, wrapping them in their cloaks, brought them back to the village. Ráðgeir Ráðgeirson approached, "We have taken all of value, Jarl, but there is no sign of our men."

I nodded and Rollo opened his cloak, "We have found them. Drag the boats ashore. We will give the remains of our warriors a true Viking funeral. We will burn the village and the boats. We neither forgive nor forget."

Bergil and his brothers returned just as the pyres were almost ready. They carried a helmet and a sword. I recognised the helmet. It had belonged to Cnut. Bergil opened his hand. He held in his palm a carved stone wolf. That too had belonged to Cnut. "That is Cnut's sword, Jarl." Olaf Leather Neck knew weapons better than any.

Bergil said, "I am sorry, Jarl. This warrior held us off until the rest could escape. We could not take him alive."

"It matters not. We know that two of our men died here. Which direction did the people take?"

"They headed east."

"Then fire the village and we will sail further upriver. If they have a stronghold it will be high up. Now we will raid these people!" Even as I said it I knew that I was being unreasonable but I was angry with myself for having abandoned Atticus and the others.

As the smoke began to rise from the village my men loaded all that they had taken. If nothing else we would have enough supplies to stay in the area for ten days or so.

Haaken came to me, "You think the others are dead also?"

"Don't you?" He nodded. "If we could capture one and question them we might find out what happened!"

"That would be quite a trick, Dragonheart. We do not speak their language."

"I speak enough to question them. Come we need to get as far upriver as we can before dark and then we will find somewhere to use as a base. They may not have much in this area but what little they have we will take and next time Vikings come, no matter how few, then they will run and they will hide!"

We had to row but the memory of the two skulls meant we did not need a chant. The crew were in a sombre mood. I saw, to the south of us, a mountain which was almost as high as Wyddfa. I had never seen it before and I wondered if it too had the same kind of magic associated with it. If so it would explain the power which the people who lived here had. The river wound through the steep-sided valley. There were few settlements. The only sign of them was the occasional plume of smoke rising in the sky. I now doubted that the knarr had reached this far. I could not even remember now where the mines lay. I just knew that they were somewhere upstream and, as I recalled, on the north bank. Unless there was a bridge then that meant there had to be a stronghold on the south bank. The men managed to row another five miles and then the sun began to disappear in the west. Erik spied the fork in the river and we pulled in to the bank of the southern arm.

That night we camped on the shore and lit a fire. We had taken the few sheep from the village and we cooked them up. We knew that we would be able to find more to take back when we had finished punishing the people who lived close by. I sat with the Ulfheonar and Sámr. I knew that warriors like Bergil and Ráðgeir would have liked to be a party to it but I needed the skill of the Ulfheonar.

"We are few in numbers but we still have skills."

Olaf Leather Neck nodded, "And I would like to use them before I lose them!"

"Tomorrow we will let the others raid the farms and houses along the river. We will head inland and find this stronghold."

Rollo looked surprised, "You think it will be strong enough to hold off a warband of Vikings?"

"I know not but I would not lose untried warriors without scouting it out first. Where can they go? I need us to use our skills and find them without being seen."

"And I come too?"

I smiled, "No Sámr. You are here because if our skills fail us then someone will know and can tell Erik and the others why we fail to return." I did not believe for a moment that we would fail but we could not take him with us and I would not put him in danger without me watching over him.

He seemed satisfied. "Then this is all a secret?"

"They will think we raid but, unless I am wrong, this stronghold will be on a high part of the land. It is likely to be a hill fort and it will have good defences. We scout only. I will make the decision about an attack. Germund will stay here too. His injury would slow us down."

We divided into three groups. Bergil led one and Ráðgeir a second. I led the smallest, the third. Sámr and Erik, along with the ship's boys made an armed camp. There were now just six of us, Haaken One Eye, Olaf Leather Neck, Rollo Thin Skin, Rolf Horse Killer, Aðils Shape Shifter and me. The rest had died or been wounded. Cnut Cnutson wished to come for his son was now in my crew but I had persuaded him to stay at home asking him to defend the stad in my absence. His lame leg, like that of Karl the Word, prevented him from moving as swiftly as an Ulfheonar could.

We had seen no sign of a road when we had headed upstream but we knew there had to be one and so we headed due south until we found it. This was an old Roman Road. It was not like the one we had close to the Roman wall. This was a much smaller one but it was Roman. We recognised the ditch and the cobbles. You always knew when the Romans had been somewhere for they left two things: roads and forts. I guessed that the stronghold might be a converted Roman fort and that it lay to the east of us. This was rough country. The Romans had cleared the trees on both sides of the road but they had grown back. We left the road and headed up through the woods. We wore our wolf cloaks and had not bothered with helmets and shields. We were scouting. Aðils Shape Shifter had his bow. The rest of us had our favourite weapons.

Our sharp eyes told us that we were on the right track. We saw evidence of the flight of the villagers: pieces of material caught on branches and broken branches not to mention footprints where they had left the road to make water. We found where they had emptied their bowels. That alone proved that there were few warriors with them. A good warrior hid his tracks whenever he could. Our noses told us when we were getting close to the stronghold. The trees were too thick to see through them and we dared not risk the road. We smelled their smoke and their bodies, not to mention their food. As soon as we knew we were close I waved my arm and we spread out so that there were thirty paces between each of us. It made us harder to see and we could see more of the stronghold. We would act independently. We had so much confidence in each other that we would see all that we could and then head back to the river. That was what made us Ulfheonar. When there had been more than twenty of us we could have taken any stronghold without the aid of lesser warriors. Those days were gone and soon we would be just a memory, a legend.

I was in the centre and I moved quickly through the trees. I ignored the hints of noises to my left and right, they were made by Aðils Shape Shifter and Haaken One Eye. I stopped when I saw the trees thinning and the ground ahead becoming lighter. I pulled my wolf skin up and dropped to the ground. I slithered like a snake to the edge of the trees and peered towards the walls of their stronghold. Even though I knew I had warriors close by me I could not see them. I lay still and I looked. I saw that the Romans had used an old Celtic hill fort for their fort. They had not made it from stone but wood. The people who lived there had maintained it. That was unusual. The original fort had had three ditches. The Romans had utilised just the inner one. A bridge crossed the other two. It was a small Roman fort and there was not a great deal of room inside. Many huts and homes lay outside.

The gate to the fort was open and there was no one on the gatehouse watching. As the river lay down the slope, perhaps just under a mile away people had to fetch and carry water. I had chosen, by luck or perhaps it was *wyrd*, the section which allowed me to see into the fort through the open gate. I was merely four hundred paces from it. Although my eyes were not what they were I could see everything clearly. I was in position and ready to see all that I could see. Rollo and Rolf would have made their way around to the far side of the walls. We would all have a different view. I settled down to watch.

I saw that some men carried weapons but I would not have called them warriors. The people wore simple clothes. This was not a palace. I had wondered if some chief lived here. If there was then he was a minor one. This land was often debated between Powys and Gwynedd. Occasionally it would be fought over by Dyfed too. The reason was the copper that they mined. Then I caught a glimpse, inside the fort, of a helmet and spear. They had warriors but why were they not guarding the walls? When a second appeared with a sword in his belt then I knew that it was the hall of a minor chief. He would have his own oathsworn. We would have to fight here.

The road to the river was a busy one. It was not just water which was fetched. I saw handcarts being pulled. The commerce they had could not be downstream for **'Heart of the Dragon'** was there. It had to be upstream and that meant the mine. It was late afternoon and I was desperate to make water when I saw the two guards walk from the gates. They looked around to ensure that the land was safe and then gestured. A second armed man and a girl followed. The girl looked young and her blond hair suggested that she was not of the people of this land. Even as I was speculating about her presence I saw Atticus walking behind and at the side of the girl. He was smiling and he was talking. It was obvious it was to the girl for she laughed at something he said. Atticus was alive! How?

This was where my plan let me down. We had come to scout. We were spread out. Had we been together then we could have raced close, killed the guards and rescued Atticus. Alone I could not do it. The people who lived and farmed outside would see me. The ones who had fled us sheltered here. They would be watching for Vikings. I would wait until dark. We were Ulfheonar. Night time was our world.

The girl, Atticus and their guards were away for some time and when they returned Atticus carried a basket in his hands. I had time to study him. He looked to be in good health and appeared happy. Atticus had a unique attitude to life. He made the best of everything. He had been captured. Why else would he need the guards? However, as he was not bound he must have accepted his lot. As they entered the fort I wondered why they needed three guards for one girl and a Greek slave.

I was stiff and I was desperate to make water. Both were due to my age and I cursed my body for being weak. I slithered back slowly when the attention of those near the fort was not on the woods where I hid. When I dropped below the ridgeline I stood. It was a relief which was even greater once I had hissed and steamed my water away. There was a movement ahead of me and I whipped out my dagger, Wolf's Blood. Haaken said, "Peace, Dragonheart. We both needed the same thing." I nodded, "You saw Atticus?"

"Aye, I did. I could not come up with a reason why he is here."

"It is the girl. She looks to be Angle or Saxon. You know that he has a way with languages."

"Aye, but he could not speak the language of these people. See if you can find Rollo. We will meet here after dark. The plans have changed."

"They may be heading back already."

"It matters not. This changes everything. Before we raid this fort, we rescue Atticus. That needs the knives of the Ulfheonar and not the club of the clan!"

He nodded and, like all Ulfheonar, slipped away as though he had never been there. I headed towards the river. I made my way back to the ridgeline. Before I reached it, I dropped to all fours. As the forest thinned I stopped and watched. I was Ulfheonar and knew what I sought. It was the movement of Aðils Shape Shifter's back as he breathed. If I had not been looking for it I would not have seen it. His wolf cloak was covered in leaves. Had a local seen it they would have taken it for a mouse burrowing beneath the leaves for titbits. I picked up a stone and threw it. I hit the middle of the leaves. The leaves stopped moving and so I threw another. The leaves began to move, imperceptibly at first and then, as they dropped below the ridgeline and entered the forest proper, it was quicker.

Aðils Shape Shifter stood and stretched, "I am getting old, Dragonheart. You found me!"

"I knew where you would be hiding. You saw Atticus?"

"Aye and the Saxon girl."

"This changes our plans. Find Olaf. We meet forty paces up there." I pointed to where I had met Haaken. "We will gather after dark. We use the night to rescue Atticus."

He nodded, "Then I will make water and then go and find Olaf. If he is not asleep!" It was a joke for we both knew that Olaf was a warrior through and through.

I took a piece of dried venison from my leather satchel and began to chew it. I made my way back to the place where I had met Haaken. I had marked the tree with my dagger. I added three more horizontal lines so that I could find it in the dark. I knew that Haaken would have marked his route too. That was what we did. I returned, very slowly, to my post.

The sun was setting and I thought that all of the ones who would be returning to the fort would have done so. I was wrong for a line of roped men appeared. They all had a yoke about their necks and their feet were shackled. They were the miners. They shambled rather than walked. I had to look twice but I recognised two of them. It was Haraldr Leifsson and Sweyn Alfsson. Both looked like shadows of their former selves but I knew them. From the dress and appearance of the other four, they were Hibernians. This changed everything. We would not only rescue Atticus but our two oar brothers!

As soon as the slaves entered the gates they were slammed shut. I peered at the walls as they set the watch. They had two men on the main gate. The walls looked to have no sentries. Would the two of them patrol the walls? I watched until it was too dark to see but when I saw the burning brands at the gate I saw a way to gain entry to the fort.

Haaken was already there when I arrived. "Did you see, Dragonheart? It was our men! There is a saga to be written there!"

"Let us save them first."

The last men to arrive were Rolf and Olaf. Rolf reported that there was just one sentry at the southern gate. Roman forts had four but it seemed they only used two.

"Then we have a good opportunity. Do they have burning brands at the southern gate?"

"Aye, jarl."

"Then we take the west gate. The brand will ruin their night vision. I am guessing that Atticus, as he was guarded by armed warriors, will be in the hall. Haaken and Aðils will come with me. We will go to the main hall. Olaf, you take Rolf and Rollo. Rescue our men and free the captives. We meet back here."

Olaf nodded, "Come. Let us make a start!"

We ran in two groups. If the fort was laid out as all the other forts were then we knew where the hall would be. It would be the place the Roman Commander had lived. Although Atticus would be better guarded Olaf and the other two had the harder task for they had to find the slave pens! We moved like shadows across the open ground. The old ditches actually helped us. There were no huts on the west side. They were all on the north, the riverside.

When we reached the wooden wall, I turned sideways and dropped to my knees. Haaken stood before me. Aðils Shape Shifter stepped lightly on my back and sprang on to Haaken's shoulders. He then leapt for the wooden palisade. Had they had guards or sentries then we could not have used that technique. He disappeared and Haaken and I ran down the wall to the gate. Rolf and Olaf were there already. The wooden bar had not been moved for some time. I knew this because of the time it took to move it and the slight creak when we did so. However, the interior of the fort was filled with noise. People were eating and there was much conversation. I had no doubt that the arrival of the Viking ship formed much of the talk. Finally, the door opened a little. We did not open it fully. We slipped inside and drew our swords and daggers. Aðils nocked an arrow. We parted. Olaf went to the south gate and we headed into the centre of the fort. Our wolf cloaks and blackened faces and hands would make us invisible until the last moment and by then it would be too late.

I knew that we had come too early but I wanted to take them by surprise. There were people in the fort. These were the important people. That is why they were protected by a wall and armed men. We were lucky. We were halfway to the building the Romans called the Principia before we were seen. I was so used to seeing my men that I had forgotten how frightening we looked. With our wolf cloaks and mail not to mention our savage-looking swords and daggers, we terrified ordinary people. They dived back into the building. These were not the Roman buildings, they had long fallen into disrepair, these were crude huts built of unmortared stone and wood. One man made the mistake of drawing a sword. Haaken One Eye did not even pause as he slashed his sword across his middle. The others fell back into the building and shouted something. It sounded like *'Viking!'* but I was not sure. Either way, the alarm was given and in some ways that helped us. They did not know our numbers and might think it was the whole ship's crew. The ordinary folk ran for the gates while the warriors came from the hall to deal with the threat. The battle was between boys and men! We were the men.

The first six warriors made the mistake of coming at us piecemeal. They had swords and shields but had not bothered to don mail nor find their helmets. I blocked the sword which came at my unprotected head and rammed Wolf's Blood over the top of his shield and across his throat. He died gurgling as he tried to stop his blood from flowing. The second warrior actually managed to hit me but he used the tip of his sword and it was like a punch from a weak man. My sword came down from on high and split his skull. When the others were dispatched by Haaken and Aðils the remaining five warriors saw sense and made a shield wall.

"Aðils!"

My Ulfheonar took his bow and nocked an arrow. The men held shields which were locked together but three of their heads had no helmets. The first arrows killed two instantly and then Haaken and I charged as Aðils sent a third arrow into the last man without a helmet. My sword blocked the spear of the warrior while my dagger drove up under his rib cage and into his body. The building they had been guarding lay before us. I threw myself at the door and it flew open. Inside I saw Atticus, the young woman and three servants.

"Dragonheart!"

I smiled at the Greek, "Get your gear. We are leaving."

"We must take the girl. Her name is Æthelflæd."

This was typical of the man! This is not the time for debate! "You bring her and you watch her! We have a horde of wild men to kill!"

We stepped out and I saw more armed men. These were not warriors. These were men who were protecting their families.

I shouted, "Atticus, make for the west gate! Haaken watch them! Aðils, charge!"

He laughed as he shouted, "Aye, Dragonheart!"

I raised my sword and roared. I ran at the ten or so men who faced me. They were all family men. None were willing to face the two wolf men who charged at them. They ran. "Come, Aðils, we have chanced our arm enough and the Norns are spinning! I can hear them!"

We shouted and roared as we ran back to the west gate. There was now confusion and chaos in the fort. They did not know who had attacked them. The large number of bodies suggested that it was a warband and the people fled. That was the sensible thing to do when Vikings attacked. We could probably have walked out but I kept running until we crossed the last ditch and reached the woods.

"Aðils, stay here and wait for the others. If they are not back by dawn then return to the ship." Had it just been Atticus then I might have waited but we had two girls for a second had attached herself to the one Atticus had called Æthelflæd. Atticus was no fool and he would not have had us take her for no good reason. If he had then he would be whipped!

"Aye, Dragonheart!" Aðils nocked an arrow and sent it towards the walls of the fort where one soul, braver than the rest had emerged.

"Haaken, lead us back to the ship. I must talk to this Greek fool!"

Haaken led off and Atticus smiled, "You do not mean it, lord! I am glad that you came for me. Surprised but pleased. How did you find us?"

"A long answer and it can wait. Olaf and the others are trying to rescue Haraldr and Sweyn. What happened?"

He nodded and slowed.

"Do not slow! You can talk and walk can you not? Talk!"

"Sorry, lord. We entered the mouth of the river. Haraldr said we should travel at night but I overruled him and said we might miss something. I am sorry, lord, he was right and I was wrong.,"

"And men died because of it but it was my mistake in sending you there in the first place."

"Aye, lord."

"You were attacked."

"Boats came from both sides of the river. They were fishing boats. Galmr and Cnut were slain first and then Sweyn and Haraldr were overpowered. All of us were rendered unconscious and when we awoke we were in the Roman fort. They had yokes and I found that they had a use for me. I was spared the mines. Had I not been of use to them then I would be dead."

"The Saxon girl?"

"The Saxon girl."

"That is a tale for later. Did our men work at their mine?"

"Yes, lord, it is upstream on the north bank."

"Good."

We ran in silence for a while, "Thank you, lord. I cannot believe that you came for me."

Haaken had been listening and he laughed, "That is because since you have been gone the Dragonheart died and was reborn!"

"I can see that I have missed much!"

It was dawn when we saw the ship but there was a reception waiting for us. Sámr, Bergil and what seemed like half the crew greeted us with spears. Sámr looked the most upset, "We thought you all dead!"

I smiled, "No, but we have brought someone back from the dead. Atticus take the women to the prow. There is a canvas there. Sámr, go and help him. These girls look terrified. Give them some shelter and privacy. Atticus they are your responsibility. I am going to see where Olaf and the others are."

We did not have to wait long. Even before the sun had become hot we heard them. My four men approached. They were in a circle and protected Haraldr, Sweyn and four other captives. Haraldr dropped to his knees and kissed my mail byrnie, "Jarl, you came for us. I swear I will give my life for you."

"Rise, Haraldr. A jarl has a responsibility to his men. This is not over. We return later to destroy the fort."

He stood and his eyes became hard and cold. "I will come with you!"

"You are weak!"

"Nonetheless, Sweyn and I will return with the Clan of the Wolf. Those people need punishing."

I nodded. He needed to see the end of this hill fort. We fed them and armed them and then I prepared to leave. "Sámr, you stay here. Atticus needs to know why I did not come sooner and you need to find out why this old Greek fool has saddled us with two girls!"

Haaken and I were weary but we could not show weakness and, after we had donned our helmets and grabbed our shields, we headed back to the hill fort. They thought we had fled and people had returned to their walls. When my warband appeared, it was like a wolf pack surrounding a herd of deer. They ran. They ran without order. With the sight of the captives, emaciated and beaten my men needed no encouragement. Any who stood before us were slaughtered. The women, children and the old escaped. Their men did not. The flight of so many meant that the gates were open and we simply ran in. The defenders had poor mail, weapons and helmets but we took them anyway. The Ulfheonar had killed their best warriors in the night. What they did have and in great quantities were both copper and the blue stones. We found them in the hall. Along with the chests of gold and silver, we had enough so that we did not need to find the mine. We torched the wood of the fort. It had survived since the time of the Romans but it did not survive Jarl Dragonheart and his Clan of the Wolf.

Chapter 3

When we reached our drekar I was weary but neither Haaken nor I would be able to rest until we had the whole story of the girl and Atticus. As we had walked back from the torched fort we had spoken with Haraldr and Sweyn. Neither had been concerned with taking treasure. They wanted to see it burned. They spoke of beatings which had led to other miners dying. Some had been killed in the mine while the lack of food had taken other slaves. The ones who had survived had been on their last legs.

"They were expecting more slaves, Jarl Dragonheart. We learned to understand some of their words and their King, Rhodri ap Merfyn, has claimed most of the other kingdoms hereabouts. He is an ally of King Beorhtwulf of Mercia. The girls are something to do with him but they kept Atticus from us. We could not speak with him."

"I am sorry that I did not come back for you, Haraldr Leifsson."

"I am just amazed that you found us."

"I think we were meant to find you. Had they not put the heads of Cnut and Galmr on the spears we might just have sailed upstream to find the mine."

Haaken said, "Do not judge the Dragonheart too harshly, Haraldr. He went to Valhalla and returned."

I looked to the heavens as Haaken told the two of them of our voyage to Miklagård and my operation. He exaggerated everything.

When he had finished Haraldr shook his head, "You are wrong, Haaken, I did not think badly of any save myself. I captained the knarr and I allowed them to capture us. We should have sailed at night and as I was the warrior I should have ignored Atticus. It was not his fault." Haraldr's amazement was in his voice and his eyes as he turned to me, "You saw Valhalla?" I nodded. "And you saw my father?"

"Aye and the others who were dead. When I did not see you then there was a chance that you were still alive."

"I would not have thought of that."

"I am jarl and have lived long enough to know what is possible and what is not."

While the treasure and loot were stored beneath the decks of the drekar and men prepared food, I sat on the south bank by the burned-out village and spoke with the survivors. Germund and Sámr sat with us. Sámr had already told Atticus my story and now we heard his.

"I was destined for the mines until they discovered that I could speak languages."

"You could speak the language of these people?"

Atticus smiled, "Yes, Haaken One Eye. When I was a slave that was what I did. I translated for my master. It saved my life for I would have lasted barely seven days in that mine."

Haraldr said, "Less!"

"Just so. A month after I was captured I discovered the real reason for my survival. They brought Æthelflæd and her servant Nanna." I looked at the two girls and saw that they were not girls. Both were women; very young women but women nonetheless. "Æthelflæd is the daughter of Æthelstan, the King of the East Angles. The Mercians captured her in battle and she is the surety that the East Angles bow the knee to Mercia. She was to be wed to a Mercian eorledman. When Æthelstan dies then the Kingdom of the East Angles would become a Mercian puppet." He smiled at her. "She deserves better. With neither brothers nor sisters and her mother dead she is all that King Æthelstan has. It is no wonder he allowed himself and his people to be subjugated."

I nodded and yawned. I was tired, "And now we can sail back to the Land of the Wolf. Kara will care for the girls and perhaps she can dream their future."

I began to rise but Sámr rose and said, "No, great grandfather. We have to return them home to their father!"

I looked at him. "We have to get to our home."

Sámr stood his ground, "Why? We have more food than we need. We could sail to Miklagård if we chose. We have barrels of ale and animals as well as dried and salted meat. If we sail home and then travel to Cyninges-tūn a month will pass. Her father will worry. What if this was Gruffyd? What if this were me? You would not want another half year of not knowing. Atticus was a slave and Haraldr a simple warrior yet you came to search for them. Her father cannot search."

This was where I missed Ylva and Kara. They would have offered me good advice. Sámr made a valid point. We had sailed almost a quarter of the way to Lothuwistoft. We could land there and return the girl. The question came into my head, 'why should we take the risk for a Saxon?' I knew that I was tired and tired men never make good decisions.

"I will sleep on this. We sail down the river on the morrow. Let an old man have his rest." I turned to Æthelflæd and spoke in Saxon, "Do not worry princess, we will watch out for you. My men look fierce but they have kind hearts. You can trust all of them."

She smiled and took my hand in hers, "I know, Jarl Dragonheart. Even before you came Atticus had told me of you. He said you would come and when you did that I would be safe for if you came you would guard me with your life."

I looked at Atticus who looked a little shamefaced, "I think I know you, Jarl Dragonheart, and even now I can see that you are torn but you are right. You need to sleep."

Haaken had brightened during Atticus' story and he clapped me on the back, "And we are close enough to Wyddfa for the spirits to help you dream!" As tired as he was Haaken would talk long after I was asleep. I curled up next to the fire we had lit on the bank and, wrapped in my wolf cloak, I fell asleep. As I had expected and Haaken had predicted, I dreamed.

I was in Valhalla. I had glimpsed through the door and I knew what it looked like. Haaken was there, as well as Arturus, Cnut, Old Olaf and all the other warriors who had died in battle. The Allfather was raising his drinking horn and men were banging the table. One name was being chanted, "Sámr Ship Killer". It echoed and reverberated around the hall. It grew so loud that it deafened me and I closed my eyes. When I opened them, I was a hawk flying high above Úlfarrberg. I saw sheep on the fells and, as I passed over the Grassy Mere and the Rye Dale I spied farmers and their families toiling in the fields. I crossed over to Cyninges-tūn and as I soared and then dived I saw the grave of my wife. Next to it were three more graves. There was a new hall where once mine had stood and I saw children playing by the Water. I swept around the hall and saw young boys practising to be warriors. A fully grown Sámr strode out of the hall which I saw now was the one in which I had lived with Erika. It had been improved and enlarged. Sámr wore my mail and, at his waist he carried the sword that was touched by the gods. He looked in the sky and, seeing the hawk, he waved. He turned and spoke. I could hear his words but a moment later a heavily pregnant and now fully grown Æthelflæd emerged. I began to climb and soar. I flew high in the sky towards Old Olaf and then felt a pain as an arrow was sent into me from below. I began to fall. The ground raced towards me but I did not reach it for all went black.

I woke and the sun had not yet come up. I rose and went to make water in the river. Wyddfa brooded to the north and, when I had finished, I saw the other mountain to the south. Atticus had said that it was called Cader Idris and the people who lived in Powys believed that spirits lived there too. I had slept between two holy mountains and it was no surprise that I had dreamed. Most of the dream I understood. Sámr was my heir. He and Æthelflæd were meant to be together. But I did not understand why I had been slain above Old Olaf. However, what was clear was that I should take Æthelflæd back to my land. There Sámr would take her as his wife. He would not be happy that we were not taking her home but he would understand in time.

I went to the fire and poked a log within to liven it up. As it flamed I put more wood upon it. Atticus ghosted next to me. "You dreamed, lord?"

"I dreamed. I saw Sámr and Æthelflæd, they were together and had children."

He smiled, his teeth white in the firelight, "I did not dream but I could have told you that. When first they laid eyes upon each other I saw that they were meant for each other. I am a Christian but I have come to believe in this thing you call *wyrd*. Your coming here was meant." He shrugged, "I have had to question that which I believe. This idea of webs and threads explains much that the teaching of Jesus does not."

I laughed and poured some ale from the skin into a horn, "Good. Then we sail home."

He shook his head, "If you wish Sámr to be happy then we have to go to the land of the East Angles, lord. If you do not then Æthelflæd will pine for her father."

"But if we take her back and she stays with her father then I will lose Sámr and my dream will not come true."

"You know that you have to follow the threads, lord. They draw you to the land of the East Angles. If you do not go then it will nag at you and eat you from within. If you went home what would you do? Sit and watch the sun set behind Old Olaf? That is not the Dragonheart. You came for me, Haraldr and Sweyn but that was the lure which your Norns put in your path. They started your feet upon this path and you must follow it."

"You are becoming quite the pagan, Atticus. This might be dangerous for you."

"I am content. I have lived longer than I believed possible. I should have died many times but I have not. When I die and go to heaven then I shall be content. I have seen more of this world than a slave could expect. And you have been to your heaven. Death holds no fears for you, Dragonheart."

"But what of those who came with me? I hold their lives in my hand."

"You always do and they chose to follow you. Even if they fall then they know they will go to your heaven. They would follow you to the edge of the world!"

"Put some food on to cook. You have given me much to think about." He smiled as he took a skillet and began to slice pieces of cold lamb. He had done that which Aiden normally did. He had planted a seed and I could feel it taking root inside me. I had a good crew. We had lost no men and the land of the East Angles was not far away. I would speak with Erik and then decide. He was a shipmaster and I valued his advice.

Erik Short Toe woke and rose just before dawn. As we were anchored he had no need for a watch and he and his crew took advantage of the fact that there were armed men all around the ship. I waited until he had made water and then approached him. "Erik, how are we set for a voyage to the land of the East Angles."

He did not look surprised. He had sharp ears, "The girl?" I nodded. "At this time of year, the seas are calmer and it would not be difficult. We have spare rope and sails. Thanks to this raid we have food aplenty and we have live animals we can take." I waited for he had not finished. "Is it worth the risk to you, Jarl Dragonheart? We all know that you are fond of Sámr and you would be risking him too."

"I have thought all of that through but the Norns have mixed the threads of the girl and my great-grandson. You know, better than most, the perils of attempting to fight the Norns." He nodded and drank from the ale skin. "Besides this may aid us. We bloodied the nose of the King of Mercia last year. If we help to make the East Angles be a thorn in his side then we weaken him."

Since our victory we now had more families farming the fertile land north of the Belisima. The stronger our hold the less likely that the Mercians would take it from us.

Haaken rose and strode over to us. He broke wind so loudly that the noise woke Sámr and the girls. He laughed, "That is the problem with good food, jarl, it gives my rear end a voice as loud as my other! Have you decided?"

I saw Sámr looking expectantly at me. "We sail for the land of the East Angles."

Atticus turned and spoke to the girl. She ran up to me and hugged me, "Thank you, Jarl Dragonheart. My father will reward you."

"I do not do it for the reward. Sámr wishes it and so…"

She looked at Sámr and I saw what Atticus meant. They had the same sort of look on their faces as Gruffyd had when he had first seen Ebrel. The Norns had, indeed, been busy. I waved over Haraldr. Already he looked better after plenty of food, ale, a good night's sleep and the companionship of the clan. "Ask the Hibernians what they wish. We sail to the land of the East Angles but when we return to the Land of the Wolf we can take them to their homeland."

"I will ask them."

"If they wish to leave us now we can leave them at the mouth of the estuary. We have weapons and food." One result of the raid was that we had captured both mail and helmets, swords and shields.

We took our time leaving. We slaughtered four more sheep. That left us but four to keep alive. We gathered food for them. The slaughtered sheep were skinned, jointed, salted and placed in a barrel. We had taken both from the men at the fort. Then we set sail down the river. We needed no rowers for the current took us and the twisting river was easier to navigate at slow speed. The sail was furled halfway. When we reached the sea, we would travel much faster.

I watched the men as they divided the spoils of war. Bergil, Benni and Beorn Hafþórrsson looked disappointed. They were all big men and the mail we had captured did not fit them nor the helmets. They had to make do with the swords. They were not the best of swords. The Saxons and the Franks had the best swords or they could have one made by Bagsecg and his family. The three brothers all had coin for we had taken much from the men at the fort.

As we sailed Atticus asked, "Do we trade the copper and the beryl?"

"Beryl?"

He nodded, "It is the correct name for the blue stone." He nodded towards the pommel of my sword. "I recognised it as soon as I saw your sword."

"We will trade half of the copper but the blue stone, the beryl, is precious to us. That we will keep."

"Then Lundenwic will be the best port to use." I gave him a quizzical look. "Since the death of Egbert, Wessex wanes. Lundenwic is a free port now. The Danes raided and left, the men of Essex are a spent force as are the men of Cent." He smiled. "Visitors to the fort talked. They thought me an educated man and sought my opinion on many matters. Their King, Rhodri ap Merfyn brought the girl to the fort on his way to Aberffraw. He was boastful of his Mercian ally. The Mercians push east and south leaving Powys safe. The Danes battle Mercia. It is why Æthelstan is necessary. He fights for the Mercians and he bleeds so that the Mercians have a secure border."

Atticus always had a good mind. I trusted his judgement. As we neared the sea I spoke with the Hibernians. Their leader was Conan Mac Finbarr. "Jarl Dragonheart, we would sail with you. We have swords and helmets but there are few of us." He smiled. "Haraldr told us of your prowess in war. We will join your crew until we reach Hibernia once more. We were dead but for you and your crew. If we can serve you for a short time then it will be some way towards repaying you. We need to become stronger if we are to have vengeance on the snake who betrayed us."

"Then join us and welcome. Good men with a sword and shield are always valuable!"

As we cleared the mouth of the estuary I said, "Erik Short Toe, lay in a course for Lundenwic. We will try that Danish den of thieves once more."

It took three days to reach An Lysardh and the approaches to Syllingar. We had neither volva nor galdramenn. All were fearful and men clutched their amulets while they prayed to the Allfather to protect them from the wrath of the witch. I had seen my death. It was an arrow. Yet I was fearful for Sámr. We all breathed a sigh of relief as we turned east and headed for Wihtwara. The Norns had forgotten us. Or so I thought. I was wrong. The wind which had helped us sail south now worked against us and we furled the sail and the men rowed. We used shifts so that only half the crew rowed at any one time. The rescued captives insisted upon rowing and so we could change our rowers frequently. The seas were not totally flat but Ran had been kind. Even so, we needed a chant to bond the new men and those with more experience.

Haaken had a wicked sense of humour and a sense of the dramatic. He chose the saga of Sigeberht.

The Dragonheart looked old and grey.

He fought a champion that cold wet day.
A mountain of a man without a hair
Like a giant Norse snow bear
Knocked to the ground by Viking skill
The Saxon stood and struck a blow to kill
Saxon champion, taking heads
Ragnar's Spirit fighting back
Saxon champion, taking heads
Ragnar's Spirit fighting back
Old and grey and cunning yet,
The Dragonheart his sword did wet
With Ragnar's Spirit sharp and bright
He sliced it down through shining light
Through mail and vest it ripped and tore
The Saxon Champion, champion no more.
As he sank to the bloody ground
Dragonheart's blade whirled around
Sigeberht's head flew through the air
Dragonheart triumphant there
Saxon champion, taking heads
Ragnar's Spirit fighting back
Saxon champion, taking heads
Ragnar's Spirit fighting back

The new men enjoyed the saga and we sang the same one for a whole day. At night we hove to. Three days after An Lysardh we passed Wihtwara. We had been attacked there before by Saxon ships waiting to ambush the unwary. That had been in Egbert's day when they had a strong king. Now his sons fought amongst themselves and sought power. Wessex was still a valuable throne and all of them desired it.

As we neared Hæstingaceaster I thought of what we might find in Lundenwic. There would be news of the Saxon kingdoms. Atticus had information but it was half a year out of date. Much could have happened. There would, of course, be danger. A free port meant that those who sought to make great profit would gather there. It was why we would visit. One man would control it all. That was in the nature of things. Æthelflæd was of value. The Mercians had shown that. She would need protection. I waved over Sámr, Haraldr, Sweyn and Germund. "When we are in Lundenwic then you four shall guard the girls. I do not want them off the ship if we can help it but there will be great danger there."

They were all happy to be their guards. Lundenwic held no lure for them. With our charge protected then I could trade. I would take Haaken and the Ulfheonar as well as Atticus. We had the sharpest minds and ears. We were not only trading we were seeking knowledge and that was equally valuable.

I was always amazed at the traffic on the river. We did not have to row as the wind which had slowed our eastward progress now aided us. The wolf on the sail showed the world whose ship it was. I was the wolf of the north! Other ships moved out of our way. There were many more drekar on the river but we were the biggest and all gave us a wide berth. The old Roman fort of Lundenburh was now almost in ruins. Battles and raids had rendered its walls indefensible. We had been partly responsible for that. It accounted for the freebooting nature of the city for it could not be defended against a determined attacker.

We nudged into the wharf which lay to the west of the ruined fort and was close to the Roman Bridge across the river. As soon as we tied up hawkers, chancers and thieves approached us. They were not afraid of the wolf. Ráðgeir Ráðgeirson and the Hafþórrsson brothers descended to the wharf and cleared them. They made a camp on the wharf daring any to question their right to do so. I saw no other large drekar and assumed that whoever ruled here had either given up the sea or sent his men to raid. That suited us too.

"Ráðgeir Ráðgeirson, take charge here. Have half of the copper brought on deck and the sheepskins. We will trade."

Erik said, "We have sealskins too and some slate. We brought it as ballast."

"We will trade that too."

"And I will slaughter the last of the sheep. There is no grazing here and they will only get thinner. We will cook these, jarl, for we cannot leave until tomorrow's tide."

"You are shipmaster. That is your decision. We will spend as short a time as we can here in this burgh."

Only Atticus was not armed and mailed. Next, to the Ulfheonar, he looked tiny. He walked in the midst of my mailed men. He pointed to a mass of people to the north of us. "I am guessing that is where trades take place."

I nodded, "You negotiate and we will look fierce. When we have traded we will find out how the men of the East Angles kingdom fare."

People moved as we passed through the crowded market and, in equal measure, shouted for our attention. My ship and my sword marked me as Jarl Dragonheart and men used my name as though they knew me. They were trying to sell me their wares. I was of an age where I needed very little and ignored them. We made for the merchants with scales. Atticus had brought a piece of ore. There were three such men. One was dismissed immediately for I saw him using his finger to cheat the customer he was serving. The other two were a Saxon and a Jew. Atticus went to the Jew. Although an unpopular race amongst the Christians, Greeks knew their worth and, generally, their honesty.

Atticus smiled and gave a slight bow, "I am Atticus the Greek. We have ore of this quality. What sort of price could you give us?"

The Jew gave a slight bow to me and said, "I am Isaac of Eoforwic. I will examine it for you." He took the ore and held a piece of glass over it. I had rarely seen glass and wondered what purpose it served. He licked the copper and then placed it on his scales. He had a wax tablet and he took his scribe, it was poised over the tablet when he asked, "How much more do you have?"

Atticus pointed to a nearby barrel of salted fish. It was the type we used most often, "Four of those."

The Jew's eyes widened, "That is a good amount." He scribbled down a number on the tablet and showed it to Atticus. It was a clever move on the merchant's part for it told him if we could read. Only Atticus could read.

He shook his head and turning to me said, in Saxon, "I fear the market is not yet right in Lundenwic, Jarl. We will take our cargo to Dorestad. There the price is better or, perhaps, the merchants are more honest."

The Jew feigned outrage, "My prices are the best in Lundenwic!"

Atticus smiled, "And that is why we will sail to Dorestad. There the prices are higher."

"And you need to cross the sea to reach them. There are many dangers!"

Atticus beamed and said, even more loudly, "When you sail with Jarl Dragonheart of the Clan of the Wolf it is others who fear the sea! Good day."

The Jew had not recognised me and I saw his face change, "Jarl Dragonheart, I did not recognise you. I am sorry if I caused you offence." I maintained a stoical expression. He scrubbed out the marks on the tablet and put down a second amount.

Atticus looked at me and nodded. I smiled, "Then we have a deal. Have your men bring the gold to our ship and they can fetch the barrels. We are moored at the end of the wharf close to the London Bridge."

"Of course, jarl!"

As soon as Atticus had said my name a ripple ran around the market. All eyes turned to me as we left. Atticus said, quietly, "I liked that last touch, Jarl Dragonheart. This way the Jew has to fetch the cargo!"

Now that word of who I was spread we were we found that we were offered the best prices straight away. When the deals were concluded we headed away from the market towards the inns and taverns. Part of our business was concluded and now we needed to find out how the land lay in East Anglia. We headed into one tavern and they must have been forewarned for the owner ejected four Frisians who had been nursing their beer.

"Jarl Dragonheart, welcome to the Wheatsheaf. I have the finest wheat beer in Lundenwic."

We would be served the best for the owner would be able to tell other customers that he had a legend who used his inn. The beer came and it was good. Atticus paid him and I said, "Sit friend, we would speak with you."

"Of course, Jarl Dragonheart. What is it you wish to know?"

"Firstly, who runs Lundenwic now?"

"It is a Dane, Einar Red Cloak. He has the hall in Lundenburh. He and his men are on their way back from the land of the East Angles. There has been war in that debatable land."

My ears pricked up. "How do you know he is on his way back?"

"He sent a messenger. They won a great victory on the borders with Essex. They fought at Beamfleote and the Saxons fell back north to their capital at Beodericsworth."

"Who leads the Danes?"

"Ivar Wartooth. He is said to be descended from a King of Sweden."

I ignored the claim. Every Dane and Swede who came to Britannia claimed to be a King of somewhere. The truth was most of them were just chiefs of warbands who sought a kingdom. "You are Saxon, yes?"

"I am a practical man, Jarl Dragonheart. Lundenwic changes hands more time than a Saxon penny. I serve whoever rules this burgh; Dane, Saxon, Norse, it is all one to me."

I smiled. I liked this pragmatic little man. "Then make an educated guess, will Æthelstan King of the East Angles survive?"

The man shook his head. He spoke quietly so that only we could hear, "He is doomed. His ally Mercia sits behind his borders and the Danes are as numerous as fleas on a dog. He is doomed. It does not help that he has a cousin Æthelweard who fights alongside the Danes. When Ivar Wartooth wins then he will have a Saxon for the throne!" More men had entered, "I must go, Jarl. Business is good."

I gave him a silver coin, "More beers and this," I slipped him a second, "is to ensure your discretion!"

"Of course."

When the ale came I said, "That changes our task."

Rollo Thin Skin shook his head, "It ends it. We were trying to take the girl back to her father so that they could be together. He will not be there for us to find! You know yourself, Jarl Dragonheart, that once the Danes get their teeth into something they do not let go. They are tenacious. At best Æthelstan will be a prisoner!"

"Then we rescue him."

"Why?"

I turned to Rollo Thin Skin, "Because my great-grandson and she are enamoured. If we abandoned her father it might drive a wedge between them. Rollo, you need not come with me. The Norns have spun and the threads of the two young people are bound. You know as well as any that we cannot cut the thread of one without the other."

"I did not say that I would not come. I just wondered why. Now I know then I am content."

"Atticus, you have maps in your head. Should we head north from here to get to Beodericsworth?"

Haaken answered for him, "Jarl, you know as well as any that to reach Beodericsworth from here we would have to pass through the Danish army. We need a port."

Atticus nodded, "The one-eyed storyteller is right. The shortest journey would be from Gippeswic. If memory serves it is twenty odd miles."

"Then we would need horses."

"And the girl"

I looked at Atticus, "The girl? Are you mad? It will be hard enough getting to Beodericsworth with men but with a girl who cannot defend herself then it would be impossible."

"She needs to see her father. If he cannot be rescued or will not be rescued then she might not believe you besides would her father trust a Viking?"

Annoyingly he was right. "We will be leaving on the morrow. That gives us tonight to choose the men we would take."

We finished the ale and headed back through the market. As we passed Isaac of Eoforwic his servant approached, "Lord, my master would have a word." I heard the terror in his tremulous voice.

I smiled, "Of course."

The Jew stood and approached me. He spoke quietly, "Jarl Dragonheart, after you left two Danes came. They seemed interested in where you were moored. They are the oathsworn of Einar Red Cloak. His men began arriving back in Lundenwic early this morning." He gave an apologetic shrug, "Men have spoken of little else since your ship arrived."

I nodded, "Thank you, Isaac of Eoforwic. I would send your men sooner rather than later."

"Of course and thank you for your understanding." I slipped him a silver coin as we shook hands.

"What was that about, jarl?"

"Trouble, Haaken. The Danes are interested in us and that never bodes well. I hope the men who went to buy ale are back on board. Lundenwic is a den of thieves!"

Haaken laughed, "Said the Viking who has stolen more treasure than every Dane and Saxon leader combined!"

It made me smile for he was right. I was pleased that we had concluded our business so quickly. As soon as the ore was taken from the ship then we could edge into the middle of the river and anchor there if we had to. I saw the barrels of ale being rolled towards the gangplank and Erik had the ore barrels already waiting on the wharf. He would ensure that the beer barrels and other supplies were well-balanced. When we were at sea it was he who would determine which barrel was to be broached. Too many ships had sunk because of an unbalanced load. It was Erik who distributed the rowers. He had an eye for such things. It was one of the reasons why we were one of the fastest ships afloat.

I saw Sámr and Æthelflæd waiting anxiously for my news. They would have to wait for the safety of the ship was my prime concern. I waited until Erik had stowed the barrels. Just as I approached him I heard the sound of feet as Isaac's men came for the barrels of ore.

"Erik there may be trouble. There are Danes in this city who may wish us harm. Could we anchor in the river and await the tide?"

He shook his head, "I am sorry, Jarl. Outside of Miklagård, this is the busiest port I have ever seen. Some of these captains are incompetent. We might be rammed. I would rather stay tied to the wharf and have armed men ready to defend us."

He made a fair point. Even while I had been talking to him ten ships had sailed upstream. The bridge was the point at which the larger vessels would have to turn. It was not worth the risk. I waved over Ráðgeir Ráðgeirson and Bergil Hafþórrsson. They were the two most reliable men after the Ulfheonar. "Divide the men into two watches. One stays on board and the other near to the fire. There may be trouble from Danes. I hope that there will not but let us be prudent."

They nodded. Bergil said, "I never trust Danes, Jarl Dragonheart!"

Just then I saw the crowds part as a column of men, spears over their shoulders, came through the market. I saw Isaac's overseer hurrying his men to get out of the way.

"It looks like we have trouble now. Organize the men and I will greet these Danes. Have half of the men armed with bows." I turned to Sámr, "Keep the young women hidden. It will be safer for all!"

He nodded and he and Germund hurried them to the safety of the canvas at the prow. I went to the gangplank and walked down to the cobbled wharf. I heard heavy feet follow me. That would be Olaf and my Ulfheonar. Without even looking I knew that he had Rolf carrying their two-handed axes and Aðils Shape Shifter his Saami bow.

The twenty men halted and spread out. They did not point their spears at us but I could see that they were at the ready. Half of them had mail and all wore a good helmet with a fine sword and a well-made shield. The shields were all painted red and when they parted I saw why. The Dane who approached had a red cloak. His helmet had an ostentatious plume and it was made of horsehair dyed red. That showed that he was not a true warrior. Such a plume would be an invitation in a battle. I also saw that he was young. He was younger than Bergil Hafþórrsson.

"You are Jarl Dragonheart?"

"I am." My Ulfheonar spread out on either side of me.

"I am Einar Red Cloak and this is my port. There is a charge levied!"

"I heard it was a free port."

"Free for men to come and go but we make a charge for the safety of our facilities and the protection of those who use our port."

He sounded like a clerk! "Thank you for the offer but we do not pay men to do our fighting. We are real warriors and we fight for what we have. Besides we leave on the morning tide."

He was an arrogant little man and he waved an imperious hand, "You leave when I say!"

I laughed, "Really? How many sea battles have you fought, Einar Red Cloak?"

For the first time, he looked a little less confident, "That has nothing to do with this. My uncle Ivar Wartooth has fought in many battles and he has charged me with levying a tax on all those who use his port."

"Ah, so this is not your port. You are the clerk who collects the coins!" I heard Haaken laugh. It was not a subtle laugh. "You get no coins from us, now leave. We wish to use the wharf for a feast this night."

"You are not allowed to light fires upon the wharf."

Olaf Leather Neck was growing impatient, I could tell. He pointed to the fire my men had lit when we arrived. The pot with the mutton bubbled away. "You are wrong, it seems. Go away little red cloak for I am bored."

His men were growing impatient and a few spears were lowered. I said, quietly, "If spears are levelled at me I will take it as a discourteous act and blood will be spilt!"

I know not if it was Olaf's insult or my words but he was angered and he coloured, "Spears!"

I raised and lowered my hand so quickly that it was a blur. There was the loud crack of arrows hitting shields. Ráðgeir Ráðgeirson and Bergil must have ordered the men to hit shields. At thirty paces they could not have missed.

"How dare you!"

"The next arrows will not find wood they will find flesh!"

One of his men said, "Lord, we can take these old men. Just give the word."

I said, "Aðils!" In one movement he raised his bow, nocked an arrow and sent it into the forehead of the man who made the suggestion. As the dead body hit the cobbles there was a stunned silence. Blood began to trickle towards the river.

"That was one of my guards!"

"As Olaf said, we are bored. Do we shed more blood here or will you leave us to drink some ale and eat some mutton?"

The dead man had decided for him. The others held their shields high and showed no inclination to take us on. "This is not the end of the matter!"

Haaken said, "It is for us!"

They dragged away the body of their comrade. All along the wharf, the other captains all began banging their shields. We had done that which they had wished to do. I turned to return to the ship. I nodded at Ráðgeir Ráðgeirson and Bergil Hafþórrsson. They would organize our defences. I turned, once I was on board. "I would rest now. When darkness comes we will have visitors!"

I took off my cloak and walked toward the prow. Sámr and his charges rose along with Germund. "Germund, we need to make this shelter a little stronger. Go and buy an old barrel. Let us see if we can make a cabin." I gave him a couple of coins. When we were alone I said to Æthelflæd, "Your father has just lost a battle. He lives and is heading to Beodericsworth. Do you still want to join him?"

"He needs to know that I am alive and then he can make peace with the Danes. He is a practical man, Jarl Dragonheart. He knows he cannot defeat the Danes. He fights them only because he thinks I am a prisoner. Many men will die unless we can tell him. I am sorry but we must find him."

I nodded. She was right. "We will land at Gippeswic."

"That is a royal burgh and the headman is one of my father's old hearthweru, Oswald of Northwic. He will help us."

"Good and I hope that you can ride. We will have to sneak through the Danish lines to reach your father. Sámr, when Germund returns make a wolf's den for the ladies. There may be trouble this night and I would have you and Germund protect them. I will have enough to worry about without two young ladies and my great-grandson."

Once again Æthelflæd grabbed my hand, "Thank you, jarl. I beg you not be hurt on my account."

I ruffled Sámr's hair, "It is my great-grandson I worry about! He is my future. He will be the Clan of the Wolf."

As we would be leaving early Erik had everything ready so that we could cast off quickly. The sail was ready to be unfurled. We were just secured by two ropes and the ship's boys who would loose them knew who they were. There would be a high tide just before dawn. We were laden and so we needed as much water beneath our keel as possible. By the time we reached Grenewic, it would not be a problem but until then it would.

I wandered down to the prow and saw that Germund had cut a hole in the side of a large barrel which had been cut in two. Upended it gave protection from the elements and from swords. I was happier. If an attack came then they would be safe. Coming back down the ship I saw that Bergil's half of the crew were resting while Ráðgeir's were waiting along the landward side of the drekar and by the fire. Their weapons were close to hand. I went to the steering board and sat with my back to the rail. The Danes had done a good job of destroying the old Roman fort but I wondered if it would come back to haunt them. Had this been my clan we would have repaired the walls and gates. We would have made it impossible for an enemy to gain entry without bleeding upon the walls. I closed my eyes as I tried to picture how I would make it even stronger. I must have fallen asleep for when Haaken One Eye woke me it was dark.

He yawned as he said, "Lundenwic is asleep."

"Did the Danes come?"

"Not yet but I sense that it will not be long. Bergil and his half of the crew are on watch."

I stood. Perhaps it was the fact that I had slept longer than I had expected but I was a little unsteady on my feet. I put my hand to the gunwale on the steerboard side. I glanced over and saw three small drekar. They were river boats. They were approaching us with purpose. It was the Danes! I hissed, "Danes! Get the men to this side." I grabbed a spear as Haaken scurried down the drekar to wake up the sleeping crew. I saw Sven Ship Sealer. "Bring Bergil and his men but do so silently."

I could have shouted the alarm but I wanted the Danes destroying. The three boats had been packed with men. There were sixty or so Danes coming. Olaf and Aðils were the first to join me. Aðils had an arrow nocked. Olaf grinned as he swung his axe. I drew the sword that was touched by the gods and we waited. Men appeared like wraiths alongside us and gradually the steerboard side filled up. There was a slight bump as the first of the small drekar pulled next to us. They would have to leave men sculling in order for the boats to stay next to our hull. As the first hand came up I shouted, "Now!"

Olaf swung his axe and severed the hands of the first man. He screamed as he fell backwards. He crashed into the boat sending two men into the river. I leaned over and swung my sword. I connected with the side of a Danish head. Aðils sent an arrow into the man at the steering board of the nearest ship. As he fell overboard his dying hand dragged the board with him and allowed the current to tug it away from the side of our ship. Those who were clambering up the side of our drekar slipped into the river. As they fell the drekar tipped and began to ship water. It would soon sink. The men who wore helmets and had swords at their sides would die. Their only chance was to rid themselves of helmets, swords and daggers. When they did that they would be helpless. Aðils switched targets and began to loose at the steering boards of the other ships. Some Danes had managed to get aboard our drekar. I ran towards Rollo who was using his sword to great effect.

Shouting, "Ragnar's Spirit!" I raised my sword and brought it down on the Dane who was trying to stab Rollo in the side. His sword actually touched Rollo's mail but the metal byrnie held and I split open the Danish skull. When Ráðgeir Ráðgeirson brought his men from the wharf it was all over. Those still alive discarded helmets and weapons and threw themselves into the river. They would take their chances with Ran! Bergil and his brothers were like men possessed. They hewed, stabbed and slashed. Soon the only Danes left on the drekar were dead ones. We heard cries and frantic splashing as Danes tried to reach the south bank. They failed.

As we walked along the deck, dispatching the ones who were not quite dead, I heard Bergil complaining, "Give me a decent-sized Dane or I will never find any mail to fit me!"

For some reason that made me laugh and I clapped him on the shoulder, "When we reach Cyninges-tūn I will have Bagsecg make you a byrnie and it will fit! It might take all the iron we possess but it will be done."

Chapter 4

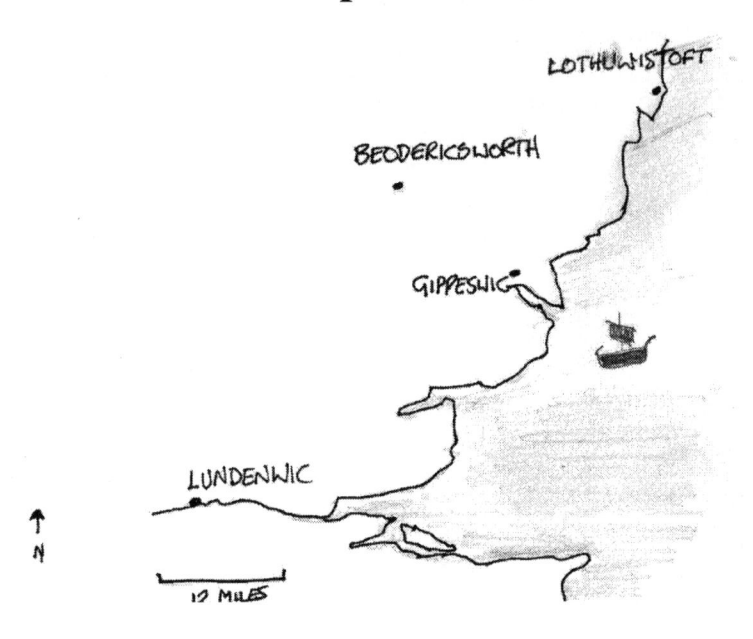

We reached the mouth of the river by noon. We had had the wind, the current and the men were in a mood to row. We were all eager to be away from the stench that was Lundenwic. If I never saw it again it would be too soon! The wind which had taken us from Lundenwic now was against us. Erik said, "The men fought in the night and are tired. We will sail north and east. We can still use the sail. Then we can tack around and approach Gippeswic from the northeast. We will have the wind pushing us that way even though we appear to be sailing in a circle. It will take a day, jarl but you will need the men once we land. They need to recover from the battle." He looked at me, "You need your rest."

He was right. "Very well." I took off my mail and walked to the upturned barrel in which the two girls resided. Sámr, Germund and Atticus were outside. I said, simply, "The winds are against us we have a long circular sail ahead of us."

"I will fetch food." Germund limped off to the mast.

"How are the girls? Did they take the news badly?"

"Æthelflæd is strong and Nanna, her cousin, believes that their god will save the King."

I was not so certain. The Danes had overwhelming numbers. Our only hope was to get there so that Æthelstan could make peace with the Danes but from what I had heard Æthelweard was already ready to take the throne. Why should the Danes make peace when they could kill the opposition and have their own man ruling the land for them?

"When we land you will stay with the ship, Atticus."

He frowned, "With respect, my lord, I should be there with the girls."

"Why? We speak their language and it will be hard enough travelling with two girls without a Greek who can do little if danger comes. I will be taking few enough men as it is. This is not open for debate." He nodded and I softened my voice, "Atticus, you have put yourself in danger enough. I would not want to carry the guilt of your death with me."

He smiled, "You are probably right, lord. It is just that I wished to see this through to the end."

Sámr said, "I will be coming. Before you say anything great grandfather I have fought alongside these men before. I am a warrior. Unlike Atticus, I can ride and I can fight. Baldr has taught me to ride. More, I have an interest in Æthelflæd; more than an interest. I will take her for my bride."

I nodded. He was determined, "What if her father says no?"

I could see that he had not considered that. He looked astern at the birds following the ship. Their cries, men said, were the cries of the men who had not gone to Valhalla. For that reason, we did not harm them. They had an existence without purpose save to follow drekar and call to their comrades. The cries of the birds seemed to give him an answer. "Our threads have been spun and they have become entwined. Let us see what the Norns have planned. Æthelflæd's father's decision has yet to be made. He has not met me." He smiled, "I will comb my hair and Atticus can trim my beard. I shall wear clean clothes. I will convince him."

"Good. You have thought this through. Then I suggest you teach them our language."

"I have begun already."

Germund came back with food and ale. I was now hungry and I joined them. While Sámr, Germund and I attacked our food Atticus picked at his like a bird. He had grown accustomed to drinking ale but he preferred wine.

When we had finished Atticus said, "What will you do with the beryl when we reach your home, lord?"

"We prize them. They will be divided amongst the crew and we will give some to Kara and her family. There is power within them."

Atticus shook his head, "They are blue stones, lord. They are pretty and when polished glisten in the sunlight but powerful? I think not."

"You are wrong. The icy blue is like the ice on the mountains and glaciers of Norway. I did not live there long but I remember those glistening blue tongues creeping down the mountain. They protected the people of that land." I could see I had not convinced him. "Above the fire in my hall, you remember the old rusted sword?"

"The one like the Roman spatha?" I nodded, "Aye, lord."

"That one has the blue stone. The sword has lasted more than a thousand years. The ancient peoples who lived before your White Christ understood the power of the stones. Ragnar's Spirit is powerful not just because of Thor's thunderbolt but because of the stones."

Atticus still found the story of the sword hard to believe, "It was lightning which struck your sword, lord. This god called Thor was not involved."

I knew I could never convince him but I tried. "Thor used his hammer, Mjøllnir, to strike my sword and to harden it. The sparks which flew were the thunderbolt sent by Thor."

Atticus smiled, "Then we will never agree on this lord but I thank you for the opportunity to debate. A slave rarely gets to argue with his master. It usually results in a beating."

"And you are not my slave. I freed you."

"Yet you will not let me come with you to Beodericsworth." He shrugged, "I will wake the girls. They have slept long enough."

I stood and stretched. "Another reason for not taking Atticus is the fact that I am uncertain how many horses we will be able to get. I am not even certain that this old retainer, Oswald of Northwic, will be at Gippeswic. If his King needs men he may already be with him."

"Who will you take then, apart from me and the Ulfheonar?"

"Bergil and his brothers have shown themselves to be resourceful. I would take Ráðgeir Ráðgeirson but I need someone I can rely upon to watch the ship. Lars Long Nose and Siggi Eainarson would be handy men to have but the rest have little experience."

"There is always Haraldr Leifsson and Sweyn Alfsson."

I shook my head, "They are not yet fully recovered."

"The Norns spun threads. Haraldr Leifsson and Sweyn Alfsson were kept alive. I believe it was for a purpose. Atticus was kept alive to watch the girls but Haraldr and Sweyn? Their work is not yet done."

I laughed, "You are a volva eh? Where did you get such wisdom?"

"When Ulla War Cry fell into the ocean near Syllingar and I visited the cave of the witch. I now see things that others do not. Often it is through a grey mist but I see things."

"Have you told others of this power?"

He nodded, "Ylva. She helps me often. It was she who taught me to interpret the grey, murky pictures I see."

Just then the two girls emerged. They smiled. "It is like a little cave which Germund has made for us, Jarl Dragonheart. It is cosy in there. It smells of beer but I am used to that now."

"Good. Your comfort is important to me."

Atticus said, "And with that in mind, lord, we need to give the ladies some space they will need to make water." He waved us away like a housewife moving chickens. As we headed down the ship I smiled. I had missed the fussy little Greek.

As the day progressed and we turned our circle the wind changed a little and helped us. The Allfather liked circles. Life was a circle and he ringed the world with a circle. Erik had chosen the right course. The men were fresher and would be prepared for whatever awaited us in Gippeswic.

I had heard Sámr's words and so I sat with Haraldr and Sweyn. "You two look better than when we found you at the fort."

"Good food and the sea air helps."

"Aye," said, Haraldr, "and the companionship of the Clan of the Wolf."

I tapped the leather jerkin Haraldr wore. "You shall have mail when we reach Cyninges-tūn."

"I am not sure that I would be able to bear it yet."

That was what I had worried about. "When we land I will take a few men to ride to Beodericsworth. My great-grandson thinks I should take you two. I do not think you are strong enough and I would not risk two such brave warriors."

They looked at each other and then Haraldr spoke, "When I left Cyninges-tūn I was young. My body had just grown to be a man but inside I was like Sámr is now, I had growing to do. We were meant to endure the labours of the mine. I now have stronger arms than I once did.

We were taken because the Norns had spun. Our comrades died and we did not. We had hoped to go home but we all know that we cannot until the threads which have been bound together are either unravelled or cut. I grew inside too. My mind is stronger. We would go with you, Jarl Dragonheart. You do not go to make war. You take a small number of men to move quickly and be unseen. Sweyn and I are not Ulfheonar but we know how to be both silent and remain hidden."

I looked into their eyes and saw their steely determination. "Then make certain that you are armed and prepared for a hard ride through land which may be hostile."

It was dawn the next day before we saw the coast appear. The light from the east reflected on the breakers along the beach. Erik determined that we were too far north and so we sailed down the coast. The people of this land had been raided many times. I knew that the sight of a drekar coming down the coast would alarm them. For that reason, we had no shields along the side. I hoped they understood the significance of that. We came in peace. The day's delay had cost us. We could ill afford a day trying to convince them that we came in peace.

I walked aft, "Æthelflæd, does this Oswald of Northwic know you?"

She nodded. "Until four years since he served as Captain of my father's guard. He saw me each day."

"Then I will need you to come with us. He will need convincing. What happens if he is not there?"

She looked worried, "I know not. Why should he not be there?"

"You have been away for a year and much can have happened. He might be fighting alongside your father."

"Then I know not what we shall do."

Sámr shook his head, "Great grandfather, the pot is half full and not half empty. Stop worrying about things which may or may not be. The Norns have spun this web and our threads are entwined. If Oswald is not there then we shall think of something else!"

The entrance to the river was wide and posed no problems for Erik. We headed north along the ever-narrowing river. We saw huts and fishing boats drawn up along the banks but we saw no people. They were hiding. Then we spied the town but the gates in the walls were closed. Spear points glistened on the fighting platform.

Olaf Leather Neck grumbled, "Our usual welcome! You think they would know that without shields we come in peace."

Atticus shook his head, "I fear that in this part of the world they have been raided too often to take the risk."

There was a wooden quay but knarr and small ships were tied up. Their crews were inside the fort. "Moor us next to the nearest knarr and we will cross over the ships. Lady, you and Nanna will need to come with us. Atticus and Sámr, come too. The rest stay aboard."

Haaken laughed, "Aye we would not have them fill their breeks at the sight of Olaf Leather Neck!"

"Aðils, watch for danger. I would not have anyone killed; if you have to then worry them."

He laughed, "Aye, jarl. It will be as though they have nicked themselves while shaving."

Atticus helped Nanna and Sámr helped Æthelflæd. I wore mail and went before them. If they used stones or arrows I would afford them some protection with my body. I stopped one hundred paces from the gates. I shouted, "I am Jarl Dragonheart from the Land of the Wolf. I have brought back Princess Æthelflæd. She was captured and held hostage. She is returned."

I stepped aside to reveal the two girls.

Æthelflæd, her voice sounding thin and reedy, shouted, "Oswald of Northwic, it is I. These men look fierce but they can be trusted."

I saw heads come together and then there was a delay. I was patient. They would have to unbar the gate. If this Oswald knew his business then he would have used logs to jam against the gate. Eventually, the door opened and a white beard emerged. He limped. He wore an old mail byrnie and, on his head, he had a simple round helmet. He strode over to us, peering into the sun. He shaded his eyes. When he was just ten paces he broke into a shambling, limping run, "It is you! God be praised. You have been delivered!"

She threw herself into his arms, "These men rescued me."

He took off his helmet and, holding it in his left hand, offered me his right, "I am sorry for the suspicion. We cannot tell the difference between Norse and Dane but I have heard of you. When I saw the wolf sail, I wondered why you were raiding over here."

"As much as I would like to talk, Oswald of Northwic, time is pressing. The Danes are hurrying to end your king's reign. If we can get his daughter to him then he may be able to sue for peace."

"It may be too late for that."

"Nonetheless we will try. Have you any horses?"

"Eighteen, the King took the rest."

"Then I will take some of my men and escort the Princess to her father."

"My two sons and I will come with you."

I was relieved. It would make life easier if we had a local lord with us. "My ship will stay here. If your town is attacked they can help to defend it."

"I will fetch the horses and my sons."

"Atticus, go to the ship and tell them what is happening. Send the Ulfheonar, Bergil and his brothers, Haraldr and Sweyn and Germund."

The horses were not the best I had ever seen. We used the weaker ones for the two girls. Most of us were mailed. There were just five who were not. For the first ten miles, the road followed the river. I could see that although they could ride Nanna and Æthelflæd were not confident riders. Sámr and Germund stayed by their sides. Oswald's two sons were warriors. They had long byrnies and carried axes. I wondered why they were not fighting with their King. They rode at the fore with their father. I noticed how flat the countryside was. It was as unlike my land as it was possible to get. I could see how the Danes had been so successful; we could have sailed our drekar another four miles upstream.

We stopped after a couple of hours for the horses needed the rest and the two ladies were in some distress. They did not complain but I could see that they were relieved to be off the back of their horses. I chose that moment to talk to the three Saxons. "Will the King be behind his walls?"

Oswald nodded. "When the King was defeated he managed to fall back in good order. He sent his thegns, men like my sons, back to their own burghs. An open battle was pointless for the Danes outnumber us. He said to wait behind our walls. The Danes do not like sieges and soon they would tire and go back to raiding."

It was not the way I would have done it. "And will we be able to gain entry to the town?"

"That I know not. The last we heard the Danes were investing the land south of here. That treacherous cousin of the King, Æthelweard, is with them and suborning many of the eorledmen and thegns. The King's power is diminishing day by day."

"Now that he has his daughter back he could negotiate."

"No offence, Jarl Dragonheart, but negotiating with a Dane is like trying to convince a pack of hungry wolves not to eat you."

I smiled, "Then it is lucky you have brought your own wolves with you!"

"I wondered at the wolf cloaks. Are you the ones they call shape shifters?" I saw him clutch his cross as he asked the question.

"Aye, we are Ulfheonar, wolf warriors."

He looked at his sons, "Then had you come for war…"

"Your town would be ours already."

"In that case let us get to the King as quickly as we can."

We rested, a little longer than we would have done without the ladies and then hurried on. I discovered that the Saxons were not as good at scouting as we were. I had sent Aðils to ride next to Oswald's sons and it was fortunate that I did so. He sensed something. Reining in he held his hand up and grabbed his bow. I could see that the Saxons had seen nothing for they looked bewildered.

"Sámr, Germund, Harald and Sweyn, stay with the ladies. The rest with me." Even as I dug my heels into the horse I was drawing my sword. I heard the bowstring as Aðils sent an arrow into the woods which lay to the right of us. There was a cry and suddenly a warband of Danes burst forth. They were all on foot. Even on a horse, Aðils was deadly with a bow and two fell in rapid succession. We reached the three Saxons who still sat on their horses. They had no stiraps and sitting on a horse and trying to fight a Dane was a certain way to an early grave. We threw ourselves from our horses and ran towards the Danes. It was then that Oswald and his sons dismounted. I did not take my shield from my back and I held Ragnar's Spirit two-handed.

There were twenty Danes. Three had mail the rest did not. I saw one red shield which I recognised. It was one of Einar Red Cloak's men. Even as he recognised me he stopped, turned and fled. It was too late to ask Aðils to slay him for my archer had dismounted and was rushing to aid us. The first Dane had an axe and shield. He was also mailed. I was almost sixty-nine years old and yet I had not forgotten how to fight. I allowed him to swing his sword. I watched its arc and I spun away and brought my sword around to his back. His speed had carried him beyond me and his swing had held him there. His mail held but I had hit with a swinging blow which always carries more power. He gave a grunt. I reversed the sword and brought it to the other side. This time it came away bloody as I sawed it backwards. He dropped to his knees and I took out Wolf's Blood and slit his throat.

Bergil and his brothers had no mail but they were ferocious fighters. They all hated Danes and it showed in the reckless way that they fought. Bergil still had no helmet although his two brothers had taken two from the fort we had captured. Rolf, Olaf and Rollo were relentless as they used their axes and swords to hack through the Danish ambush. Haaken One Eye looked deceptive with his empty orb and white hair. Men thought him easy to defeat but nothing could have been further from the truth. He had incredibly quick hands and a cunning mind. When the last three ran down the road Aðils used his bow to slay them in succession. The last hit was when the man was a hundred and fifty paces away.

"Bergil, you and your brothers take what you like from the dead and then we move."

Oswald said, "We have defeated them. We will be safe for a while."

I shook my head, "We will not for one of Einar red Cloak's men escaped. If the Dane is near then Wartooth is not far away and he has a large warband and reason to hate me. We move!"

We left the Danes where they lay. The three byrnies were taken and slung over the horses. We hurried west. When we were a mile or so from the town Oswald stopped. "If the Danes are here then they will be to the south of the town. There is a river north of here. We can ford that and enter by the north gate. It is getting on to dark. With luck, we can sneak through any of their scouts."

I nodded, "No disrespect, Oswald, but I would like Aðils, Rollo and Rolf as the scouts. They have senses you and your sons do not possess."

"I am not offended. How your archer knew the Danes awaited us I have no idea. I am just grateful."

We pushed the horses as hard as we dared. Æthelflæd and Nanna had seen the dead bodies and endured the hardship of the saddle without complaint. It was dark by the time we found the road which led to the north gate. Once we saw the walls my three scouts allowed Oswald and his sons to take over. Aðils, Rollo and Rolf had stopped each time there was danger and we had reached the outskirts of Beodericsworth, unseen.

Oswald shouted up to the guards on the walls, "Open the gate. It is Oswald of Northwic and I have good news for the King."

The voice replied, "Then you are doubly welcome for we need your swords and we are in desperate need of good news."

The gates swung open. My men and I waited until the two ladies had entered before we rode in. A sentry shouted, "These are Vikings! It is a trick!"

Oswald said, "These are not Danes and they are friends. Now take us to the King quickly! Our news might end this war."

We dismounted and I hung my shield and helmet from the saddle of the horse. "You stay here with the horses. Feed them and see if there is food for us. With luck, we can leave tomorrow. I will go with Sámr and the ladies."

They nodded. The Ulfheonar were masters at foraging. They would find food, ale and beds.

Oswald turned to his sons, "You two stay with them. We want no trouble with the garrison."

Sámr and I received strange and hostile looks as we headed through the town. I saw men being treated for wounds in the street. Oswald asked, "What happened?"

"The Danes made a sudden attack today just as Eorledman Wiglaf was entering the burgh from the west. They were badly cut up. They were our hope. We have less than two hundred spears. The addition of another fourteen is invaluable, even if they are Vikings!"

I was not insulted but Æthelflæd was, "Peace, you ingrate! These men have risked their lives for me. I will not hear them insulted."

I smiled. She had spirit. Sámr had made a good choice. Would her father think so?

There was a large hall and there were many warriors outside of it. Some were sharpening weapons while others were having wounds tended. I said, quietly, "Sámr, keep your hands from your weapons. These men have lost comrades today and they will lash out blindly."

"Aye, Jarl."

Oswald's voice boomed, "Eorledman coming through." Luckily the Saxons parted. Perhaps they saw us as prisoners, I know not but they allowed us through without reacting to our dress and weapons.

I heard voices and they were raised. "Majesty, we have less than three hundred men and of those but two hundred are warriors. The warband which arrived from the south to join the attackers today is bigger than our entire garrison."

"What else can we do? If we surrender then we will be put to the sword."

Oswald stepped in, "King Æthelstan, here is your daughter. She is no longer a hostage."

Æthelflæd ran to her father and threw herself into his arms. The man who had been speaking to the King said, "And is this a Viking prisoner?"

Oswald said, "That is ungracious of you, Æthelberht. This is Jarl Dragonheart and he is the one who rescued the princess and brought her to her father."

"Is this some kind of trick? Why would a Dane help us?"

I moved closer to the man who was half a head shorter than I was, "Friend, do not call me a Dane again or there will be bloodshed. I am Jarl Dragonheart of the Clan of the Wolf and if I were you I would remain silent. I have journeyed far and I need food, ale and a bed."

I thought for a moment his hand would go to his sword but he thought better of it.

The King said, "Thank you, Jarl, and I apologise for my men. We lost shield brothers today! Now I can go on the morrow and see if we can salvage peace from this."

I was not confident but I nodded. "We will leave in the morning if that meets with your approval. I have been away from home longer than I anticipated."

"I would have you wait until I have spoken with Ivar Wartooth."

I did not want to and I was about to refuse when I saw a pleading look from both Æthelflæd and Sámr. My great grandson needed time to speak with the King. "Very well. Sámr, I will wait outside. It will be safer for Lord Æthelberht."

Oswald chuckled, "And I will come with you."

Once outside the Eorledman said, "You have balls, Viking, I will give you that."

It was my turn to smile, "I was born to a Saxon father, a mother who was of the old people of this land and brought up a Viking. There is little that I have neither seen nor done. I may be old but I can still use my sword."

"You were the one who killed Sigiberhrt in single combat were you not?"

"I was."

Oswald turned, "We have a champion amongst us. This is Jarl Dragonheart of the Clan of the Wolf. It was he who killed Sigiberhrt in single combat."

One of the younger warriors shouted, "Impossible! The Dragonheart has to be a hundred years old! My grandfather told me tales of him and his son stealing King Ebert's wife!"

I laughed, "Aye that was me but my son is long dead and his grandson now rides with me. I am old but I still know how to hew heads."

Unlike Eorledman Æthelberht the warriors had heard of me and knew me to be a Dane killer. I was plied with questions about the Danes I had slain. "You killed Eggle Skull Taker too." I nodded. "Then with you and your men, we will defeat these Danes!"

"I brought but a handful of men. I brought back the King's daughter."

"She is no longer a hostage?"

Oswald said, "No, for the Jarl and his men rescued her."

A cheer went up as the news was spread. I was plied with offers of drink and undying friendship. I was able to detach myself from the slaps on my back and the praise. The Danes would have sentries and they would hear the euphoria. They would think we had been reinforced. Perhaps there was hope for the King. I know not how long we drank. As a leader, I knew that this was good for the men. When we had entered there was an air of depression and doubt. Now there was hope.

Nanna came for me, "Lord, the King wishes to speak with you." Oswald made to come too but she said, "Sorry, my lord, just the Dragonheart."

I entered. All had gone save Sámr and the two ladies. "Your great-grandson has asked to marry my daughter."

"Aye, I know."

"She has seen but thirteen summers and is my only child."

"And Sámr has seen just fourteen so it would seem they are well-matched."

"He is Viking."

"With Saxon blood from me and his grandmother who was King Egbert's wife. We can go all around the town walls but we will still end up at the same place. Either you give your permission for them to marry or you do not. There is no middle ground. Sámr will accept your judgement. He will not be happy about it but he has given me his word."

The King laughed, "By all that is holy but you are a man. For myself, I am happy for my daughter to choose a man with whom she is obviously enamoured and an alliance with your clan might help us but I fear I am about to lose my kingdom."

"Aye, you are."

"Bluntly honest."

"If these are all the men that you have then it is a matter of time before the Danes defeat you. Your cousin is with them."

He looked surprised, "Æthelweard?" I nodded, "How do you know?"

"It was common knowledge in Lundenwic and your daughter heard it in Powys." She nodded too.

"Then whatever I do I have lost." He turned to Sámr, "If you swear to watch over my daughter and her servant then you may marry her. That way she will have a future."

"Father! What of you?"

"I am still King and I cannot allow my men to be slaughtered."

Sámr said, "You could come with us!"

I knew that he meant well but it could not be. From what I had seen of the King he had honour. He would not abandon his men.

The King shook his head. "We will see. Tomorrow, Jarl Dragonheart, I would be honoured if you would come with me to speak to this Ivar Wartooth. Perhaps your presence might persuade him not to continue the war."

"I doubt that, King Æthelstan. When we were in Lundenwic his men tried to take my ship. He lost many men. I will come with you but I fear it might aggravate the situation."

"I would still have you with me."

"Then I will go to speak with my men. They will need to know what is afoot. Come, Sámr." He looked longingly at Æthelflæd. I smiled, "If things go well there will be time enough for that in the future."

Æthelflæd impulsively grabbed him and kissed him. It was as chaste a kiss as I had seen. Sámr looked surprised and then he followed me still touching his mouth. As we walked back to the others I reflected that his mother had been a captive too but that had been far from here. I had been a captive as had my mother. Perhaps we became what we were because of the hardship we endured. It made us stronger people.

My men had saved food for me and I ate and drank by the stable. It was one of the few places we could find enough space for us. Bergil and his brothers were happy for they had new mail and it fitted. They were a little distracted as I told them what had happened.

"We cannot win, Jarl, you know that."

"Of course I do, Olaf Leather Neck, but if you were the King what would you do?"

"I would not have got into the position in the first place."

Haaken One Eye shook his head and laughed, "Olaf, you have no children and you are not a Saxon. There is not one thing about the King's position that you could possibly understand."

"There you are wrong! When the Dragonheart had his granddaughter taken he sailed after her. He went into the bowels of the earth to wrestle with a witch. He did not obey someone else and hope that his family would be safe! You are right I am not Saxon. I do not worship the White Christ. This blind faith makes for bad warriors. The Allfather helps those who help themselves. Until the Saxons have a leader who is willing to be as ruthless as we are then they will lose."

I smiled. The silence was almost oppressive. "You are quite right, Olaf. Tomorrow you can watch the horses while we go and speak with these Danes."

I saw the others hide their smiles, "I did not say I would not come! I will be there! But we cannot win!"

"True, so long as we do not lose then I am happy. Germund, you will have the horses saddled and ready by this gate. If events go against us I would not be trapped in this rat hole. We run to the coast." He nodded. He was reliable. "You will need to gather as much food and skins as you can find. And remember we may well have the two ladies with us. You and Sámr will have to watch them."

"It is good that we did not bring Atticus. We would have to watch him even more carefully." Haaken was right. Atticus would have slowed us down even more.

"Aðils, we shall need you and your bow tomorrow. I will be with the King. You will be the eyes in the back of my head. Haraldr and Sweyn, you watch out for Sámr and the two girls. If there is violence then leave my side and get those three to safety." I saw Sámr look up. "That is right, Sámr, you will be with the girls. If all goes well then we may not have to run."

He nodded, "But you believe things will go badly."

"I do."

Haaken nodded, "So it will be the Ulfheonar and the Hafþórrsson brothers who have to fight the Danes."

Bergil showed that he had been listening, "Aye, Haaken One Eye, but now we shall have mail and a helmet."

Haaken nodded, "But the Dragonheart hopes that we do not need to fight. I would like to see that!"

That night, as I curled up in the straw of the stables I wondered how I had got myself so far from home, fighting for Saxons against Danes! The Norns had spun well!

Chapter 5

We were awake before dawn. We ate well and prepared our weapons, mail, helmets and shields, as a poorly fastened strap could be disastrous. "Sámr and Germund, make sure we have water skins, ale skins and food on the horses. If we have to leave quickly it may take some time to reach the sea."

"Aye, Jarl Dragonheart. Be careful!"

"Always! I have a wedding to attend!"

We marched through the town. When we reached the hall, the King was there with his Eorledmen. I saw Oswald and his sons. They had with them a standard bearer and a warrior with a horn. The King was dressed in a polished mail hauberk with a leather jerkin beneath. He had a fine sword at his waist. His shield bearer carried his shield. His helmet was a little too ornate for my taste. It had a face mask but also a pair of small wings. In battle that would be a hazard for the King.

"Jarl, you and Oswald will walk with me."

"Aye." I nodded to my men. They all knew what was expected of them.

The King nodded to the warrior with the horn. He sounded it three times. The gates opened and we marched out to face the Danish horde. I recognise Ivar Wartooth and Einar Red Cloak. There were other shields I had seen on battlefields but I did not know the names of their owners. Only the Saxon hearthweru were mailed. Some only had a short vest made of mail while many had a short byrnie. The warriors to fear were the ones with the byrnies which reached down to the tops of their boots.

The King waited fifty paces from the gates while the Eorledmen and thegns with their oathsworn formed ranks. When they were gathered he had the horn sounded twice and marched forward. This time only the King, his personal guards and the Ulfheonar moved. A party detached themselves from the Danes. One was obviously a Saxon. I took that to be Æthelweard. I saw that he kept Einar Red Cloak between him and us. He was afraid. We moved together until ten paces separated us. Most of them were chiefs or jarls but there was one warrior who stood behind Einar Red Cloak. He did not look like a jarl. He looked like a killer. He had a shield on his back and a two-handed axe in his hand. I saw him grinning at me and I knew what was coming.

King Æthelstan spoke first. "Ivar Wartooth, I have called this truce because I no longer wish to fight you. Know that King Beorhtwulf of

Mercia kidnapped my daughter and held her hostage. I was forced to make war on you. Now we can be allies."

I had not met Ivar Wartooth before but I recognised him before he spoke. He had filed teeth and tattoos on his arms. From his pigtails hung bones. I suspected they were from animals but he would boast that they were men's. He had a long sword and a scale byrnie. His helmet had a pair of eyes made from some green stone above his own. He liked to intimidate his foes.

When he spoke he almost spat his words out, "That is very generous of you, King Æthelstan, but you shall not have the title long. Surrender to me now so that King Æthelweard can assume the throne. I promise that I will make the deaths of you and your eorledmen quick."

The King kept his voice remarkably calm. "Æthelweard, you were always a weasel. I see that you take shelter behind a Dane. Are you frightened of me?"

Æthelweard jabbed an accusing finger at the King. "And what of you? You shelter behind that pagan! You will rot in hell for that!"

I found it incongruous that the King was being accused of consorting with pagans when he had immersed himself in them.

"Ivar Wartooth, I would rather not fight this day. My daughter has been returned and I would celebrate. You do not want this half-man as your king. The Eorledmen and thegns will not follow him."

"Then they will all die." Silence fell. "So we fight?"

The silence seemed to grow. I could feel men fingering the weapons behind me. It was like a pile of dry kindling waiting for the first spark. When the spark struck the whole pyre would ignite

Einar Red Cloak stepped forward, "We have a champion here. Jarl Dragonheart has a special sword and prides himself on his skill. Let him fight my champion, Sigismund of Frisia."

This had all been arranged before the meeting. I could see that now for Ivar Wartooth smiled, "If your Viking can win for you then you may rule this land for me."

Æthelweard shouted, "But what about…"

"Silence! Your cousin is right, you are a weasel. Now keep quiet while real men talk." He stepped back. "What say you, Dragonheart?"

The King said, "But the Dragonheart is three times your champion's age."

The Danes said not a word. The two just looked at me. Sigismund took his axe and licked it. Blood came from his tongue. He was trying to frighten me. "You give your word, Ivar Wartooth?" I chose my next words carefully and I raised my voice so that all men could hear. "The Norns are spinning and the gods are watching."

"If you win then King Æthelstan keeps his throne. His men will all be spared."

"Then we fight."

The Danes formed a half circle and we formed the other half. Haaken said, quietly as I prepared, "He looks like a hard warrior."

I smiled, "Really, a champion who is a hard man? Who would have thought? Watch for treachery. You can always tell when a Dane is lying. His mouth is open!"

The King did not look happy. "I owe you much already. How can I repay this?"

"It is not you, it is the Norns. They have spun and I must fight."

"He looks bigger than you."

"He is and he is probably fitter and quicker. By rights, this should be a foregone conclusion and I will die but let us cast the bones and see what the Norns have planned for me."

Sigismund shouted, "Come, old man! I am anxious to use that magic sword of yours."

I hefted my shield and twirled my sword. I stepped towards him. He began whirling the axe around his head. He was using it one-handed. He was strong. The Danes began banging their shields to intimidate me. They failed. The Dane had an open helmet and I could see his eyes. He could only see my face mask. It was not much of an edge but I would take it. I was old. I could not lose the years but I could still move and I had my best weapon; my mind. I had not become fat as most men who grew old for the operation to take away the evil in me had made me lean. I felt fitter than I had ten years ago but he would not know that. He had seen my wispy white hair and seen the old gnarled hands. He thought he would defeat me.

His eyes gave him away. They widened and I knew that he would strike. As he swung, a mighty blow, I danced to my left and the axe hit the ground. I swung my sword at his back. I hit hard and although his byrnie held I had hurt him and weakened the mail links.

He roared in frustration, "Stand still you flea!"

I could have responded but I needed all my breath and concentration. He suddenly swung around. The axe was at chest height. I dropped to one knee with my shield above me and the axe thudded into the boss on my shield. I had a shield studded with metal and when his axe struck it jarred and stuck. I was close to him and, as I stood I stabbed him in the foot with my sword. It helped me get to my feet and, as he pulled his axe away I punched him in the mouth with the boss of my shield. He roared with pain and anger. Blood poured from his nose and his foot. I knew that the blow would have made his eyes water. As he stepped back I swung my sword at his left shoulder. This time the mail links did not hold. There was more movement in the mail around the arms and, if it wasn't maintained then it would weaken. He had not looked after his mail. I made his arm bleed.

The Danes had gone silent and I heard, from the Ulfheonar at first and then the Saxon lords, "Dragonheart! Dragonheart! Dragonheart! Dragonheart!"

I forced myself to look for the killing blow. The Frisian gave it to me. Throwing away his shield he grabbed the axe in both hands and ran at me swinging it in a figure of eight over his head. If he expected me to run he was mistaken. I dropped to one knee and held the shield over me. As the axe came down I rammed Ragnar's Spirit up under his byrnie. It entered his lower stomach and his momentum drove it deep within him. When the axe struck it was held by dying arms. It lacked power. His body collapsed on me and I heard a cheer. I pushed his body from me and stood.

Ivar Wartooth shouted, "Kill them all! Slaughter them!"

I was the one in the greatest danger for I stood over Sigismund's body and the Danes were closer to me. My men raced to protect me with their shields. I braced myself for the onslaught. It was the men with the red shields who came at me. I had been the one responsible for the deaths of so many of their shield brothers. I fended off one spear with my shield and a second with my sword. A third was wielded by a veteran. He stabbed at my leg and I felt the spear sink into my flesh. Then two axes scythed down as Olaf and Rolf Horse Killer chopped across two of the spearmen. The blood which spattered on the veteran made him glance away and I rammed my sword under his arm. I tore it out and was blood-spattered. He sank to his knees, dying. Bergil and his brothers were with Haaken on one side of me and as I glanced to the right I saw Haraldr and Sweyn. They had disobeyed me, "Haraldr and Sweyn, get to Sámr!"

I heard, "Aye Jarl!" and then the next men ran at us.

"Shields!" We pulled our shields around. They were not locked with each other but there was a wooden wall before us. Spears shattered against the shields which shook. I stabbed across my shield and my sword went into the cheek of a young Dane. He fell back. I saw Einar Red Cloak exhorting his men forward. Suddenly an arrow flew and found the centre of his face. He fell back and the wounding of their leader weakened the resolve of the Danes attacking us.

Bergil and his brothers, now wearing mail, suddenly roared and launched themselves forward. Rolf and Olaf swung their long axes in circles and the Danes fell back. I glanced over my shoulder and saw that the King's standard was down. "Clan of the Wolf, fall back to the King!" Bergil continued to hack and slash at the Danes. "Bergil! Obey me!" He stood stock still and then fell back with his brothers. We stepped back together. The Danes were warier now. They had seen their champion and Red Cloak fall. Even though their leader was not yet dead he was hurt. There were easier targets than the small band of Vikings who kept stepping backwards swinging their bloody and deadly weapons before them.

There were dead Danes behind us and it was difficult to maintain our line. I glanced down and saw the bodies of the standard bearer and the warrior with the horn. The King's shield bearer lay dead. Two of his housecarls supported the bloody body of the King who struggled to be free of them, "Let me die honourably!"

Oswald of Northwic and his sons appeared from behind. All around us was a savage battle as the Danes fought Eorledmen and thegns. The Saxons lacked numbers but not heart and they were holding them. Oswald shouted, "Take the King within the walls! The jarl's men are at the stables and they have horses." The two housecarls dragged the King away. I saw that he had been cut many times. Oswald and his sons squeezed next to me. Behind them were more thegns. Oswald smiled, "This will be my last fight, take my King back within the walls and to your home, Jarl. The Danes have won but I will have Ivar Wartooth before I die!"

I saw that the Danish leader was leading a wedge towards us. I nodded, "Ulfheonar, we join Oswald to charge and then fall back. Bergil, you and your brothers clear us a path back to the walls! Aðils cover us!"

We formed a wall and Oswald shouted, "For King Æthelstan!"

We all stepped forward together and the Danes charged at exactly the same time and when we met there was a clash which sounded like Thor's thunder. Spears shattered as they broke on our wall. We knew our business and the axes and swords of the five Ulfheonar were deadlier and more effective than the Danish spears and axes. As a spear shattered on my shield I stabbed at the Dane's thigh. When I felt bone, I twisted and the Dane screamed. I head-butted him and he fell to the ground. Haaken One Eye knew how to fight and with his empty orb terrified most enemies. The young Dane he faced seemed mesmerized and his spear just glanced off Haaken's helmet. I heard him laugh as he skewered the Dane, "There I have metal within and metal without!"

Rollo Thin Skin used his shield as an extension of his left arm. He punched with it as he slashed sideways with his sword. Spears rasped against his mail but as the men who wielded them were dying the blows failed to penetrate. It was Rolf and Olaf who caused the most damage and to add insult to injury they were using their Danish war axes better than the Danes.

We cleared a hole in their front line which allowed Oswald and his sons to face Ivar Wartooth. Oswald shouted, "Thank you, Jarl! Now save my King!" He and his sons launched themselves at Ivar Wartooth and his standard-bearer.

"Ulfheonar, fall back!"

We turned and allowed other thegns to pass into the space we had just occupied. I saw that the Saxons were surrounded. Bergil and his brothers, backed by Aðils were fighting with a handful of thegns to protect the backs of the men trying to get at Ivar Wartooth.

Olaf turned to Rolf, "Let us show these nithings how real men use an axe!"

"Aye!"

"Ulfheonar coming through!"

Bergil and his brothers parted. Aðils sent two arrows into the faces of the nearest Danes and then the swinging Danish axes began to sweep away the Danes like fallen leaves from a doorway. We had momentum and using my shield I joined Haaken as we ran at three Danes who had stepped away from the deadly axes. The edge had gone from my sword but the three Danes had no mail. I used Ragnar's Spirit like an iron bar. I heard the Dane's right arm break as the sword smashed across it. I punched hard with my shield at the middle one and then rammed the tip of my sword into the thigh of the one with the broken arm. He fell writhing to the ground and as he fell knocked another Dane to the side. Rollo slew him.

And then we were through. We had cleared a path and the gate lay just fifty paces from us. "Get inside!" I turned and saw the Danish standard fall but the Danes had now surrounded the Saxons. I heard the thegns and Eorledmen keening their death song. They were Christians but at the end, they were still warriors and knew how to die well.

We entered the gates and I shouted, "Close and bar them!"

The men who stood there had helmets, shields and swords. "But our lords!"

"Can you not hear their death song? This is over. Bar the gate and then flee through the north gate. Your lords are buying you time to escape. The Danes will be full of fury when they enter for they have lost their leaders."

He nodded.

I said, "Aðils, come with me. The rest of you get to the stables I will not be long." We hurried to the fighting platform as the Saxons placed everything they could behind the gates. I pointed to the battle. I could see Oswald and his sons. Around them were a handful of thegns. Even as I watched I saw Oswald slay Ivar Wartooth but then his two sons were slain by Danes. They died protecting their father's back. Oswald lifted Wartooth's skull. Just at that moment, Einar Red Cloak, his face bathed in blood from the first arrow, thrust his spear through the brave Saxon. "Kill him!"

Aðils pulled back on the bow and then released. Just as Einar raised his spear in celebration Aðils' arrow struck him in the chest and knocked him from his feet. This time he would not rise!

"Now we go."

The north gate was open and the people were fleeing. I wondered how many would make it. We had done all that we could. When we reached the stables, I saw that my men ringed someone lying on the ground. They parted for me and I saw that it was the King and his daughter held his hand. There was a widening pool of blood. He smiled, "I have hung on until you came. My enemies have done for me. Thank you for what you did. Ivar is faithless but you knew that anyway. Care for my daughter. I give her to you." He pointed a finger at the housecarls, "Harold and Edward, I release you from your oath. Find a life! Æthelflæd, I am sorry I…"

And then he died. She prostrated herself on his body.

"We have no time. Sámr, put her on a horse. The rest of you mount." I pointed to the spare horses, "You have served your lord well. Take the horses and live."

"Aye jarl. We will go to Northumbria. There are kin there."

"Aðils, fire the stables. I would not have the King's body be despoiled and it will slow the pursuit."

Even as I mounted, painfully for the wound in my leg had not been tended, I heard the battering of axes on the south gate. Soon the Danes would enter. Any who had not escaped now would not be able to soon. Sámr was watching Æthelflæd, but Germund was watching me. He saw blood dripping from my wound. "Jarl, you are wounded!"

"It is nothing and it will not kill me. If we stay here then we may well die! We ride!"

I heard the whoosh as the flames caught and Aðils rushed out leading his horse, "Hurry, Jarl, this will burn fiercely!"

Sámr and Germund had led the two ladies through the gates and so we dug our heels into our horses. We were the only horsemen save for Harold and Edward. The rest were those on foot. They were taking just what they could carry on their backs. As I glanced back I saw that the wind was taking the fire south. It would delay the Danes. It was sad but the Kingdom of the East Angles was gone. Their nobles and their king lay dead. The puppet who would be placed on the throne would have none to rule. This was the start of the Danish kingdom in the east.

The road led north and we followed it. The Danes were to the south and soon would be in the east. In many ways, the safest route home would be across the debated border between Northumbria and Mercia but that would leave my ship stranded and there was no guarantee we would make it home. I caught up with Haraldr and Sweyn, "Why did you disobey me?"

They hung their heads in shame. Haraldr said, "It was the blood of battle, jarl. We saw you and the others in need of help."

I nodded, "That may be the right thing for another to do but you are Clan of the Wolf! Do penance by riding at the rear. Keep us safe. Aðils, ride with me."

"We will."

Passing Bergil and his brothers I said, "Stay at the back with Haraldr. If we are followed then let me know." I made my way through the others until I reached Olaf at the fore. He glanced down and saw the blood dripping from my leg. "I know but the blood has slowed. When we stop then Haaken can repair it. We have more pressing problems. The short way to Gippeswic is due east and south but the Danes will be there. After what we did to them they will be out for vengeance."

Aðils said, "Then why not head north and east to Lothuwistoft? It is a port and we may be able to steal some boats. Even if that fails it will be safer travelling south."

He was right. "Ride ahead and find the road which heads east. We will stop at noon."

Olaf had taken a cloth from his tunic. He handed it to me. "If you will not stop then at least tie this around the top of your leg to slow the bleeding. If a young warrior behaved as you, Dragonheart, you would have him on night watch for a month!"

As I tied the cloth tightly about my leg I smiled, "Then as that is one of the few benefits of being jarl I will take it!"

"You were lucky, you know. That Frisian was a powerful man."

"If you had been wielding the axe then I would now be dead but I saw weakness. He was a show-off. He tried to impress his masters and he saw an old man. Would you have fought me one-handed?"

He laughed, "Of course not. I would have shortened my grip and used the blade to hook your shield. It does not look as elegant or heroic as swinging an axe but it gets the job done."

"And that is why I knew that I would win. And Wartooth was punished for breaking the oath. Oswald killed him."

"Then it is *wyrd*!"

The road we rode was a Roman one and at every milepost I loosened the tourniquet and then tightened it. Olaf had been right. The loss of blood had made me feel light-headed. Most of the people were heading for a small settlement called Theodford. It was a crossing for the river. Aðils rode back as we approached it. "There is a road east. It passes through Watlingsete. The people there will not hinder us."

"But the bridge?"

"Possibly."

"Then, Olaf, we ride hard across the bridge and keep it safe for the others."

"I like not fighting from a horse, jarl."

"And you will not need to. The sight of our horses with us on their backs should be enough to scatter them. We will rest there and water the horses. If the Danes follow us then this will be a good place to hold them. The ladies have ridden far enough!"

My men galloped off. I dug my heels in to make my horse go faster. Sámr and Germund took the ladies' reins and match my speed. The four had been silent since the death of the King. Sámr was sensitive enough to know that there was little he could say. He just had to be there ready for when she did speak. I heard the thunder of hooves on the wooden bridge ahead. I could not see my men because of the huts on this side of the river. I heard no clash of steel. They had driven them hence. Our ride had outrun the refugees from the battle but soon they would follow us.

We stopped on the far side of the bridge and dismounted. Haraldr, Sweyn, Bergil and his brothers took the horses to be watered. Sámr and Germund found an empty hut and took the ladies inside. Rollo and Rolf took out the food we had brought.

Haaken said, "Sit and let me see that leg."

When we cut open my breeks we saw that it was a long and deep cut. "We need to seal it with heat or sew it."

"We have no time to light a fire. Sew it."

"Aye."

Olaf poured vinegar on the wound as Haaken prepared the needle and gut. The vinegar stung and hurt. That was a good thing. It cleansed the wound. Then Olaf smeared honey all over the cut. It slowed the bleeding and would heal the cut. When Haaken began to stitch I gripped the pommel of Ragnar's Spirit. That always helped. Even so, the loss of blood made me feel light headed. I forced myself to stare at the bridge and study it. By the time he had finished Rollo and Rolf brought over food and ale.

"We have found some fresh bread too, Jarl." He handed me a large piece.

"Have the ladies eaten?"

He smiled, "All have eaten, Jarl, except for the wounded! Eat!"

Aðils had been watching the road from the far end of the bridge, "Some of the Saxons are approaching."

"Let them across. We had better get ready to move."

Olaf said, "The horses need a little more rest, Jarl."

I nodded absentmindedly as I could see that the refugees were running now. More, they were leaving the road. "Get your weapons!"

Just then Aðils shouted, "Danes on horses."

"Get your bow. The rest, with me. We make a shield wall at the end of the bridge." I grabbed my shield and donned my helmet. As soon as I put weight on my leg it hurt. There were stitches in it.

"You should stay here, Jarl."

"And let others bleed for me? Come. We cannot ride off for they would dog our tail. We need to hurt them and make them fear us. How many can you see, Aðils?"

"No more than thirty."

Haaken said, "That makes sense. They would not have more horses than that."

"Then we need to kill half of the warriors. How many arrows do you have, Aðils?"

"Fifteen."

"Then use them well."

I could now see that the Danes were using their swords to clear the road of those Saxons too tardy to move. My sword needed sharpening and I felt weary but a real warrior would fight with a stick and two broken legs if he had to. We formed two ranks and I saw that Haraldr had found some spears. They poked over the top of our shoulders. What I did not know was what the enemy would do. There were three possible choices. They could dismount and send for more men. They could dismount and advance to fight us or they could use their horses to charge us. I did not want the first two options and so I stepped forward and shouted, "I am Jarl Dragonheart and I do not fear faithless warriors who follow a foresworn leader. Ivar Wartooth broke his oath. You are not men, you are nithings!"

I stepped back between Olaf and Haaken. Aðils stood on the bridge's parapet. They had been a hundred and twenty paces from us when I had shouted and Aðils could have sent arrows in their direction but he wanted to make certain that every arrow counted. When they were ninety paces he sent three arrows in rapid succession. All found men. As one Dane fell he kept hold of the reins in his dying hand. He dragged his horse's head down and it brought down the next three riders. Already they were in disarray but that merely made them angrier and they roared as they charged us. Danes do not ride well and they certainly do not fight well on horseback. Rolf and Olaf stepped forward and both swung the axes in unison. The two double-handed axes covered the width of the bridge and when three horses baulked the riders were thrown from the saddle. One hit the parapet and there was a sickening crunch as his head was crushed. Haaken and I stepped forward and slew the two fallen Danes.

Aðils now had his rhythm. His arrows found flesh for the Saami bow could penetrate mail at ranges of less than eighty paces. Behind me, I heard Bergil shout, "Let us at them, Jarl! We can slaughter them!"

Olaf snorted, "Do not let that mail go to your head. The Jarl is right to let them bleed. They cannot hurt us and Aðils Shape Shifter can thin their ranks."

When Aðils sent his last arrow into a Danish skull there were just eight riders left. They retired out of arrow range and then conferred. Four of them rode off. I turned to Bergil, "Now you may have your wish. Take the horses of the dead Danes and go with Haraldr and Sweyn. Kill them or make them flee!"

The five of them ran to grab the reins of the dazed horses. They mounted them and set off after the four Danes who remained. The four Danes made the mistake of procrastinating. They could have run or they could have charged. They did neither until it was too late. As they turned to flee, for they heard the rage in my five men as they charged, my warriors' horses had gained speed and were almost upon them. I turned and went to the hut where Sámr and Germund waited in the doorway.

"How are the ladies?"

"What do you think, great grandfather? Æthelflæd has lost her father and Nanna her uncle."

"I meant are they ready to ride? We have a long journey ahead of us and I rely on you two to let me know if they need a rest."

"I am sorry. I forgot that you have much on your mind and you are wounded."

"It is nothing. We will ride when Bergil and the others return. This will not be easy, Sámr. We are alone in this land and every man, Saxon and Dane will turn their hand against us. Until we see Whale Island we are in danger."

When my men returned leading four horses then I knew we would not be followed. Of course, they could easily work out our destination but we had the initiative and it was up to me to keep one step ahead of the Danes. The Norns had spun an incredibly complicated web. When I had sat on the top of Old Olaf I could not have envisaged where the path would lead. Had I done wrong by bringing Sámr? I knew why I had brought him; I wanted him to learn to lead. If he lay dead with a Danish Axe in his body then he could not lead.

Part Two
The Long Road Home

Chapter 6

By the time we reached Watlingsete, the girls could go no further. Their thighs, unused to the saddle, were rubbed red raw and Nanna was in tears. We were lucky in that the villagers who lived there were Saxons and when Æthelflæd told them who she was they were happy to share information with us. There were no Danes between us and the sea. Like Gippeswic the port was a burgh and walled. The people inside would be suspicious. As we sat around a campfire eating a simple stew the villagers had made I explained to Æthelflæd the precarious nature of our position. I used a piece of kindling to draw a crude map in the soil.

"We are here. My ship is there. We could go across country but the Danes will have a net spread wide to catch us. They may think we head north. The town where Oswald hailed from, Northwic, lies there. Instead, we go east to Lothuwistoft. I am going to try to get a ship and sail to Gippeswic. We will need you to help us gain access to the town."

She did not cry but tears rolled down her cheeks. "I know not if I can do that. I did not think that my father would die."

"Nor did any of us but sometimes the sisters spin and we end up with a situation we do not like."

"Sisters?"

Sámr said, "Remember, Æthelflæd, the Norns about which I spoke."

"It is heresy to speak of them!"

I put my arm around her tiny shoulders, "Had I not come for you then you would still be in the fort on the Blue River. You would only know of your father's death when Beorhtwulf sent men to marry you off to one of his Eorledmen."

She looked genuinely shocked. "He would not do that."

"Your father believed so. It was one of the many reasons he wished you to marry Sámr; that and the fact that you were meant to be together. Be strong. I have good men around me. I believe we will reach my ship."

"And then we will be safe?"

"I will not speak an untruth; I do not know. We take one step at a time." I handed her some salve in a jar. We used it for the new rowers. It eased the pain and redness when they rowed in the salt water. "Rub this on the parts which cause you pain for we ride before dawn."

The extra horses we had captured had helped us. With less than twenty-five miles to go, I believed we would make Lothuwistoft. I was just uncertain where we went from there. Once again we rose early. We needed to move quickly towards Lothuwistoft. I had raided the port many years earlier but I could not remember much save that they had a quay and wall around the houses. This time we would not be fighting our way in, we would be talking our way in.

We made the twenty odd miles in half a day. It would have been faster with just warriors but Æthelflæd and Nanna had slowed us down. It was not their fault. We were warriors. We had done this before. We were seen before we reached the walls and, at the sight of our armour and shields, the gates were slammed shut. Sámr looked the least warlike of us and he rode, bareheaded and with open hands, towards the walls. Æthelflæd and Nanna rode just behind him. This would be a test of the Saxons' state of mind. I hoped that they would not wish to antagonise Danes. It was hard for Saxons to differentiate between us.

Olaf said, gloomily, "And if they do not allow us in what then?"

"We ride all afternoon and into the evening until we reach Gippeswic."

"The young women will not make it. They have done well enough but I do not think they can go further."

Germund said, "Olaf Leather Neck is right, Jarl. The only way they could ride would mean not sitting astride and they would fall off."

Haaken laughed, "Then if they will not help us we shall take the town and make them!"

I saw that the Saxons were talking with Sámr. His body was not riddled with arrows but it was taking some time to persuade them. We could see the sea and I saw that it was high tide. I realised that even if they did allow us we would probably have to wait until the next tide to head south and that would mean travelling at night.

After what seemed a lifetime the gates began to open and Sámr waved us forward. As I approached him he looked pleased with himself. "You look smug. Why?"

"Not only have I got us inside the town walls I have us a ship to take us south."

I was impressed. "How did you manage that?"

"I promised them coin before we sailed."

"Coins?"

As we rode through the gates he said, "And the horses we ride. We will give them the coins we took from the Danes who ambushed us. It is worth it is it not?"

His face looked crestfallen and I realised that I had sounded like Olaf Leather Neck. I smiled, "You have done more than well. This way I do not need to worry about finding a navigator."

I found that the horses and the coin also bought us a hot meal and ale. The ship was prepared for us. It was a large fishing ship. Most fishing ships were simple affairs with a crew of four or so. This one was just a little smaller than a knarr. The captain, Ethelbert, told me that they sailed far into the ocean to fish. Sometimes they stayed out for two or three days. They were able to make larger catches. The captain was resourceful. We left in the early evening as the sun was setting in the east. The wind was not in our favour and lacking oars we had to tack back and forth. It took until dawn to reach Gippeswic. The younger warriors, the ladies and my great-grandson all slept but the Ulfheonar and I watched. The Danes had drekar. Admittedly most were on the Tamese but a rider could have reached there. We knew that there were many Danish drekar in Cent and on the Tamese. How much would they want Jarl Dragonheart?

The captain had made as much from this one voyage as from a whole week of fishing. It was no wonder he looked pleased as we tied up next to my drekar. We had had no trouble and by nightfall, he would be home. While my men boarded our drekar and Erik prepared for sea I went with Æthelflæd, Nanna and Sámr. Oswald of Northwic had been the Eorledman. They needed to know that their King and Eorledman had lost. I spoke with the thegn who ruled the town while Æthelflæd and Nanna spoke with Oswald's wife. I had the easier task.

The thegn was philosophical, "If we have a King who is supported by the Danes then we can go on as we have done for centuries. Life here is quiet. The men fish and they farm. Eorledman Oswald was happy to have this as his domain. He had tired of war." He gave me a sad smile, "We Saxons are not like you Danes and Norse. We do not enjoy war. We can make war and we can fight but your people enjoy war and that is why you will win. It will remain that way until we have a Saxon King who can fight the way that you do."

"And that can never be while you worship the White Christ."

"Perhaps. The old warriors have told me of the code that warriors fought by. We have lost that and we have lost our freedom." He tapped his head, "In here we can remain free."

"Good luck!"

"I wish to thank you, Jarl Dragonheart. When your ship came I feared the worst but Oswald had heard good things of you. He said you were a hard warrior but one with a sense of honour. Your attempt to save the King speaks well of you. Your men all behaved well. They paid for all that they needed. When others speak harshly of Vikings the men of Gippeswic know that there is one clan which is to be admired."

As we set sail in the early afternoon I felt sad. I had fought Saxons foremost of my life and yet I was part Saxon. I now knew that the Saxons were not my enemies. I had Norse enemies, Danish enemies, Hibernian enemies and Saxon enemies. It was not the people I fought it was their leaders. It was the ones like Ivar Wartooth who sought power. I had never sought power. I wanted peace for my land. That would be my legacy to those that followed me. They would have a land which they could defend.

The winds did not help us but we had oars and most of the crew had sat doing nothing for days. They rowed and they sang. With the battle against the Frisian still fresh in their minds, my Ulfheonar chose the most appropriate chant.

> *The Dragonheart looked old and grey.*
> *He fought a champion that cold wet day.*
> *A mountain of a man without a hair*
> *Like a giant Norse snow bear*
> *Knocked to the ground by Viking skill*
> *The Saxon stood and struck a blow to kill*
> *Saxon champion, taking heads*
> *Ragnar's Spirit fighting back*
> *Saxon champion, taking heads*
> *Ragnar's Spirit fighting back*
> *Old and grey and cunning yet,*
> *The Dragonheart his sword did wet*
> *With Ragnar's Spirit sharp and bright*
> *He sliced it down through shining light*

Through mail and vest it ripped and tore
The Saxon Champion, champion no more.
As he sank to the bloody ground
Dragonheart's blade whirled around
Sigeberht's head flew through the air
Dragonheart triumphant there
Saxon champion, taking heads
Ragnar's Spirit fighting back
Saxon champion, taking heads
Ragnar's Spirit fighting back

Erik took us well out to sea so that when we rounded the coast of Cent we could pick up winds from the south and save the oarsmen. It would also keep us far from the Danish ships which would be hunting **'Heart of the Dragon'**.

Erik had left the barrel cabin in place but made it more secure by using large wooden nails to hold it in place. Sven Ship Sealer had lived up to his name and used pine tar to make certain that the barrel was watertight. The voyage home might take a whole moon or more. Atticus had made the interior cosier with furs and sheepskins. He was thoughtful. He fussed over the two Saxons and Sámr. When he discovered my wound then he berated me much as a mother would a child who had misbehaved. He glared at Haaken One Eye.

"Let me see the wound! Haaken One Eye can tell a good tale but as a healer, he leaves much to be desired."

Haaken feigned outrage, "Just for that you shall not be in my saga about the rescue of the princess."

"And for that, I am profoundly grateful."

When he saw the wound all jests and banter went for there was a smell. "Jarl this is putrefying."

Haaken looked shocked, "But I used honey and vinegar."

Atticus sniffed the wound, "It has gone bad. Did you ensure that all the material from the breeks was removed?"

Haaken looked confused, "It was material! That cannot hurt!"

Atticus nodded, "Then I know the cause of the poison. The question is can I heal it?" We were far out to sea and surrounded by hostile enemies. I saw Atticus weighing up what to do.

"Could you take the leg?"

"I could but there is no guarantee that would work and I would have to cut so high that I would risk having you bleed to death. No, I shall cut it open. We need a fire."

I saw the look of despair on Erik's face. Fire was the enemy of all ships. He did not object for I knew that he would risk anything to save my life. Instead, he said, "Arne, Beorn, fetch as many pails of sea water as you can. Find as many empty barrels and fill them too."

Atticus said, "Fear not, Captain. I am not Haaken the Clumsy. I will light the fire in a pot. That way it will be hotter. When we have finished with it we will cast it overboard. Your ship will be safe."

Haaken felt guilty about his botched surgery. He brought me the ale skin, "Here Jarl, you will need a drink if this Greek butcher is going to hack at you!"

I saw that Atticus was unbothered by the comments and I drank. "What will you do, Atticus?"

"Open the wound, drain the pus and see if I can find fibres from the cloth. If I am able to then when I burn and seal the wound it will heal well. If we had maggots then they would perform the same function. I confess that this will hurt."

"My life has been a series of hurts, Atticus."

"Then I will do my best to be as painless as I can," he said gently.

I saw Æthelflæd, Nanna and Sámr. They had come to watch. I smiled, "A rarity, entertainment while we sail for you to watch. Here will be a tale to tell your children."

Half of the crew were rowing and the rest were gathered around the mast watching too. The veterans knew that this could be them someday and the pain might be lessened if they saw another endure it. It took time to get the fire hot enough. While he was waiting Atticus prepared the thin, sharp bone knives and tweezers he would use. A pot of water sat on top of the fire pot. It helped to increase the heat of the fire. When the water was bubbling he took it from the fire and dropped in his instruments saving one pair to pick out that which he would need.

"I am almost ready. Lie back. Haaken and Germund, hold his shoulders. Sámr, sit on his feet."

"You have no need I shall not move."

"If the blade slips then I might cut an artery and then you would be dead. Germund, Haaken, hold his shoulders." There was authority in the Greek's voice.

I looked up at the sky above me; clouds were scudding by. We were too far out to sea for the gulls and I missed the call of the dead. I was not afraid of the pain but I did not like not being able to see what was happening. This was preferable to the last time I was cut open when I had entered the dream world. Here I felt as though I had some control. I felt a prick as the sharpened blade began to cut the stitches. I heard a gasp from above me. That was not Atticus that would be one of the I. My men had seen flesh torn open before now. I felt something warm slipping down my leg. Atticus' fingers were soft and gentle and yet when he squeezed the wound I felt a sharp pain and despite myself found my legs trying to move.

Atticus grunted, "And that is why you hold the Dragonheart. Sven Ship Sealer, pour some vinegar over the wound. Try to wash it out."

The pain from the vinegar was excruciating but I gritted my teeth and did not move. I felt something moving inside my leg. It felt like an insect!

"Ah, ah, there it is." Atticus' face appeared above me and he held a pair of bone tweezers. There was a bloody strand there. "That is what Haaken One Eye missed. I will continue to search. I do not want to do this twice." The insect moved in my leg again. "Now we can heal. Vinegar and then, Sven Ship Sealer, be ready to hand me a brand from the fire."

I knew that this would be painful. Atticus seemed to take an age. I was anticipating the fire but he did not ask for it. "Get on with it, Greek! I have laid here long enough!"

"Unlike Haaken I am trying to make the wound as neat as I can. I am folding the flap of skin back over. You will have a scar but I would make it as neat as I can!"

"Just get on with it! I am too old to worry about scars."

"As you wish. Sven!"

In a flash of searing pain, he applied the flame. My back arched involuntarily. There was a smell of burning hair and flesh. I heard a little scream from Nanna and that somehow made the pain lessen.

"Good. It is done." Atticus came and lifted my head. He poured some ale from a horn down my throat. I needed it. It was honeyed. "Now lie back and sleep. I have put something in the ale to make you sleep. Sleep is nature's way of healing. I do not want you moving about."

I was going to object but I could not keep my eyes open and I slept. It was dark by the time I awoke and there was no sound of oars. All that I could hear was the creak of the ropes and the occasional snap of the sail. I tried to move and I heard Atticus above me. "I will help you up. I wish you to keep your weight from your leg." His hands came under my arms and I put my weight on my good leg.

"I need to make water."

"That is a good sign. Use me as a crutch. I will take you to the leeward side."

I saw that the crew were asleep and Arne Eriksson was at the steering board. He smiled as I passed him. I did not like the hopping motion I had to adopt. After I had made water Atticus led me to the steering board where someone had cut a small barrel in half. "Here is your seat. We thought you would want to be by the steering board. I will fetch you some food and ale and then I will sleep. Sven Ship Sealer will act as your servant until I wake. You are under orders not to move from here without help!"

"Whose orders?"

He smiled, "The crew have appointed me as your captain until you are healed. I have gone some way to repay you for saving my life. It is early days yet but had I not operated when I did then you would have died."

"From a little cut like that? I have endured far worse and lived!"

He shook his head, "In the east, they use expensive fine silks beneath their clothes. They are clean. Your breeks were filthy. I doubt they had ever been washed."

"They are for fighting!"

"Nonetheless they nearly killed you. The other wounds you suffered had no foreign material in them. You healed. This is a lesson, Jarl Dragonheart. We threw away your dirty clothes with the fire in the pot. You have clean ones on now. When we reach your home, we will have more clothes made for you and you will wear clean clothes each time you go to battle."

"It is a waste!"

"It would be a bigger waste to lose the jarl who holds this clan together." He lowered his voice. "Is Ragnar ready to take over the clan?"

I spoke quietly, "I am not certain he ever will be and before you ask nor will Gruffyd. Sámr is my heir."

"And he is young and not ready yet. We have to keep you alive, Jarl, despite yourself."

I watched him walk unsteadily through the sleeping rowers to the prow. Sven Ship Sealer brought me my food and ale. Erik's son, at the steering board, said, "He has not moved from your side. Each time you stirred he pounced to ensure that you were not distressed. Such devotion is touching Jarl. And he is right, the crew said that he will determine when you are able to rise."

"We will see about that. Where are we now?"

The Tamese is astern of us. After talking with Olaf and Haaken my father feared that the Danes might send ships after us. He wanted sea room and so we are using this wind to take us well south of the coast. We will head due west when dawn comes. We hope to lose the Danes in the vastness of the sea."

As I devoured the food and ale I wondered at that. Men could plan and plot but the Norns' threads and webs could ruin those plans. Until we saw Whale Island then we would be in constant danger. I would follow Atticus' advice but if trouble came then bad leg or not I would be on my feet and I would be fighting.

When dawn came it was a grey and overcast day. The seas were livelier than they had been. I was already unhappy about being forced to sit at the stern but I would do so until I was needed. My leg ached and when I had risen to make water I had made the mistake of putting my weight upon it. I sent Sven for a spear and I used that as a staff. It was easier.

Erik took over at dawn and he said, "The wind is from the north and west, Jarl. It will add time to the journey but I will continue to use it and head south and west. It will be safer than heading due west for there may be Danes there and we cannot keep the men rowing."

"We have enough supplies?"

"We bought from the people of Gippeswic and we can use rainwater. That is one advantage of these northern seas. You can guarantee rain!"

"Just so long as we get home. They will be concerned about our extended voyage."

He shook his head, "Kara, Ylva and Aiden will have dreamed. They know you are not in the spirit world. So long as Jarl Dragonheart is alive then there is hope. They will not be overly concerned."

It took two days for the winds to turn in our favour. We had a lively two days of gusty winds, troughs and crests. When we did turn Erik determined that we were too far south. If we had just turned west we would have risked Syllingar and no one wanted that. He headed north and west for Wihtwara. Since Egbert's death, Wessex was not the threat it had been. We had seen not a ship nor a bird since we had left Gippeswic and it was as though we were alone on the sea.

Atticus decided that I could walk about the deck. I had done that before while he was asleep. At first, it had been hard but, as we headed north-west I was able to discard the spear and I could limp about the ship. That enabled me to speak with the crew. The young warriors who had left the Land of the Wolf had grown. We had lost not a man. Their only battle had been with the men at the fort but they had acquitted themselves well. It boded well for the future. The mail won by the Hafþórrsson brothers had made them all eager for such treasure. While the Ulfheonar and those who had gone ashore were keen to get home the majority of the crew hoped for more opportunities to gain glory, riches and mail.

I wondered, later, if their wishes had reached the ears of Odin for, as we headed north and west he sent a storm to test Erik's skill as a mariner and the craft of Bolli her shipwright who had built her. We had to reef the sail and the crewman the oars as we were tossed from one crest into a trough so deep that the Saxons thought the sea would swallow us! Their little nest at the bow proved to be priceless for within they were safe. Atticus took shelter there too.

Sámr showed how much he had grown for he took an oar. He was now much stronger. Not yet a fully-grown man he was becoming one. I was the only one who did not have to row and I stood gripping the steering board with Erik and his son Arne Eriksson. It lasted an afternoon, a night and part of a morning. The reefed sail was damaged and there were severed stays and sheets. As the wind abated we hove too with a sea anchor and while the rowers ate the ship's boys and Erik's crew began their repairs. The sail had to be stitched. In a perfect world, we would have replaced it but the spare was in the hold. It was late afternoon by the time we were able to continue north and west. The scudding clouds and our erratic course meant that Erik was uncertain as to our exact position. We sailed all night under reefed sails. We passed the wreckage of ships which had not been as soundly built as ours.

As dawn broke we saw the thin grey line that was Wihtwara and then Lars Longsight shouted from the masthead, "Danish drekar ahead, five of them!"

The Danes had been clever. They had not chased us. They had allowed the storm to bring us to them. We now had to work out how to get by five Danish drekar!

Chapter 7

"Arm yourselves! This day we fight!"

Erik said, "They have been waiting for us. They have spread out so that, even with the wind behind, they can cut us off."

I stroked my beard, "They do not know me and they do not know you."

"Everyone knows of the Dragonheart."

"But not as a sailor. They see me as old. What if I was nervous and you were a young frightened captain? What would we do?"

Erik had sailed with me for many years and we understood each other. He nodded, "We might try to sail south."

"And they would close with us and cut us off."

"Then we would try north."

"What would a young frightened captain with an old jarl who had lived too long do next when the four foxes were surrounding the helpless duck?"

"He would run out the oars and try to outrun them."

"Then that is what we do except that we want them as close to us as we can." While the crew armed we worked out how to escape this most deadly of traps.

As the crew waited and the five Danes closed with us Erik shouted, "Take in a reef. Arne, I want us sloppy! Make them think we are panicking."

His son had listened to our discussion and shouted, "Aye, father, we will pretend to be Saxon!"

"Prepare to come about!" Normally we made gentle manoeuvres for savage ones lost you speed. He put the steering board hard over and we lost speed as he headed south.

Lars Longsight shouted, "They have changed course. They are attempting to cut us off."

We sailed that course until the five Danes, with furled sails could be seen more clearly. They began to spread in a line to stop our escape.

"Prepare to come about!" Erik put the steering board the opposite way and we almost stopped.

As we began to move again, I shouted, "Ready with oars!"

"They are matching us, Captain. They are closing with us for they have raised their sails now."

"Where is the largest gap, Lars?"

"Between the second and third ships from the north."

We sailed that course until the Danes were just half a mile away, "To your oars! Lower the sail! Prepare to come about!"

The savage manoeuvre caught out a couple of men. Einar Red Nose fell against the mast fish. We turned so that we faced the wind. We effectively stopped. "Steerboard row, larboard backwater!" Even as the Danes flocked to surround the seemingly helpless ship we turned on a silver penny. As soon as we had the wind we leapt forward.

"Now row as though your lives depended upon it!" My words acted as a spur and our men rowed as one. Haaken chose a fast chant.

> ***The Angry Cubs and the Wolf Killers Bears***
> ***Sailed together, through dangers shared***
> ***Through battles hard against their foes***
> ***They forged a link, a bond which grows***
> ***Cubs and bears forged from steel***
> ***Cubs and bears to no man kneel***
> ***When Egbert came they held their walls***
> ***When others fled they still stood tall***
> ***With Ironshirt and Wolf's blood***
> ***They drove the Saxons through the wood***
> ***Cubs and bears forged from steel***
> ***Cubs and bears to no man kneel***
> ***And now they sail, brothers in arms***
> ***Protected by the volva's charms***
> ***Cubs and bears forged from steel***
> ***Cubs and bears to no man kneel***
> ***Cubs and bears forged from steel***
> ***Cubs and bears to no man kneel***

We had tricked them. Our confused manoeuvres had made them think that we had lost our wits and now we would turn with the wind behind, men at our oars and the Danes packed together to destroy us. Using the wind Erik headed north-west towards the second and third Danish drekar. The second drekar had a red-painted dragon. It was old paint for it looked browner than red. They had every man at their oars and no sail. Even as we watched the one to the north tried to turn and her oars clashed with the second one. We were approaching each other rapidly. The five Danes had to watch out for each other. Already two of their drekar had slowed because of the collision of oars. Erik was heading towards the gap. The captain of the third drekar, I saw it had a black dragon at the prow, turned to cut us off. The gap which had been there was closing.

Erik was quick thinking. "In oars!"

The wind's speed was such that we hardly slowed and the Danes were moving quickly. They were trying to close the gap and use the power of their oars. The red dragon ship was being pushed towards the black dragon ship.

"Brace!"

Our keel smashed through the oars of the two drekar. I saw, from my vantage point at the stern, broken oars spearing men. Others were struck in the head and felled. We were so close to the red dragon ship that I saw that the red dragon at her prow had a skull for a head. An archer who was attempting to loose at us was knocked from his feet and he fell below the turning dragon ship's prow. I looked astern and he did not rise. And then we were through.

"Now row!"

The Angry Cubs and the Wolf Killers Bears
Sailed together, through dangers shared
Through battles hard against their foes
They forged a link, a bond which grows
Cubs and bears forged from steel
Cubs and bears to no man kneel
When Egbert came they held their walls
When others fled they still stood tall
With Ironshirt and Wolf's blood
They drove the Saxons through the wood
Cubs and bears forged from steel
Cubs and bears to no man kneel
And now they sail, brothers in arms
Protected by the volva's charms
Cubs and bears forged from steel
Cubs and bears to no man kneel

Cubs and bears forged from steel
Cubs and bears to no man kneel

The Danes to the south were undamaged and they were able to turn but it took time and we had the wind and oars. We headed north-west for that would mean they had further to come if they were to catch us. The other three drekar would follow but all three had lost rowers. We now had to lose the other two.

Atticus, Sámr, Germund and the Saxons came down to the steering board.

"It is safer in the prow."

"Great grandfather, we are safer here! You have beaten them!"

"Not yet!"

Atticus frowned, "I fear you have made a mistake, Jarl Dragonheart! That is the island they call Wihtwara ahead. We will be trapped!"

"Not so, Greek. You might know your way around a body but Erik and I know our way around this island. There is a narrow passage between the island and Hamwic. They risk colliding unless they sail in line astern. The wind will help us and we can sail through the passage between the island and the mainland. We hope to build a lead and lose them by dark."

"That is many hours away!"

"And as soon as we clear the island we rest half of the crew. We will see who the real men are, us or the Danes!" Atticus was clever enough to work it out and he smiled. "Now you five can help by taking ale and water to the rowers."

To those who did not know it, and I suspected that would be the Danish captains, it looked like a trap. The waters narrowed. We had raided Hamwic and the island. Erik knew the waters but Sven Ship Sealer was at the prow and he would shout when he saw the deadly white-capped water which marked rocks and shoals. Travelling at this speed, it would take a moment's misjudgement and then it would be a disaster. The gap looked narrow but we had sailed these waters and knew that with a wind from the east a drekar could take advantage of the channel to cut off a large area of sea.

"Rest half the rowers! Drink, eat and find bows! This will be a long chase!"

I turned to look at the drekar following us. One had a serpent prow. That was the ship which was leading. The one behind had a dragon with a skull for a face. Both were the larger of the five drekar. The other three would still follow but they had lost crew, way and were smaller. They could hurt us if some disaster befell us and that was not out of the question. We had An Lysardh and Om Walum to pass. If they were still with us then the Sabrina and its precocious tide could catch a ship unawares. I was under no illusions. The Danes had ambushed us and done it well. There was little point in brooding about it. The only way we could have avoided them would have been to sail further south and that would have risked Syllingar. This was unavoidable. The Norns had seen to that.

Now that we had halved our rowers the two Danes began to catch us. That was to be expected but when we changed rowers we would maintain our speed. The Danes would lose speed. My worry was that they had more ships at the western end of the channel. That could prove disastrous.

We cleared the channel and found open water a couple of hours before dusk. We had changed rowers twice. The nearest Dane had crept to within three lengths of us but then began to lose way as a new set of rowers powered on.

"Do we lose them after dark?"

"Can you lose them, Erik Short Toe?"

"I can try but these are no fools. That trick we pulled did not hurt them as much as we hoped. I will keep close to the coast. If they try to use the wind to get ahead of us then they risk Syllingar and inshore is treacherous. I will sail as close as I dare to Karrek Loos yn Koos. Perhaps they will try to use the channel."

I laughed, "If they did then the gods and the Norns would be working together." Karrek Loos yn Koos had a causeway which was revealed at low tide. At high tide, it looked like a navigable channel.

We were extending our lead and dusk would soon be upon us when Lars Longsight shouted, "Danish drekar to the south-west. It is a mile off the larboard bow."

I turned to Erik and my heart sank. They had us trapped. All that the Dane needed to do was place his ship before us. If we turned north or south then the ships chasing would have us. It mattered not that the crews of the three Danish drekar would be tired; we would be outnumbered three to one.

Erik looked at the pennant and at the Dane, "Jarl, we can still escape. If I sail directly for the Dane he will have trouble matching our move.

We can lay alongside him and disable him. Then we could head north and east still with the wind."

"What about the ones following?"

"The Dane ahead of us cannot see them and they are falling further back. They have exhausted their crews. If you can destroy one Danish drekar then we can head into the western seas. Darkness will fall and we will escape."

It was a risk but I spied a chance. "Change rowers." It had been the experienced crew rowing and they had only rowed for an hour or so. They looked surprised. "We are going to take the Dane ahead of us. I will only use half a crew they will be led by the Ulfheonar. Our aim is to board her, disable the ship and sail away before the other Danes can catch us."

My men began banging the deck with their hands. They approved. The Clan of the Wolf hated running!

The five drekar who were following were spread out. Two were keeping together but the other three were struggling to keep up. The fleet was more than a mile away. I strapped on my sword and dagger. They had been sharpened once more. I held my shield and helmet. I would need my helmet but not necessarily my shield.

"Erik, lay us by their steering board."

"Aye, Jarl."

"Boarders, with me." The twenty-odd men who would be boarding followed me to the bow. When we were there I explained my plan. "Ráðgeir Ráðgeirson, you take half of the men and cut the stays and sheets on the mast. Bergil, you and your brothers, along with Sweyn and Haraldr will come with the Ulfheonar. We kill the men around the steering board and cut the withies!"

Haaken said, "That sounds disappointingly easy."

"Let us board first and see how easy it is. I do not want to be caught by the other Danes. Be ruthless!"

"Aye, Jarl Dragonheart!"

Each man had his own ritual before battle and all of the warriors who would board prepared as though there was not another man on board. My ritual was simple. I tied my mail hood and then my helmet. I banged my helmet to see if it moved. I slid my sword and dagger from their scabbards and then hefted the shield onto my back. If I could I would avoid using a shield. Then I kissed the wolf hanging around my neck and finally I took out Ragnar's Spirit and kissed the blue stone. When we reached Cyninges-tūn I would have one of the blue stones we had taken from the fort placed in the centre of my helmet. It would look good and would add to my protection.

The Dane who was our target had a good captain. He kept the wind and sailed a parallel course. It would allow him to move quickly and counter any move we made. He did not have men rowing and was relying on the wind. That was a mistake for our rowers gave Erik Shot Toe more options. Erik cleverly aimed our ship towards the steering board of the Dane. He thought we were trying to slip by and head for the western ocean. He turned and presented us his stern. We had him.

Haaken turned and began to chant our fast chant. The rowers would not have much longer to row and he wanted all the speed that they could manage.

Push your arms
Row the boat
Use your back
The Wolf will fly
Ulfheonar
Are real men
Teeth like iron
Arms like trees
Push your arms
Row the boat
Use your back
The Wolf will fly
Ragnar's Spirit
Guides us still
Dragon Heart
Wields it well
Push your arms
Row the boat
Use your back
The Wolf will fly

It was as though *'Heart of the Dragon'* was a steed who had been kicked hard. We almost left the water as we leapt forward and gained two lengths on the Danish drekar. The Danish captain was confused. He turned to larboard and that meant we could board him.

"Benni and Beorn, have the grappling hooks ready!"

I was not sure how many ships they had boarded before. I gave them the easier of the tasks. They were strong men and just had to hold us against the Dane. We would do the rest.

"Aye, Jarl!"

The move by Erik had thrown the Dane into disarray. He did not know which side we would attack. When Erik feinted to the larboard he tried to copy us and Erik slammed our prow into his steering board. Half our work was done for us for the steering board was shattered. A large splinter drove up through the helmsman. Benni and Beorn hurled their hooks and Haaken and I leapt the narrowing gap! It was reckless but effective for the Danes were not ready. My sword went through the back of the warrior who was just rising after the collision. I did not aim the sword. The sword killed of its own volition!

"Clear the stern! Ráðgeir Ráðgeirson, destroy the mainmast."

My men hurled themselves down the centre of the ship. The Danish captain had had his men spread out on both sides. That suited us. The Ulfheonar, Bergil and his brothers, Haraldr and Sweyn had the easiest of tasks. We slaughtered all those on the steering board. Then we hurried after Ráðgeir Ráðgeirson. Although he was outnumbered he had men who were desperate for treasure and glory. I stayed at the steering board. My leg ached and I would risk further injury if I joined them. I spied some seal oil. I poured it over one of the coiled ropes and took out my flint. There was a tallow candle lying by the steering board. It would be to help the steersman at night. I took out my flint and struck it until I had a spark. The candle lit. The stays and sheets were severed and Olaf and Rolf had used their axes to weaken the mast. I saw the other Danes hurrying to rescue their comrades.

"Back to *'Heart'*!"

My men were well-trained and they hurried back. I saw that the ones without mail had dragged mail, swords and helmets from the dead. As the last man passed me I hurled the candle to the oil-soaked rope. Flames leapt up and then spread across the deck. I hurried back to my ship. One Dane had been feigning death. He rose with a seax in his hand. Suddenly an arrow flew. I saw Sámr at the prow with his Saami bow. I landed on our deck and the ropes were severed.

"Let loose the sail!"

The wind caught us and the flames. The Dane was quickly shrouded in flames and smoke as we headed due west.

"Take to the oars! Let us show these Danes that we can row and fight!"

The men were filled with the joy of battle and they took to their oars with such enthusiasm that they needed no chant. Haaken, of course, gave them one! He could not resist basking in his own glory and so he began his saga.

The Dragonheart sailed with warriors brave
To find the child he was meant to save
With Haaken and Ragnar's Spirit
They dared to delve with true warrior's grit
With Aðils Shape Shifter with scout skills honed
They found the island close by the rocky stones
The Jarl and Haaken will bravely roar
The Jarl and Haaken and the Ulfheonar
Beneath the earth the two they went
With the sword by Odin sent
In the dark the witch grew strong
Even though her deeds were wrong
A dragon's form she took to kill
Dragonheart faced her still
He drew the sword touched by the god
Made by Odin and staunched in blood
The Jarl and Haaken will bravely roar
The Jarl and Haaken and the Ulfheonar
With a mighty blow, he struck the beast
On Dragonheart's flesh, he would not feast
The blade struck true and the witch she fled
Ylva lay as though she were dead
The witch's power could not match the blade
The Ulfheonar are not afraid
The Jarl and Haaken will bravely roar
The Jarl and Haaken and the Ulfheonar
And now the sword will strike once more

Using all the Allfather's power
Fear the wrath you Danish lost
You fight the wolf and pay the cost
The Jarl and Haaken will bravely roar
The Jarl and Haaken and the Ulfheonar

Until we got up our speed the Danes were catching us but soon they tired and we watched nightfall and the Danish drekar burn. Eventually, blackness enfolded us and we saw nothing. The chase was over and they had lost!

Chapter 8

The men were exhausted and we still had the wind. We stopped rowing and Erik took in a reef. The men ate and drank. Two men had not returned from the Danish drekar. Einar Ulfsson and Petr Jorgensen had died on the Danish ship. As their bodies had been by the steering board then I hoped that they had been burned and not despoiled by the Danes. Atticus saw to the wounds of the men while Æthelflæd and Nanna fetched food.

"Sámr Ship Killer, I owe you a life."

My great-grandson shook his head, "You have kept me safe this whole voyage. I have never been in danger and yet you have put yourself in harm's way at every turn. You owe me nothing."

Æthelflæd handed me a piece of hardening bread while Nanna poured me a horn of ale. She smiled and said, to Sámr, "Your great-grandfather is doing as my father did, Sámr. He is ensuring that his blood lives on. That is true is it not, Jarl Dragonheart?"

I smiled. The last days had seen a change in Æthelflæd and Nanna. They both looked older. Æthelflæd had become more confident. Once we had reached our ship and set sail it was as though she had wrestled with her grief and hope had won. I wondered if, even though she was Christian, she had something of the volva in her.

"That is what all parents do. I lost your grandfather when he was relatively young, Sámr. Your uncle died that day too. It tore the heart out of me. I swore that I would never watch another child of mine die. Now that you have a bride then you can father children and you will learn of the weight which comes with a newborn babe. Light as a feather they weigh as much as the world. They are your future and your past for they carry within them the blood of all who went before." I turned to Æthelflæd, "Did you know that his grandmother was a Saxon noblewoman? Elfrida, Sámr's grandmother, had been married to King Egbert of Wessex. He had married her when she was younger than you. From my blood, he has the line of the old people who lived here when the Romans came and a Saxon too."

She looked at Sámr, "You did not tell me."

He shook his head, "I am at fault then for I am proud of my heritage and you are right, Jarl Dragonheart, about parents but you seem to carry the weight of all of our family upon your shoulders."

"I do but when we are at home, in the Land of the Wolf, I have help. Kara, Aiden and Ylva can read my mind and they can help."

He said, bluntly, "But not my father."

"Your father chose a land away from Cyninges-tūn. My son Gruffyd did too. that is their choice and I know that if there was danger then they would come to my side."

Sámr rose, "Æthelflæd, you will learn that these men who fight alongside my great grandfather, the Ulfheonar, are closer to him than any family."

Haaken had been listening and he laughed, "That is because we know all of the Dragonheart's secrets. He has to be close to us. That way his secrets remained buried."

Olaf snorted, "The Dragonheart's secrets? With you around the whole world knows every detail of the Dragonheart's life. Fear not, Sámr Ship Killer, there are no secrets. If we are closer to the Jarl than his family that is because we all swore an oath. The dead Ulfheonar who went before us would not let us enter Valhalla if we did not protect him. I am grateful that your arrow was true and that you saved his life. His work is not yet done."

Olaf rarely spoke so much and, unlike Haaken he did not speak to fill the silence. Was he right? Had I still work to do? I wrapped myself in my wolf cloak and stared at the stars above my head as we headed north and west. The King of the East Angles had failed in his quest. He had tried to keep his lands safe. The puppet who danced in the hall of Beodericsworth was not the ruler of the East Angles. The Danes had clawed a foothold in Britannia. Northumbria would fall next and then Mercia. King Beorhtwulf of Mercia had failed in his attempt to keep the Danes from his door. When he had kidnapped Æthelflæd he had made a grave error. It would cost him and his people. We had not taken the Land of the Wolf from any people. The ones who lived there when we arrived, Pasgen's people, still lived there and prospered. They were indistinguishable from the Norse I had brought. Raibeart, his one surviving son, still sailed the seas in a drekar. The question which filled my mind, as we headed for the treacherous seas of Om Walum was would my people survive my death? Would I live long enough to see Sámr become jarl?

When dawn broke we were still half a day from An Lysardh but the seas were empty and Erik had managed to keep us far from Syllingar. Until we rounded the rocky cape then we were still in danger but each mile we went north increased our chances of avoiding the wrath of the witch. She still bore me a grudge. Erik was unhappy with the damage we had incurred when we had hit the Dane. We had promised the Hibernians to take them to their island home. That meant the open sea and Erik wished to check the hull before we did so. I knew that he was not being unduly fussy. He knew his ship and I trusted his judgement. We were already so many days late in getting home that one more day beached would not hurt us.

"With your permission, Jarl, we will land at those empty beaches at Carrum."

I remembered them. We had gone there with Danes to fight King Egbert. That seemed a lifetime ago. "Aye, Erik, that would be a good place."

I remembered the many dead we had left there and of those jarls who had followed us back to the Land of the Wolf. Most had used my land as a place to recover and gain men and mail to help them to raid. I liked to believe that they took the heart of the wolf with them when they sailed. There were many Vikings but not all of them had honour. Those who sailed with me did.

We reached a suitable beach at dawn the next day. An Lysardh had been almost benign. We chose a beach far from any signs of habitation. We would not be raiding. We offloaded all that we could from the drekar and then the crew hauled her, bow first on to the sand. Using spare spars and wood which had washed ashore on the beach we chocked her so that she was upright and then Erik and his son began to examine every uncia of the keel. Although we would not be raiding my men took the opportunity to forage. Sámr and Æthelflæd found the time to walk together, hand in hand along the empty beach. I nodded to Germund who followed but out of earshot. Atticus saw an opportunity to search for some herbs. He found the food on the boat bland and in lieu of spices he found greens and herbs to enliven it. The experienced warriors, like the Ulfheonar, just slept on the warm sand.

Taking off my sealskin boots to paddle in the shallows I saw Nanna by herself and thought she looked both sad and lonely. I wandered over to her. "Would you like to walk with me along the beach? I like the feel of the water next to my skin."

Her face brightened, "Yes, Jarl. If it is not too much trouble." Since Sámr had come into Æthelflæd's life Nanna had been gradually pushed away from her cousin. Far from home, her life would be difficult. She slipped her sandals from her feet and hitched her skirt up into her belt.

As we walked I chuckled, "I remember when I had seen barely five or six summers and I was in the Dunum checking the nets. That was the day the Vikings came and captured me. That was the day I became a slave."

"And that makes you smile?"

"It does for it changed my life for the better. I would not be Jarl Dragonheart if Harald One Eye had not taken me and my mother."

"Ah, you had your mother. Then you were not alone."

"Your family is Æthelflæd?" She nodded. "And she will be taken from you when she marries Sámr?"

I saw tears spring into her eyes. Sometimes we have thoughts and they are not painful until they were voiced. I had voiced her fears and the tears tumbled. We walked in silence and I allowed the tears to cease.

Then she spoke, "My mother died giving birth to what would have been my brother. He died too. I was sent to live with Æthelflæd and her family. When my father was killed by the Danes I became a sort of half-sister to Æthelflæd. Then, a year after my father was killed we were taken to that place you found us. If it had not been for Atticus then I think we would have gone mad. He is a kind man and funny. He kept us amused. Events happened so quickly. I had no time to mourn."

"And now you fear a life among barbarians in the land of the Wolf." She looked up guiltily as though I had read her mind. "I know that is how people see us but it is not true. Atticus was a slave. I freed him and he chose to live amongst us. Life cannot be that bad can it?"

She smiled and wiped away a tear, "But you have mountains and wolves."

I laughed, "We are the clan of the wolf and we do not fear the wolf. There are many things to admire in wolves. When they march they go at the speed of the slowest and weakest. The leaders are ready to defend the pack with their lives. So it is with our clan. We do not discard the old; we cherish them. Had you and Æthelflæd been of our clan then we would not have rested until we had rescued you."

She stopped and looked at me, "Sámr said that you went into a witch's cave and wrestled with a dragon to see your granddaughter. Is that true or was he trying to impress Æthelflæd?"

"Sámr does not speak that which is not true. The witch took the form of a dragon and Haaken One Eye's white hair is evidence of the battle for he was there with me. And Sámr was taken by the same witch when Ulla

War Cry fell from our ship. I say this not to frighten you but to reassure you. I do not say the Danes and the Mercians will not come to our land but if they do then their passage home will be marked by their bones."

We spoke for the rest of the morning and then I realised we were far from the drekar. We turned and headed back up the beach. By the time we had reached it Atticus had a large pot of stew bubbling away. With the greens, shellfish, salted meat and herbs it was an appetising smell that masked the smell of pine tar being heated.

Sámr and Æthelflæd looked guilty as we returned and Æthelflæd rushed to her cousin's side. Sámr said, "She was lonely?"

I nodded, "And fearful of her future."

"She needs not be. She can live with us."

"She is now a woman. You and Sámr will want privacy. Nanna needs her own life. When you marry Æthelflæd then Nanna becomes your responsibility too. You will have to find or approve a match for her."

He looked shocked, "But I am barely a man myself. My beard is not yet fully grown." I knew what he meant. It was not yet long enough to make it into pigtails like other young warriors.

"You have stepped on this path, not of your own volition for the Norns wove the threads but now that you walk this path you leave your own life behind." We sat on a couple of rocks and I saw the significance of his impending marriage sink in. "Will you live at Whale Island?"

"No!" The answer came so quickly that I knew he had already thought of this. He smiled and said more gently, "No, for I wish to make a new start. I thought to make a home by the place you and my grandfather's mother lived. The east side of the Water is beautiful but it is your hall."

I felt a shudder down my neck. This was my dream. "The hall is yours if you wish it but none has lived there for many years. It will need work."

"But not as much work as building a new hall."

"Then it is yours. There will be none to work the land yet and you have no oathsworn."

"They will come in time and I have coin. Raiding with you has brought me a small chest of coins. When we visit Dyflin we can visit the slave market there. If we live alone for a while then we can get to know one another."

I nodded. Atticus handed us bowls of food. He could see that we were deep in conference. He was a sensitive man and he said nothing but his eyes were knowing. I sipped the hot broth, "Good stew." He smiled and went to fill the bowls of the others. "It is good that you get to know one another and that brings us back to Nanna."

He suddenly saw that his plans conflicted. He could not be alone and have Nanna living with them. "She could live with you."

I shook my head, "I would not mind but that would not be right. Uhtred, Atticus and Dragonheart are three old men. Would you inflict three flatulent old men on Æthelflæd?"

He laughed, "No I would not."

"The solution I see is for her to live with your Great Aunt Kara. They have a house of women and Ylva knows the pain of being alone."

"It will be hard for Æthelflæd to be parted from her cousin."

"That is life, Sámr. There are no easy solutions and those that think the gods will grant them all that they desire will be disappointed."

Erik and his crew found a couple of splits in the strakes. They repaired them and gave them a coating of pine tar. He came to me and smiled, "We can leave on the morning tide."

"Then head for Dyflin. We will land the Hibernians there and see if they have slaves in their market."

There was a time when my daughter would have been there with Moon Child and her husband Thorghest the Lucky. They had been slain by Hibernians and they were still unavenged. I knew not who ruled in Dyflin nor the identity of my family's killers. A visit to Dyflin would solve many problems. As men found places to sleep I waved over Conan Mac Finbarr.

"Yes, Jarl Dragonheart?"

"Tomorrow we set sail for Dyflin. I do not know if that is the place you would choose to land."

He shook his head, "The place you call Veisafjǫrðr would be better. You have to pass it to get to Dyflin anyway."

I was curious, "Why Veisafjǫrðr?"

"We were not slaves as long as your men. Our lord was loyal to the Jarl Thorghest. When he was killed along with our lord we tried to flee to Veisafjǫrðr. Our chief was tasked with slowing down the attackers and we were captured. They did not kill us but sold us to the King of Gwynedd. If we have kin then they will be at Veisafjǫrðr."

"You know that the wife of Jarl Thorghest was my daughter."

"I did, Jarl Dragonheart. I did not mention it before for I did not wish to make you sad. You seem to have enough problems without memories of the past."

I smiled, "This is the work of the Norns. I wondered why we found and rescued you. It was the threads of the Norns. You were bound to your chief and he was bound to Thorghest. We are all part of the same tale. We will take you to Veisafjǫrðr. I will be able to scout out those who killed my family. We will have vengeance!"

As we sailed north I questioned Conan Mac Finbarr about the Hibernians who had killed my son-in-law. "Their chief is Niall U Néill and his clan is the Uí Néill. He calls himself king but he is little better than a bandit. He might have remained as a minor chief in the north of the land of Hibernian had he not found an ally in a Viking called Garðketill the Sly. His name is well deserved. Jarl Thorghest did not find out his true name until it was too late. He claimed to have served with Hrolf the Horseman and the Raven Wing Clan. As many other jarls had come to Dyflin with such a story he was believed. The others had all been loyal warriors who served Jarl Thorghest. It was he who opened the gates of Dyflin and allowed in the Uí Néill. It was Garðketill the Sly who stabbed him and then butchered your daughter and grandson."

My eyes narrowed, "You saw this with your own eyes?"

He shook his head. We were not within Dyflin's walls. We were Hibernians and some of the Vikings in Dyflin mistrusted us. One of the hearth-were found us and, with his dying breath told us of the treachery. Our chief was Donnchad Ua Conchobair. He would have been king for Jarl Thorghest promised him, warriors, to retake his throne. That was why he led us to try to save Dyflin. We managed to hold the gates so that women and children could escape. Some wounded warriors went with them. Then our chief fell and we were captured. They slaughtered all those with wounds and the other twenty they sold as slaves. That is my sad story and now there are but four of us left. Our wives and families will be slaves of the Uí Néill."

"And what will you do?"

"The same as you would have done, Jarl Dragonheart, we will try to rescue our families and kill Niall U Néill."

"Four of you?"

"We are better armed now, thanks to you, and we have watched how you fight. I believe we are better warriors. It may be we go to our deaths but it will be an honourable death and not the one endured by those who died in the mines. Besides, there are others who hate the Uí Néill. We can gather an army."

I spent the last day as gentle winds pushed us north by west, with the Ulfheonar. I told them all that we had learned. Olaf Leather Neck nodded, "Thorghest the Lucky was an ungrateful warrior who owed everything to you. He deserted you but he married your daughter and I hate betrayal by any. I think that in your heart you would have vengeance. If you seek my axe then you have it. I will go to Dyflin and slay these oath breakers."

Haaken One Eye said, "You know that you have all of our swords and axes. This whole crew will follow you but you know that you need more than one drekar to do this."

"I do but I seek your advice on the best way to raise the men we need."

"Ragnar and Gruffyd have the same blood as Erika. If they brought their warriors then we would have enough."

"And my other jarls?" I was thinking of Raibeart, Asbjorn, Ketil and Ulf.

"We saw the Danes in Lundenwic. They are on the rise. Eoforwic is now Jorvik and the King of Northumbria does their bidding. None will forget what you did to Ivar Wartooth. You have to leave enough men in the Land of the Wolf to deter those who seek vengeance." Aðils Shape Shifter was the quietest of my Ulfheonar but he was the most thoughtful. He alone had thought through the events of the past days.

"Then we speak to those in Veisafjǫrðr and find a way to bring these killers to justice; Viking justice will save this land through Viking bravery."

Veisafjǫrðr was the closest I had seen to a Norwegian fjord and I could see why Vikings had settled there. We sailed in without shields and we were given a welcome for my sail was as good as a standard! I landed with the Ulfheonar and the Hibernians. They looked like Vikings for they wore Danish war gear we had captured. We were taken to the hall of Mánagarmr Long Stride. He was a tall man and had the longest legs I had ever seen. He was well-named. He was also young. I put him to be the age of Ragnar. He had done well to rule such a fine stronghold as Veisafjǫrðr.

"Jarl Dragonheart, I have been expecting you for some time. I am sorry that your daughter and grandson were butchered by the same men who slew my father." I could not tell if he was annoyed with me for having delayed in coming. I would not explain. I did not need to.

I smiled, "I have many enemies and many debts to pay. Blood debts are always paid. There are two enemies I believe; Niall U Néill and Garðketill the Sly."

"Aye, they are still together and have a stranglehold on Dyflin. No ships are allowed to trade without the permission of the King, for that is his new title. He charges high taxes. When other ships tried to come here his drekar captured them. Now no one comes to Hibernia for trade and they have become pirates."

I shook my head, "Then, for that alone, they should pay." I waved a hand at Conan Mac Finbarr. "These are Hibernians sold by the Uí Néill. These four will gather an army of their countrymen. I will return to the Land of the Wolf and bring my own men too. Will you and your men join us to defeat these treacherous dogs?"

He beamed, "I have waited a long time since my father died. Aye, Jarl. It will be an honour. I can bring more than a hundred spears."

"This will require coordination. It will take time for me to gather my men. We will attack in two moons' time, at Tvímánuður. I will send a ship to tell you precisely when. Conan will know the man I send." The Hibernian looked at me. "It will be Bergil Hafþórrsson. Any other who comes lies and should be held for they will be trying to deceive you."

We stayed one night for I was worried that there might be drekar waiting to ambush ships leaving the port. I wanted to leave before dawn and sail from the darkness. We saw the enemy but it was not until noon that we were almost home. Our speed and their nervousness meant that they would not risk the wrath of the Dragonheart. I could see Old Olaf ahead of us when Lars shouted, "Six drekar to the west."

I stared but all that I saw from the steering board were the sails. They were so far away that they would not catch us but my cautious departure had been the correct decision. The presence of so many ships meant that they would see our approach. My plan to send Bergil with the message to our allies would have to be rethought.

Sámr and his bride-to-be were both nervous. Astrid was a lovely lady but Sámr was her firstborn. Sámr and Æthelflæd did not know how she would react. I had almost forgotten the marriage since I had spoken with Conan. The tricky entrance to the harbour allowed all who wished to come to the harbour to meet and greet us. I saw Ragnar and his wife. Gruffyd was not there.

As Jarl, I was the first to descend. Ragnar clasped my arm. His face was not joyous, as I would have expected, it was serious, "Gruffyd went raiding a week since. That is why he is not here to greet you. He took Mordaf with him. Ebrel is not happy!"

Astrid hugged me warmly. She had a great affection for me. I had rescued her from a hard life. I pointed, "Your son Sámr needs to speak with you before I do. When you are done, Ragnar, I need to speak with you."

I could see he was intrigued but I left them. Ulla War Cry was waiting to greet me. "Great grandfather, see how much I have grown."

He had indeed and was almost a man. He was not far behind Sámr. "You have grown and have you practised with your sword?"

"Every day. Can I come with you on your next raid?"

"That depends upon your mother and your father." We turned as there was a squeal of joy from Astrid. She was hugging Æthelflæd. "I think tonight may be a good time to ask her."

I waited in the courtyard which Ragnar had built by his hall. It was a pleasant place to watch the sun set and I had barely sat down when a servant brought a foaming horn of ale. "Good to see you back, Jarl Dragonheart. I could not help but notice the limp. In the wars again?"

I laughed, "Olaf Red Hair, I am always in the wars."

We had drunk much ale since leaving home but none tasted as good as that brewed in the waters of the Land of the Wolf. I was on my second one when Ragnar arrived. He had with him Haaken and Olaf. "The other Ulfheonar went home to see their families. Haaken says we go to war again?"

"As usual Haaken does not know when to keep his mouth closed."

Haaken was unconcerned at my ire, "You would have told him all that I did. The difference is my words flowed like the ale you quaff!"

Olaf shook his head, "I am surprised this one does not talk in his sleep!"

"And if I did then it would be worth listening to!" You could not put down Haaken.

While we waited for the ale I said, "She is a lovely girl, Ragnar. Your son has done well."

My grandson nodded, "I know and Astrid has taken to her. A princess eh?"

I nodded, "A princess without a country." I wondered if I ought to speak of Sámr's decision to live near me. I decided not to. Sámr's words had been for my ears. He would break the news when he was ready. That was part of his growing up.

When the ale came I explained what I had discovered. Ragnar needed no persuasion. I then asked him the question which seemed to fill his hall. "And where is my son and Einar Fair Face?"

"They took their drekar to raid Om Walum and the monastery at Karrek Loos yn Koos."

My eyes widened, "Then I hope my son's eyes are not bigger than his belly. That is a hard nut to crack."

"Aye, grandfather, but a rich one."

"Then he will not be back in time to raid Dyflin with us?"

"But he will be back and Raibeart is keen to raid. He has two drekar."

I nodded. "And I have two. If you bring your three drekar then that will give us three hundred spears."

"That will be enough."

Astrid came with her arms around Sámr and Æthelflæd. Tears of joy were on her face. She hugged me, "How can I ever repay you, father of our people? Your generosity goes on and on. You saved me and now you have not only saved my son but found a perfect wife!" She hugged me and kissed my cheek. Then she pulled away and wagged a finger at me, "And it is time you hung up your sword! When these have children, they will be your great, great-grandchildren!"

I was not frightened of any opponent but that thought truly terrified me.

Part Three
Dragonheart's Vengeance

Chapter 9

I stayed one night at my grandson's hall. Olaf and Haaken left with me the next day. We had much to do. Erik and Bolli would prepare the drekar for sea. *'King's Gift'*, *'Wolf'* and *'Running Bird'* had not sailed for some time. They would need to be hauled from the river and given a thorough overhaul. There would be weed to be scraped and hulls to be sealed. Sheets and stays would need replacing. I had spoken to Raibeart and he had confirmed his wish to raid. Astrid and Ragnar would come with Ebrel and Bronnen to my home for the wedding ceremony. I would marry Sámr and Æthelflæd.

As we headed north Nanna and Æthelflæd were wide-eyed at the beauty and savagery of my land. The land of the East Angles was flat and featureless. When we emerged from the woods and saw Old Olaf reflected in the Water they gasped at its grandeur. While they took in the imposing savage beauty of the Land of the Wolf I dismounted and went to the Water as I always did. I took off my boots and walked in its chilly waters. It was how I knew that I was home. When I mounted my horse, I wanted to gallop to my home. I had seen Valhalla but my Water and Old Olaf were a close second.

The men who had gone directly to Cyninges-tūn had warned the people of my stad of my imminent arrival. The fishing boats on the Water had sped north to tell them of my proximity. The gates and walls were lined and I was quite touched at the reception. Nanna and Æthelflæd were overwhelmed for they thought it was intended for them. Kara, Aiden and Ylva awaited us outside their hall. They looked genuinely pleased to see me. Ylva hugged me first and as her mother kissed my cheek she embraced Sámr.

"Well, little cousin, I hear you have found a bride!"

"How …"

I smiled, "They can read minds but I am guessing that the men who came last night spoke of your union."

Kara said, "And to welcome our new sisters we have a feast this night." She put her arm around Nanna, "You shall stay with us."

Ylva did the same to Æthelflæd, "And you too." She poked Sámr playfully in the ribs. "You will have to keep your manhood in your breeks until you are married!"

He blushed, "I have…"

Aiden shook his head, "Ignore them, Sámr. They are mocking all men. Let them have their moment!"

It was good to be home. I suddenly felt forty years younger. Here I was safe. There were no enemies and only friends. This was the one place where I could let down my guard and enjoy freedom. I drank too much. It helped the fact that I had good wine and I had been home so little lately that I had barrels which were yet to be broached. Uhtric had come to help serve and he was ever attentive. I saw Atticus frowning when I spilt a goblet of wine. Aiden laughed and my daughter and Ylva smiled. They knew me. They loved me and any indiscretions would be forgiven. I suppose Sámr, Atticus and Uhtric must have taken me to my bed. I did not remember. It had been many years since I had been so relaxed that I enjoyed my wine and I had let myself go.

When I woke I did not feel sick but I felt unclean. I had a taste in my mouth which reminded me of the meat at the bottom of a barrel. I rose. Uhtric was awake, the rest of those in my hall slept.

"Good morning, Jarl." His greeting was guarded.

I smiled, "I know I drank too much last night and if I offended any then I apologise. Light the steam hut. I will have a swim first."

"Is that wise, Jarl?"

I laughed, "Let us see eh, Uhtric?"

He laughed too. "I will watch you but as I cannot swim I will only be able to watch you drown!"

Uhtric carried my drying blanket and clean shift and I walked towards the Water. Karl One Leg was at the gate. He smiled, "You drank well last night, Jarl?"

"I am a Viking, of course, I did!" He laughed.

Dawn had yet to break but I saw, towards Grize's Dale, the first hint of grey. I dropped my clothes on the sand and walked, naked, into the water. The shock made me shiver and I enjoyed the feeling. I sank down and the attack of cold water made me gasp. I seized the moment and dived beneath the surface. This was my Water. This was where Erika, my dead wife's spirit lived. I was as safe here as anywhere. I opened my eyes and pushed the water behind me. It was murky. I had lifted the sediment. When I broke surface, I took in a large gulp of air. I dived down to the bottom. Spying a white stone, I lifted it. I hovered above the bottom and floated. It was as close to flying as I could manage. When I thought my breath would burst I dropped the stone, kicked up from the mud and broke the surface. I lay on my back and I sculled up and down the water until Uhtric shouted, "Ready, Jarl!"

I swam to the shore and walked from the Water. I saw the angry red scar where Atticus had ripped the poison from my leg. Had I not saved him then I would have died. *Wyrd*! I saw the other scars including the one the doctor had made in Miklagård. The wounds crisscrossed my body like a web! Uhtric opened the curtain and I stepped into the heat of the steam hut. It was not yet at its height. It would be soon. Uhtric did not enjoy the steam hut. "I will fetch your ale, Jarl. Shout if you need me."

I smiled, "You mean if I think I am dying?"

Uhtric was convinced that I would die in the steam hut. "Do not jest about such matters, Jarl!"

I enjoyed getting into a steam hut that was not at its hottest. You could anticipate the pleasure to come. I poured some water on the coals and felt the heat as the steam surged around me. Perhaps Astrid was right. I might be able to stay at home more often these days. I enjoyed swimming in the Water and having the pleasure of a steam hut. The thought of drinking when I chose and doing this each morning was enticing. The curtain was raised and a naked Sámr joined me.

He grinned, "I thought I would see what you, Aunt Kara, Uncle Aiden and cousin Ylva find so enjoyable about this!"

I smiled. As much as I wanted to be alone there was no better company than Sámr. "Sit and enjoy."

"Should I leave the curtain open? It is a little hot!"

"That is the point. Just breathe easily and close your eyes. This is a place for contemplation rather than talk."

I saw him nod. The hut was dark but my eyes were accustomed to the dark. If he became distressed then I would shout for Uhtric. I had no need to fear. He controlled his breathing and actually began to smile. I closed my eyes. I saw, when I closed them, my dead wives, Erika and Brigid. Both had been as different as could be as wives and yet I had loved them both. Both deserved a better husband than me but I had had a clan to protect. They both understood that. Erika still occupied my dreams but I had not spoken to Brigid since she had died. She was a Christian. That was her curse.

"I can see why you like this, great grandfather."

I opened my eyes. I had been about to enter the spirit world. I did not mind. When I died I would have the spirit world for eternity. Now was Sámr's time. "When you want to use it just tell Uhtric."

He nodded, "I could see into your mind." I nodded. "I will marry a Christian. Will I be cursed?"

I laughed, "You read part of my thoughts. Brigid was cursed because she was a Christian and did not enter the spirit world. Make the most of your time with Æthelflæd. When you or she dies then you will not be able to enjoy her thoughts. I still enjoy speaking with your great-grandmother, Erika. She had the power which Kara enjoys."

"Did you not try to convert Brigid?"

"You choose your path, No one decides it for you. The Norns spin and we follow their path. My grandfather chose a Christian. Yet Elfrida was different to Brigid as a Dane from a Norse. We never know what the Norns plan. They enjoy toying with us and weaving webs which are so complex with threads which circle the world." I smiled. "Who would have thought that we would find Æthelflæd and Nanna when we went to look for Atticus?" I closed my eyes. "When Ebrel told us of Gruffyd I felt the Norns at work. When we fled the Danes, I thought about heading for the monastery. Perhaps if I had we would have found him."

Sámr said, "He might not have wished that."

I opened my eyes, "What makes you say that?"

He hesitated and I inclined my head for him to speak. "Gruffyd is desperate to be you, great grandfather. He wishes to impress you. I would not have chosen to raid the monastery for we have coin and treasure enough. I could see why your son did. He married a princess."

"As will you."

He shook his head, "When I laid eyes on Æthelflæd I did not know that she was a princess. She is a princess without land and she does not wish for the title. She believes that it was her father's title which got him killed. I think Gruffyd would be king if he could."

"We have no king here."

Sámr looked suddenly wise as he said, "And perhaps Gruffyd resents that also."

The heat built up and we sweated. I ran through all that Gruffyd had done and said when last I had spoken with him. He had much of his mother in him. She had been preoccupied by titles. Her upbringing explained that. She had had to serve a cousin who was of the royal blood and she had resented that. When my son returned I would speak with him. It was a conversation long overdue.

After we left the steam hut we swam and then after we had dried and dressed, we were ready for food. Atticus and Uhtric worked well together and the meal they prepared was a substantial one. We ate basic food when on a drekar and made up for it when we were on dry land. Sámr went to fetch Æthelflæd and Nanna. He would show them the place he would build his home. It would be a pleasant walk around the head of my Water. My land was as safe as any. Here we were in the heart of it and an enemy who wish us harm would have to be an Ulfheonar to get close. Germund would be on hand with his sword. He would be their protector.

When I had dressed and eaten I took my helmet and the best of the blue stones we had fetched back. I went to Bagsecg Bagsecgson. He had been the smith but now he no longer worked the forge. Instead, he supervised his sons. "Bagsecg, I would have you mount this stone in my helmet."

He frowned, "The stone is not as strong as metal, Jarl. When it is struck then it will shatter."

I nodded, "But the stone has powers which will protect me." I held up Ragnar's Spirit. Bagsecg had made it. "This has a blue stone and has been struck many times. It remains whole. The old sword in my hall has one and that has endured centuries."

He nodded and took the stone and helmet. "Jarl, you are getting too old to go to war. Do as I do and watch your men work. Supervise them."

"The trouble is, old friend, that my work is war and that is not something which can be supervised."

"And that is your curse."

I gripped my wolf charm, "Aye, it is."

He examined the helmet. "It would involve adding more metal. I will have to use more mail links on the aventail to balance it."

"That is not a problem."

Now that he had a problem to solve then all doubts went. "I will add a ring of metal around it and a band to encircle the whole. The helmet will be stronger."

"You will do this yourself?"

He smiled, "Of course. This is for Jarl Dragonheart. I made your sword, your dagger and your mail. Who else would do it?"

I nodded. The helmet would be perfect. It was to be made by a craftsman.

I met with Kara, Ylva and Aiden later that morning. "Did you dream?"

Aiden nodded, "We saw you and we saw the Danes. You were never in danger but the Norn's webs and threads are powerful. It seems we have made enemies of them too. They fight us. There are spells and mists which stop us seeing as far as we normally do." He looked sad. "Perhaps I am losing my powers." I saw that he looked thinner than he had. His hair was white and he looked old yet he was younger than I was. He saw my look and he smiled.

I turned my gaze towards Kara, "And the future?"

"Is unclear. You will go to Hibernia but Gruffyd and his raid on Om Walum have not pleased the spirits nor the gods."

I was confused, "Why not?"

"He is trying to change the past. His wife's father lost Om Walum. Gruffyd cannot take it. He is not the Dragonheart nor his heir."

"Sámr?"

She nodded, "He is the one chosen not only by you but by the land. You have guided him well. In the time you have left you must make him into the Wolf Warrior. You must make him the one who can control the land."

Ylva smiled, "It is not as daunting a prospect as you might think grandfather. We are here to help. I have been appointed the one to watch over Sámr and Æthelflæd. It helps that Nanna will live with us for she has powers. She knows it not yet but we can teach her. Æthelflæd loves her and love is a powerful force. When you are in the Otherworld and watching us, we will guide Sámr and Æthelflæd." She touched the hands of her parents. "When they are gone then my parents will guide me from the world of the spirits."

I thought about their words. There was a layer of meaning beneath them. "Is there danger from within?"

"There could be discord. Your son, grandsons, and great-grandsons, all have part of you within them but they have part of others too. Just as my brother, Wolf Killer, had a wilful streak in him there will be others who have one too. My half-sister, Erika had such a streak did she not? Now that she is in the Otherworld she might regret leaving this land but you cannot change the past. That is what Gruffyd and Einar Fair Face will discover."

They were right. Æthelstan had discovered that. His land was lost. The Danes had wormed their way in and would not let go.

"Then I need to make my land secure. I can protect the land from those with weapons and ill wishes but the Norns? They are your responsibility."

The three of them looked uncomfortable. Kara took my hand, "They are spinning, father and it is so complex a web that we are struggling to find where it starts and where it ends but your thread and Gruffyd's are tied to it."

"And Mordaf?"

"His too."

"But not Sámr."

Ylva said, "Sámr, Æthelflæd and you have threads which join but the start and the end are clear. That is why this wedding is good."

"All is in place for the marriage?"

"Seven nights time will see the ceremony."

"Then I have enough time to ride to speak with Ketil and Asbjorn. We will need their vigilance."

Aiden nodded, "And when you go to Hibernia I will come with you."

"You do not need to."

"It was the land of my birth. I owe my own ancestors. Had you not taken me from the island who knows what my life might have been."

"Are you trying to change the past too?"

He smiled, "No, the future. I should like to meet this Conan Mac Finbarr. He and those with him have been on a journey. They have been chosen and saved for a purpose. When you rescued them, your threads became entwined. Perhaps my powers can help to guide them too. Who knows a visit to the land of my birth might bring back the powers that I am losing."

Ylva slipped her arm through mine as I left, "And make sure that you are back before the wedding."

Baldr Witch Saviour was just a youth and had not been fit enough to come with us to rescue Atticus but he had recovered now and he was eager to come with us. We had rescued Baldr in the Blue Sea. He had been captured and enslaved. We had rescued him. His people came from a landlocked country and were horsemen. We had discovered that he was a prince of that land. As the one who had saved Ylva in the battle with the Mercians, he was held in high regard by all of my people. He knew horses and he was the one who cared for our herd. He chose two good horses for our journey. He had seen little of my land save Cyninges-tūn and this would give him the chance to see more of my land.

We headed north through the pass which led to the road to the bridge at the village of Skelwith. "Jarl, this land is so different from my own land that I wonder if I have been transported to another world."

"You do not have mountains?"

"We do but they are always in the distance. My people were horsemen. We could ride for seven days and the ground would still be flat. The rivers were not bubbling little becks that tumbled from mountains, they were great long snakes which wound across the land."

"It sounds like you miss your home."

"I should be missing my home but my family are all dead. Ylva has dreamed for me and spoken to them. They are happy I have a new family. Germund the Lame said I was reborn and he was right." He smiled, "Of course, if I try to make horsemen of you all then you will understand."

It was my turn to smile and to remember, "We rescued another slave once, Hrolf the Horseman. He was Norse but he loved horses and he loved riding. He lives in the land of the Franks and his people ride to war on horses."

He was interested and so I told him of Hrolf the Horseman. The Norns had woven our threads together but he had chosen a different path. I wondered if Baldr would leave too. He asked me about the adventure he had missed out on and I told him. "Is Sámr happy with the Saxon princess?"

I laughed, "He is marrying her!"

"When I lived with the Franks I saw that marriages were often made for the title and the power they brought. I have not seen the Saxon women. Are they pretty?"

I shook my head, "What strange questions you ask. Yes, they are pretty."

"Then Sámr will be happy. A pretty wife will keep him at home."

"You are wise for one so young."

He shook his head, "When I lived with the Franks I saw much that I did not like. Sámr is like a brother to me. We have fought together. I would have him happy."

"Then when we return you shall speak with Æthelflæd and Nanna. We will have to see if they meet with your approval."

He gave me a sideways look, "Now you are mocking me, Jarl Dragonheart. I meant no disrespect."

"I know, Baldr, I know."

We reached the Roman fort at Windar's Mere and spent the night with Asbjorn. He and his warriors listened to my tale and my plans.

"We are warriors, jarl. We would come with you."

"You were there when we defeated the Mercians, Asbjorn. You owe me nothing but I would have you watch my land. You are closer to the lands of Mercia. That is where the real threat lies. It is the Danes who are the danger now. The King of Mercia has gambled that he could use another to defeat the Danes. Now they will begin to eat into his lands. The land close to Whale Island is safer now. Our people will be able to farm there safely but the Danes are growing in Northumbria. They are growing in numbers. It is in the east where the danger lurks. Keep men watching the Eden Valley. I will go to speak with Ketil for he is the one who will know how the Saxons of Northumbria fare."

Ketil lived close to the High Divide which separated us from what had been the land of Northumbria. There had been a time when he had made an alliance with the Saxons through one of their princes. That prince had foolishly tried to take on the Danes and he had lost. Once the Saxons had been a force who were to be feared but no longer. Ketil was the son of Windar who had ruled at Windar's Mere for many years. As a young warrior he had fought bravely for me and was now rewarded with the lands which went from Ulla's Water to the Roman Wall; from Pennryhd to the High Divide. The land he ruled was a third of the Land of the Wolf.

His sons were now warriors grown and they had their own strongholds. It was one of those, Harald Ketilsson, who escorted us to his father's fort. Ketil had used a Roman Fort and made it a truly impressive stronghold. Unlike the rest of our forts, it was made of stone and was a bastion against enemies. When Ketil and his son heard of my plans they, like Asbjorn were keen to come with me.

"I am concerned about the Danes. Who rules the land to the East now?"

"King Æthelred. He fights the Danes and has had some success but these days Eoforwic is more Dane than Saxon. Carr still sends me news. Your news about the land of the East Angles now explains much of Æthelred's success. The Danes have been too busy further south to exploit their gains."

"Then King Æthelred can expect a storm soon enough. You and your sons keep a watch here." I smiled for Ketil had now grown from the scrawny warrior into a copy of his father. "You prosper here!"

He laughed and patted his gut, "Aye we eat well and we get the most from this land. The valleys produce good beef and the uplands are perfect for sheep. Ulla's Water teems with fish. It is good. One of my other sons, Erik is hersir of the land to the north and he keeps the ones who try to raid from north of the wall in check. The wall is adorned with the heads of those who would steal our cattle. They raid the Saxons instead."

Baldr and I came back by the valley of the Thirl. We had seen Úlfarrberg from the east but I preferred the western aspect. It was where I had found the wolf which had saved us from killers. I told Baldr the tale as we headed towards the Grassy Mere. "I should like to climb the mountain, Jarl."

"When we have defeated the Hibernians and taught them a lesson then we will return. I know that Sámr would like to honour Úlfarr." Wolves were never far from our thoughts. They were not an enemy. They were our brothers.

We stayed the night at the farm of Erik of Rye Dale. I took Baldr up the Scar of Nab to look at the views of Windar's Mere and Úlfarrberg. It was a tranquil spot and we sat in silence and watched the sun dip in the west. As we neared the hall of Erik, Baldr said, "Now I understand this land. It is a circle made up of mountains and waters. Each is like a stronghold. The many make the whole. You are lucky to rule this land."

"Aye, Baldr, but how do I make certain that those who come after me can keep it?" I was asking the question of myself. Gruffyd's raid had disturbed my peace. It had unsettled my mind.

When we arrived back at Cyninges-tūn Sámr's family and Gruffyd's had already arrived. My hall was filled once more. I did not mind and Atticus positively revelled in it. Astrid was a proud mother and she glowed while Ragnar looked proud. Sámr was their eldest and he had chosen his bride well. Unlike the followers of the White Christ, we did not use churches for such ceremonies. The world was our church and so we held the ceremony on the shore by the Water. Old Olaf looked down upon us and the graves of my two wives could be seen across the Water. We made a blót before I joined Sámr and Æthelflæd together. The feast was held in the open. My Ulfheonar and their families were present as well as all the warriors who had come with us to rescue Atticus, Haraldr and Sweyn. There was much ale and the food had been prepared by Atticus, Astrid and Kara. It was the best of three worlds.

I saw both Kara and Ylva exchange knowing looks as Sámr and Æthelflæd whispered in each other's ears. They looked like a pair of wood pigeons courting. It was then I saw that Nanna and Baldr were also getting on well. When we had returned Baldr had been introduced to the two Saxons and he got on well with both of them. It was, however, Nanna who had grabbed his attention. The Norns' threads stretched from the heart of the land to the north of Miklagård to the land of the East Angles. Neither was Norse but I could see that they would become part of the Clan of the Wolf.

Ragnar asked, "Did Sámr say how long he would stay here? We have a piece of land picked out for him. It is between my hall and your son's. The ground is rock free for it was farmed in the time of Pasgen."

It was not my place to say what was in Sámr's mind. I knew he had picked out his own home and it was half a day from Ragnar. I said, "He is there, ask him yourself."

Ragnar frowned. My tone and my face were enough to warn him that he might not like Sámr's answer. "Son, when do you and your bride return to Whale Island? We have a fine plot of land chosen for you."

It was then that I saw the strength in Æthelflæd. She smiled, "Father, I may call you father may I not for mine is dead?"

Ragnar smiled, "Of course. I am honoured."

"Father, we have spent some time here at the Water and we have found a place we would like to make ours." She pointed, "It is the hall where the Dragonheart first lived. When we went inside its walls, even though they needed repair, we both felt it calling to us. It was, what is the word, *wyrd*? You do not mind, do you? We would both like to live close to the Dragonheart. If it was not for the Jarl then we would not be together, would we?"

Ragnar looked at Astrid who smiled and nodded, "You are right and this means that I can visit with my grandfather more often!" He looked at me, "For I know that he has been neglected of late. We have taken him for granted. It is time we paid him the respect he deserves."

And so a difficult situation was avoided. My world was at peace and I was happy. Perhaps the absence of Gruffyd should have warned me of a storm on the horizon but I was blissfully unaware of that.

My warriors drank copious amounts of ale and beer. There were fights. Some men are like that when they drink but none resulted in bloodletting. Olaf Leather Neck was the arbiter of all disputes and when he had had enough of his drinking being disturbed his mighty fists ended the bouts. I had yet to see Olaf falling down drunk. Haaken became even louder when drunk. His wife Anya rolled her eyes but it was with affection. His daughter, Yngvild, and her husband Lars just smiled. All the clan knew what Haaken was like, none more so than his family.

Ebrel and Bronnen sat together and had their heads close by Nanna and Æthelflæd. Elfrida, Ragnar's mother, now grey and looking like the clan matriarch just smiled at them. She had buried her husband, my son, and now she saw the clan as hers. This wedding was the highlight of her year. She did not like war, she was a Christian and her joy was in her grandchildren. Sámr was her favourite although she would have denied it if pressed. The reason was simple. Ragnar was a little like his father, Wolf Killer. Sámr was identical to my son! As he had grown he had become more like Wolf Killer in build, hair, complexion, voice and mannerisms. That was truly strange for Sámr had been born many years after Wolf Killer had been murdered.

The day after the wedding I went with Aiden, Germund and Atticus to my old hall. We did not walk but took one of the many fishing boats. It was pleasant sailing on the Water. The graves of my wives were now covered in summer flowers. Forget me nots and cranesbill cascaded down. The wind which blew them made the graves seem alive.

The structure of the hall was sound. We had used seasoned oak. The walls, however, had suffered as had the roof. The hall had been one of the first we had built and we had used turf for the roof and the lower walls. Turf needed maintenance. Aiden looked at the walls and the roof and came up with a simple solution. "We use slate for the roof; the mine has produced great quantities. We do not need to sell all of it and we also have good stone. We use the better stone for the outer walls and the neater stones for the inside. We use the poorer stones for infill."

Atticus busied himself with the interior. He was Greek and did not like the communal sleeping arrangements. Erika and I had been proud when we had built the upstairs sleeping quarters. Brigid had been less enamoured for she had to climb a ladder and she did not think that was appropriate for the wife of a jarl. Atticus came up with an answer. "We build a staircase. It can run the length of the hall so that it is not too steep and then build a false wall. Æthelflæd needs her privacy. Germund and the slaves can have rooms beneath the sleeping chamber and they will be away from prying eyes too." He smiled, "Servants and slaves work better if they feel that they have some degree of privacy."

The three of them had more and more suggestions and I left. Erika and I had been happy here. It had been our first home in the Land of the Wolf and but for the attempts by the Danes to kill me and of the witches to take my daughter, I would still have been there. The old do not like change. I went to the Water and took off my boots. I rolled up my breeks. I let the water flow over my feet. I subconsciously rubbed my finger along my scar. The wound in my thigh was healing but it was a reminder of how close I had come to death. It was good that my old hall was being renewed. It would bring life back into it and Sámr and Æthelflæd would, hopefully, be as happy as I had been with Erika.

When we returned to Cyninges-tūn I had to begin the preparations for the war. I had told men that I was going to fight Hibernians and men came to offer their services. All the warriors who had sailed with us to the Blue River came forward as did many others. Those with slight wounds like Cnut Cnutson volunteered their services. Men we had rescued and saved from enemies flocked to join us. Sven Stormchaser, Olaf Ulfsson, Sigiberhrt the Scar, Hrolf Bennison, Leif Longshanks, Galmr Greybeard, Haldi Haldisson, Snorri Gunnarson, Ulf Galmrson, Sweyn Olafsson, Harald Jorgenson the list was long. Not all had mail but they were all warriors. Baldr Witch Saviour would come as would Bergil Hafþórrsson and his brothers. We might have only a handful of Ulfheonar but we had two whole crews of warriors. We would be fully crewed.

I returned to Whale Island with Astrid, Bronnen, Ebrel, Elfrida and Ragnar. With Aiden and Atticus helping them Sámr and Æthelflæd had begun to make their hall a home. Sámr would go to war. He wanted his wife safe when he did so. The drekar were almost ready for sea but there was no sign of Gruffyd and Einar Fair Face. We had no way of knowing what had happened to them. I reassured Ebrel and Bronnen, "If they have not returned by the time I have finished in Hibernia then I will sail with Aiden to find them."

As soon as the words were out of my mouth I saw the relief on their faces. Jarl Dragonheart was never foresworn. If I said I would find them, then I would!

Chapter 10

My son had not returned when we gathered at Whale Island. We could not delay our departure. I had told Mánagarmr Long Stride and Conan Mac Finbarr that we would return at Tvímánuður and that was upon us. We had Raibeart and his drekar. We had a mighty fleet. I sent Bergil Hafþórrsson with Arne Eriksson as his captain in *'Running Bird'* to tell Mánagarmr Long Stride and Conan Mac Finbarr that we were on our way. *'Running Bird'* was the smallest and fastest of our drekar. She was so swift that they would be able to deliver my message and still reach us before we had reached Dyflin.

We knew the port very well and if Garðketill the Sly had lived there for any length of time then he would know its strengths and weaknesses. He would use the drekar like a longphort. It would keep an enemy away from the walls. The river was quite narrow close to the walls and their drekar could effectively bar the town. My plan was to fix the attention of the defenders to the north so that Conan and Mánagarmr Long Stride could march their men from the south and cross the Viking longphort. We would still have the walls to take but I knew Hibernians. They were wild fighters. If we could make them attack us then we had a chance. We would land at Hǫfuð. It was almost an island and was attached to the land by a narrow isthmus. We could leave our ships there and use them as a base. It would take Conan and Mánagarmr Long Stride two days to march to Dyflin. I guessed that the two warriors were too clever not to have begun men marching north. It mattered not when they reached the river just so that they did. I had more than enough men to attract their attention.

Ulla War Cry was on his father's ship but Sámr chose to sail with me. I could see that Ragnar was hurt but all warriors chose their own leader. One day Sámr would have his own drekar and oathsworn. The day was approaching quickly. Already some of the younger warriors had attached themselves to Sámr. He took an oar and had oar brothers. It was the first step on the long road to becoming jarl. Baldr was the one who shared an oar with my great-grandson.

It took more than a day to reach Dyflin. The winds did not cooperate. Bergil and Arne joined us just ten miles from the mouth of the river. Their message delivered we knew we would have allies heading north. We landed a short time before sunset on the beach which lay on the north side of Hǫfuð. We were not trying to hide. I just wanted us to land unopposed and to make defences at the narrow isthmus. We set up camp on what must have been an island at one time. Those who lived there had fled when we approached. Their sheep and goats made for a hot meal. They would flee to Dyflin and alert the King and his Viking allies. We were unworried. I sent Aðils Shape Shifter with five of the more promising young warriors to scout. They needed to learn and Aðils Shape Shifter was the best teacher we had. It was summer and we needed no tents. As jarl, I had a fire where most of the other jarls and leaders gathered. It allowed us to hold a council of war. I explained my plan.

"We are here to draw the enemy to us. We posture and we intimidate. I want them to come to us and try to drive us away. While they watch for us they cannot see the approach of our allies. When Conan and Mánagarmr Long Stride bring their men and cross the longphort I would have it come as a complete surprise."

Raibeart asked, "Do we fight them then?"

I laughed, "Of course we do but we fight as a shield wall. We have three ranks deep and a fourth rank of archers. We let them bleed upon our shields and spears."

"And if they do not?"

"Then, Ráðgeir Ráðgeirson, I will find some other way to make them do so. Perhaps I will have Haaken One Eye give them a saga! That would drive any man to violence!" They all laughed. None were worried and it was good.

Aðils Shape Shifter and his scouts arrived back in the middle watch. I was awoken. "They know we are here, Jarl Dragonheart, and they have barred their gates. We saw the roads choked with those fleeing inside Dyflin's walls."

"Good. More mouths for them to feed. Get some sleep."

"I will. The new scouts did well. They need more help in how to find that which they seek but it is coming. I am pleased."

"Good, then so am I."

When we rose the next morning, I had the warband armed and ready to march. I sent Haraldr and Sweyn to see if they could find any small fishing boats which might have been left when the settlement was abandoned. I had an idea of how we might annoy the Hibernian King. "Aðils Shape Shifter, take charge of the archers! You will be more use there this day."

I had, on my head, my refurbished helmet with the blue stone now in the centre. Bagsecg had made a ring of metal to hold it in place and to afford some protection. Some of the copper we had taken from the mine had also been used to strengthen the helmet and as I walked the sun glinted from it making it look like gold. Along with my freshly painted wolf shield and the wolf cloak draped about my shoulders, it told the Vikings in Dyflin that it was the Dragonheart who came for them. They would have been expecting my vengeance. You did not kill the child of the Dragonheart and expect forgiveness.

As we marched I saw that Sámr had a small following. Baldr had attached himself to my great-grandson. That was not a surprise. Baldr had shown an interest in Nanna. There were other young warriors too. Germund looked out of place as he limped along with them. I had Cnut Cnutson carrying my banner. His son, Cnut Cnutson, was with Sámr and it was right that it was so. We stopped half a mile from the walls of Dyflin. They were wooden and the gatehouse was small. We could take it but I was not willing to waste men. This revenge would be a dish served cold. We had time and a secret army marching into the soft underbelly of Dyflin.

We formed our four ranks and waited. If they sallied forth then we would fight them but I did not think they would. We waited until noon. They were not coming. I marched to the front of my men. "Inside these walls are foresworn Vikings who betrayed Thorghest the Lucky. Many of you fought with Thorghest. On my command, we will march forward until I plant my standard! Then we will stop!"

Cnut appeared next to me. He held the standard in his right hand and his shield in his left.

"Let us go!"

"This is like old times, Jarl!" Cnut was Ulfheonar but it had been some time since he had marched to war. Aiden stood behind me. If arrows came in his direction then my men's shields would protect him. We needed the Vikings to see my galdramenn.

We marched until we were one hundred and fifty paces from the walls. Arrows flew from the fighting platform. We held up our shields and a couple smacked into them. I saw, from the ones which landed short, that they were hunting arrows. In theory, the men loosing from the fighting platform should have had an advantage but they were using poor bows and arrows which were even worse.

I shouted, "Garðketill the Sly, you are a foresworn villain who betrayed his lord and then murdered my family. Come now and have combat to the death with this old man! Save your men from certain death!"

There was silence and then a voice answered, "I will not waste my time! You are too few to take us, old man! Go back home and drink ale."

I laughed, "Then you do not know me. If you had a spine then you would meet us beard to beard and end this now but you are afraid. All of you fear us and you now fill your breeks!"

"Your words are just air. They signify nothing!" If he believed he could defeat us then he would have accepted my challenge. His men would now wonder why their leader did not fight a greybeard.

I turned to Cnut, "He fears us more than I thought!" I raised Ragnar's Spirit, "Aðils Shape Shifter, five flights as quickly as you can manage it!"

His men were ready and I heard, "Nock! Draw! Release!" A hundred arrows soared and before they had landed another one hundred followed. The five hundred arrows found flesh. I heard screams and cries as men were struck.

From inside I heard, "Shields!"

It was of course, too little, too late. When the arrows ceased we could hear the moans and groans from inside. My me began beating their shields and Haaken began a chant. It was aimed, not at the Hibernians but at the Vikings. It was a powerful saga which was known by all Vikings. It told of how we had managed to get inside an impregnable fortress and kill our enemies. The message would not be lost on the Vikings. They were not safe from the Dragonheart.

The Saxon King had a mighty home
Protected by rock, sea and foam
Safe he thought from all his foes
But the Dragonheart would bring new woes
Ulfheonar never forget
Ulfheonar never forgive
Ulfheonar fight to the death
The snake had fled and was hiding there
Safe he thought in the Saxon lair
With heart of dragon and veins of ice
Dragonheart knew nine would suffice

Ulfheonar never forget
Ulfheonar never forgive
Ulfheonar fight to the death
Below the sand, they sought the cave
The rumour from the wizard brave
Beneath the sea without a light
The nine all waited through the night
Ulfheonar never forget
Ulfheonar never forgive
Ulfheonar fight to the death
When night fell they climbed the stair
Invisible to the Saxons there
In the tower the traitors lurked
Dragonheart had a plan which worked
Ulfheonar never forget
Ulfheonar never forgive
Ulfheonar fight to the death
With Odin's blade the legend fought
Magnus' tricks they came to nought
With sword held high and a mighty thrust
Dragonheart sent Magnus to an end that was just
Ulfheonar never forget
Ulfheonar never forgive
Ulfheonar fight to the death
Ulfheonar never forget
Ulfheonar never forgive
Ulfheonar fight to the death

We stood until the middle of the afternoon. The defenders sent a few desultory arrows in our direction but they did no damage. Then we marched back to our camp. Sámr sought me out as we crossed the isthmus, "What did that achieve, Jarl Dragonheart?" His voice was questioning rather than rebellious. I saw his father smile.

"Their jarl told his men that he was afraid of me. He would not fight me. Remember that, Ulla and Sámr. Men like to follow brave leaders. He should have accepted my challenge and he did not. The arrows showed all those within that we have superior weapons. We killed many and wounded more. We killed men on the fighting platform. We killed warriors. Haaken chose the best chant he could. They heard the words and remembered how Jarl Dragonheart managed to get inside a wall of stone and kill faithless enemies. Aiden helped us to gain entry and they would have seen the galdramenn. The Hibernians are not the ones I sought to intimidate. I wish to weaken the real warriors, the Vikings!"

I saw that Ulla War Cry and Sámr had taken in my words and were thinking. Haraldr came up to me. "Jarl, we have found one fishing ship."

"Excellent." I turned to Aiden. "You know what to do."

He nodded, "Fill it with kindling. Put the kindling in a pot and at high tide and when the wind is right, take it close to the river and fire it."

I smiled, "Let us see how our Norse brethren like their ships being burned!"

Others, Sven Stormchaser, Olaf Ulfsson, Sigiberhrt the Scar, and Hrolf Bennison, went to help them. I drank some ale and ate some cold mutton. Then, with the Ulfheonar, I walked along the shoreline until we could see the masts of the drekar at the longphort. We sat on the sandy dunes and waited. We could see the rising tide and feel the freshening wind.

Haaken said, "If this works then the gods are with us."

Rollo said, "That cannot be in doubt for the enemy are foresworn and betrayed their lord."

We watched as there was a flickering light to the south of us. Aiden and Haraldr had cleverly placed the fire in the bows so that the wind could still blow the sails and send them close to the drekar. The narrow nature of the river and the wind ensured that the boat would have to strike one of the moored drekar in the longphort. The wind was a good one and Haraldr had tied the steering board so that the boat flew straight and true. There was silence save for the crackling of the kindling. The pot would heat and, eventually, ignite the hull, but for the moment the boat was whole and safe. It sped on its silent way. They had guards on their ships and one must have seen the glow of the fire. Suddenly the air was rent with his cries, "Fireship!"

We met Aiden, Haraldr and the others as they walked back to our camp. They stopped and turned to watch with us as the fishing boat did its deadly deed.

A longphort was a good way to defend a number of ships using a few men. That was also its weakness for if a fireship came then it was hard to untangle the vessels quickly. The fact that the attack came from the sea left them with one option only. They had to try to head upstream. We heard the alarm given and orders were given. When flames leapt up into the air then we knew that the fireship had struck. The impact would have knocked over the fire pot and spread up the mast, sail and then into the nearest drekar. The ship which was struck would be lost. Drekar in a longphort were bone dry. We saw the fire and, in its light, we saw men, looking like ants, swarming over the other ships to free them. When a second ship was ignited we could see more. There were screams and shouts as men, trying to save the other drekar were caught on board the burning vessels and had to leap into the river to save themselves. They must have been able to separate the two stricken drekar for there were no more fires. The two burning ships gradually settled lower into the water and the river began to douse the flames. The masts and sails would continue to burn for they would be above the water.

We headed back to our camp. I clapped Aiden on the back. "Once again your clever mind has helped us."

Aiden gave a sad smile, "So long as my mind works it is yours to command."

Haraldr said, "But Jarl, how will our allies cross the river?"

"The surviving drekar are upstream. They need to be moored. Wherever they are moored will be a place to cross and if not, there are fords upstream. They can cross." We neared our camp where I saw men looking at the glow in the sky. "The real victory is to the hearts of the Vikings. Two of their drekar are sunk. They have lost men on their walls and they have yet to strike a blow against us. Garðketill the Sly will have men clamouring for him to do something. Tomorrow we array once more for battle and see what effect our raid has had."

As we entered the camp we were assailed by questions. When Haaken told them what we had seen there was laughter and then a huge cheer. That would also begin to unnerve the defenders. Olaf said, "And if they do not fight then tomorrow night the wolves can howl. The Ulfheonar can strike."

There was a time when that would have been a real threat. Now, I feared, it would merely be an irritant. "Perhaps but we are perilously few. Let us save that tactic for a time when all else has failed."

When we marched towards the walls the air was filled with the acrid smell of burning. Nearing the stronghold, we saw the remains of the two blackened masts, stumps now, peering from the water. The attack had been more successful than we could have hoped for the channel was now blocked. The drekar, which had been brought back to the quay, were trapped. We stood and my men began banging their shields, "Dragonheart! Dragonheart! Dragonheart!"

Cnut Cnutson waved my standard above my head. Once again, the shining sun reflected from my helmet and, once again, it appeared to glow like gold and the single blue stone looked like a terrible eye. I was at the fore and all who sheltered behind their shields on the fighting platform would be able to see me. A desultory shower of arrows and stones flew from the walls. They landed woefully short. The wind which had taken the fire ship in from the east had strengthened. I said, "Aðils Shape Shifter, arrows!"

The wind which had slowed the enemy arrows helped ours. Some struck the walls but others found shields and at least one found flesh. They had been prepared this time. Aðils Shape Shifter and his men just sent three flights and then they stopped. There was little point in wasting arrows.

We did not have to wait until noon for a reaction. The gates opened and the defenders emerged to form ranks and fight us. We were less than two hundred paces from them. I turned to my jarls who were standing just behind me. "We will not allow them the luxury of deployment. Boar's snout! Ragnar, you will be one tusk!"

"Aye Dragonheart."

"Aðils Shape Shifter, hurt them!"

The two wedges were easy to form for all that Ragnar and I had to do was to begin to walk forward and the tusks formed behind us. Cnut Cnutson tucked in the third rank between Rolf and Rollo. With Haaken and Olaf behind me, I was as well protected as any king. The arrows from our archers made the enemy try to form up with their shields held above them. It allowed us to move closer, quickly. The Hibernians and Vikings were too concerned with getting men out of the walls of Dyflin to notice that we were attacking. They must have thought that we would await an attack. They had expected the luxury of time to deploy into lines. I began banging the pommel of my sword into my shield. The ones behind took it up and the rhythm helped us to keep in step. My leg ached a little but it did not slow me. I was Ulfheonar and I could fight even though I was in pain. I saw that the gate was filled with men trying to get out and Hibernians and Vikings jostled to fight with shield brothers. When they realised what we were doing then it was too late.

An archer on their walls must have thought that he had a chance for glory. He sent an arrow at me. I saw that its flight was true. I could not avoid it and it smacked into my helmet. I knew, from the sound it made, that it had struck the blue stone. Even as I saw him raise his arm and cheer an arrow plucked him from the walls. The gods smiled on me and Bagsecg had made a good job of the helmet. Neither the stone nor the helmet appeared to be damaged.

The intended shield wall was not ready and my shield struck a Viking whose spear was still pointed in the air. The shields were not locked and the ones behind were still trying to get into formation. The warrior wore no mail and I used Ragnar's Spirit to hack through his left shoulder. He dropped his shield and fell at my feet. I stepped on to the dying man's shield. It raised me up so that I appeared to be a giant. As I brought my sword over my shoulder I shouted, "I am Jarl Dragonheart and you all fight for a foresworn snake!" My elevated position and the long swing of my sword gave my blow a god-like strength. It split the helmet and skull of the warrior before me in two. Behind me, Rolf and Olaf used their axes to great effect. Their sweeping swings made a huge hole in their unformed line. My last strike had opened up a gap too and I saw that the gates were still open. Their men were still pouring out to fight us. We had a chance to end this battle without the need for allies!

A horn sounded and a Viking voice shouted, "Back!"

With the weight of eighty men behind me and my sword, we were unstoppable. Some of the better warriors we were fighting tried to march back into the walls of Dyflin but most just ran. I had limited vision for I was at the fore and fighting to get through the thin line of men who had formed up before me. Haaken One Eye showed that he had lost none of his skill when he back slashed across the neck of a Viking hersir who tried to skewer me. What stopped us was the sheer number of men before us. The Hibernian King must have decided to cut his losses. I saw the gates slam shut and there were still more than sixty men without. Most were Vikings. They knew there would be no mercy and they fought to go to Valhalla. Our two wedges had now broken up. Bergil and his brothers, Raibeart and Ragnar, Sámr and Ráðgeir Ráðgeirson all led their own bands of men to destroy the Vikings. Aðils and his archers had won the duel of the bow and they kept the fighting platform clear. There were Hibernians mixed with the Viking warriors. They fought recklessly and bravely without mail and often without helmets and shields. Some fought on even when a limb was severed. Perhaps they took something to make them wild or it might have been their nature but none surrendered. The only way to ensure that they were dead was to take their heads.

One of those Vikings who remained before the wall suddenly hurled his shield at us and launched himself at me. He had gone berserk. They were the most dangerous of men for I had seen them fight on when they should have been dead. Normal rules of combat did not apply. I braced myself for his attack. He held his sword in two hands and launched himself at me. He leapt into the air and brought the blade down towards my head. I barely deflected it with my shield but his weight drove me to my knees. I had the presence of mind to stab at his knee. As I saw the blade slide backwards from the wound I felt blood spurt. He did not seem to notice it and raised his sword again. I stood and brought up the edge of my shield under his chin. At the same time, Olaf Leather Neck swung his axe to hack through the Viking's mail and into his side. The blow should have killed him but he struck my helmet with his sword. My blow to his chin weakened his strike and I swung my sword sideways and took his head in one blow. Even a berserker cannot fight without his head. His corpse fell at my feet.

Haaken lifted the skull and held it above him. He began to chant, "Dragonheart! Dragonheart! Dragonheart!" The chant was taken up by our men.

Aðils Shape Shifter and the archers were our protectors and so I shouted, "Take our dead and wounded back! We have won this battle!"

There was a cheer. Men began to strip the enemy dead. There was mail, swords and gold to be had. The stripped bodies of their warriors spread out before their walls would hurt them as much as the lost battle. The wind from the east was our ally. The smell would be in their noses and fill the houses of Dyflin. It would be a reminder of their failure. The Ulfheonar were the last from the field. As we marched back I saw that Ragnar and Ulla War Cry had survived. Sámr and Baldr had blood-spattered byrnies but they lived. The warriors who had died would be in Valhalla. We did not yet have vengeance but we had made a start.

We buried our dead on Hǫfuð. They were buried with their swords and helmets. None of those who had died had worn mail. Those with mail had been in the wedges that were the tusks of the boar. When our lines had become disorganized then wilder young warriors sought glory and found death. It was ever thus. Sámr and Baldr had only been spared because of their mail. Both would be better the next time they fought.

We set a watch on their gate. They could not reach the sea and we barred their other gate. I knew that they could still send for help through the small gate to the north of the stronghold. That could not be helped. If they sent for more Hibernians so be it. We had done all that I intended and now we could wait. We had food and the weather was clement. I filled a drekar with young warriors and under the command of Arne Eriksson sent them to the river. I did not want the wrecks removed yet. The presence of **'Running Bird'** would serve to remind them that they had lost the first two battles.

The one flaw in my plan was that we would not know when Conan and the Vikings of Veisafjǫrðr would arrive. I spoke with Aiden, "Can you see them?"

He shook his head, "My guess would be on the morrow. It is tonight you need to worry about."

"You think they will try something when it is dark?"

"As do you. That is why you rest our best warriors."

"The Irish King and the lord of Dyflin have to do something. There are brave men in their walls. There are warriors who cannot live with the dishonour we have heaped upon them. Even though the sensible thing might be to wait inside the walls and hope friends come they cannot do that. Night time means our arrows cannot hurt them for our bowmen cannot see them. They will have seen the guard we leave and send men to slay them and then try to hurt us."

We held a council of war and I told my leaders of my plan. We all rested during the hours before darkness. The days were still far longer than the night and so we were well-rested. As soon as it was dark I led half of my men from the camp. Ragnar and Raibeart would command for the Ulfheonar, with wolf cloaks, blackened faces and hands slipped towards the dead bodies which lay before the walls. We moved silently and lay amongst the dead. Our wolf cloaks hid us completely. The Vikings and the Hibernians would step carefully when they came to attack us. They would not risk stepping on a body and falling. We had left our shields and helmets back at the camp. It was a risk but if my plan succeeded then we would have added another weapon to our armoury; terror.

We lay so that we could see the gate. We waited. An Ulfheonar is patient. Like a wolf pack hunting, we could take our time to guarantee success. Even though they opened it quietly, we saw the movement and the shadows who flitted out. I counted them. There were sixty of them.

They moved silently and picked their way between the bodies. The gates closed and the light from within the walls was hidden from us. As they drew near I saw a Viking warrior approaching me, he was bare-chested and carried an axe and a shield while wearing a helmet with a face mask, he paused and sniffed. Could he smell me? I was less than ten paces from him. A Hibernian came from behind and poked him in the back to make him move. He turned and raised his arm. There was discord between the allies. The two of them moved on. Another Hibernian almost stepped on me. Then they were gone. I counted to ten and then rose. I unsheathed my sword. The other Ulfheonar also rose equally silently. We spread out to form a line between the raiders and the gate. They were not looking behind them. They were searching for the men they had seen on guard.

We walked purposefully towards them. I slipped Wolf's Blood into my left hand. I saw Rolf and Olaf hold their axes in two hands. Aðils Shape Shifter had his bow. He would use that until he was seen. The men who had passed us were obviously volunteers and the best warriors from Dyflin. Defeating them would bring victory quicker. I must have become careless for the man before me began to turn. It mattered not for my sword was already slicing towards his side. Axes and swords fell as the Ulfheonar began to kill. Arrows flew. I began to howl and it was taken up by the others. Even as the raiders turned Ragnar and Raibeart led a hundred warriors to attack them. We moved in closer. Dagger and sword slashed and stabbed. I was a black shadow and the whites of their faces showed.

The huge warrior with the bare chest I had seen roared, "Treachery!" His sword took the arm of Galmr Ulfsson. Then Ragnar leapt at him and deftly ducked beneath the swinging sword and hacked into the side of the giant. Even as the Viking roared Ragnar spun around and lunged at the warrior's bare neck. When the blood spurted the giant fell. Three Hibernians tried to run back to Dyflin. I took one, Haaken a second and Rollo a third. It was over. There was silence save for the groans of the men who had yet to die.

"Take their heads and plant a row of them here. They will see their hope is gone when dawn breaks."

I was weary as I trudged back to our camp. My age was telling. Ragnar, Ulla War Cry and Sámr flanked me. "Grandfather, you do not need to do this."

I smiled, "When you have so few Ulfheonar then I do. There were at least three warriors I slew who might have done harm to my people. I am unharmed. This is good."

"But you have done so much already."

I looked at Ragnar, "And I lead the clan. Will you take over that responsibility? Will you be the one they look to?" His face gave me the answer. He looked to the ground. I saw Sámr's look. It was one of disappointment. "Then until another steps into my boots, I will continue to risk my life."

Ragnar said, "But what of Gruffyd?"

I stopped, "What do you think?"

Sámr gripped my arm, "I will take on your mantle, great grandfather, but let me grow so that I may fill your boots, eh?"

In that moment Ragnar abdicated his responsibility and handed it to his son. I had my heir and it had been achieved without a bloodbath.

Chapter 11

I slept well. None woke me for there was no need. When Dyflin woke it saw its hopes struck in the ground on the top of spears. They had tried and they had failed. We rested and waited. If Aiden was correct then we would have an army of allies arriving soon. Sámr and Baldr were there when I woke. It was late in the morning and I wondered why I had been left to sleep the morning away.

Aiden handed me a horn of ale. He smiled, "You slept well, Jarl. You must have needed the rest."

"You should have woken me!"

"Why? There was nothing for you to do. Aðils Shape Shifter and the archers discouraged the Vikings when they tried to recover their dead. The wounded were tended to and the men were fed. What else was there to do?"

I nodded and drank my ale. He was right but I was jarl and I should have been woken. Baldr asked, "Jarl, what happens if our allies cannot get across the river?"

Baldr was new to the world of Vikings. He was a horseman and swift movements were what he knew. "They will come but, if some disaster strikes and the Norns spin then we will assault their walls. We will lose more men that way but we will win."

"How can you be certain, Jarl?"

"Because their best men are dead. The ones with courage fought hard and died. The ones who are behind the walls are the reluctant warriors. They will be looking for a way out rather than a glorious death. We need patience. We have food, we have ale and we have time."

"We attack the walls?"

"If we have to. They are made of wood and they are not high. We can use arrows to keep men from the walls but use patience, Sámr. We hunt man and they are the most dangerous of prey."

We knew when Conan and Mánagarmr Long Stride arrived for there were horns in the town. There was a clamour. Our allies had done as I had asked and they were on the river side of Dyflin. They arrived in the late morning. The defenders of Dyflin were trapped. We had not lost a large number of men yet and we now had double the number to make our attack.

I went to Erik, "I would sail to the river bank and speak with Conan and Mánagarmr Long Stride."

He looked at the masthead, "The wind will take us and the current bring us out but you will not have much time. I will have time to turn us around and that is all."

"That will be enough." I waved at the nearest men. "Come board the drekar! I have work for you."

They leapt aboard and Arne and Lars cast off. I saw Sámr and Baldr race to the wharf and leap the gap to land on the deck. Sámr grinned, "You cannot leave us behind, great grandfather!"

When we reached *'Running Bird'* I saw that there was a safe channel but it ran perilously close to the river bank. Only a skilled captain could navigate it. Erik Short Toe was such a captain. There was an alarming creak as we scraped along the wreck but Erik did not seem worried. I saw that the remaining drekar were now tied next to Dyflin's wharf and they had a good-sized guard upon them. As we had already killed many men that meant the garrison was stretched thin. I saw the standards of the jarl and the Hibernians. It was a mass of men who cheered and banged their shields.

Erik pulled in close to the shore and I leapt to the bank. Sámr and Baldr followed me. Erik shouted, "I will turn us around. Do not be dainty with your words, Jarl! Time presses!"

I waved a hand and strode over to Conan Mac Finbarr and Mánagarmr Long Stride. I clasped their arms. "You have made good time. We have fought two small battles with the defenders and bested them. You need to occupy them from this side."

"Easier said than done, Jarl Dragonheart. We cannot walk on water!"

I looked across the river. "You could if you had a bridge."

"A bridge? You can conjure one?"

"No, we have one, *'Running Bird'*. When it is dark she can come up the river and you can use her to cross to their drekar."

"How do we coordinate our attacks?"

"We will sound three horns but if you are to lose the fewest number of men it should be at night. Is tonight too soon?"

Conan shook his head, "Yesterday is not too soon. We will be there!"

My drekar turned and Erik shouted, "Hurry, Jarl, the tide is on the turn and I would not risk the wreck in shallower water."

We jumped aboard. "Stop by your son's drekar. I have a task for him."

As *'Running Bird'* was beyond the wreck there was no danger. When we stopped I spoke to Erik's son, "Arne, I would have you sail upstream when it is dark and be the bridge for our men. Can you do it?"

I saw his father watch him. Both were sailors and knew the seas and rivers better than any. Arne nodded, "I have a smaller keel and I ride higher in the water. If my father could do it in *'Heart'* then I can do so in this threttanessa."

"Then wait until the next high tide." I turned to the men I had brought, "You will be the crew to row up the river!" They crossed to the drekar and my plans were made. Now I had to work out how to attack the walls! The river and Erik's skill took us back to the other drekar and Ragnar, Raibeart and the Ulfheonar awaited us as we joined them on the beach. Aiden wandered over from the shelters where the wounded were being tended.

"Our allies are here and they will use *'Running Bird'* as a bridge to attack the walls. They will do so when we sound the horn. We will be in position before nightfall."

Ragnar said, "You wish them to see us preparing to attack?"

"I do for I want their attention here and not on the river. The attempted attack on our camp gave me an idea. There was no moon and the dark was so complete that they thought to attack us whilst hidden. We can use the same idea." I waved Aiden closer. "Can we fire the gates?"

He rubbed his chin. "There are still pots which the people left when they fled. We can do as we did with the fireship. We carry the covered pots and place them next to the gates. We place them at an angle on a piece of timber which is attached to a rope. When we are far enough away we pull the ropes, and the wood comes away. The pots and the coals spill out and set fire to the gates. If we take kindling and lay it around the gates then that will accelerate the fire."

Sámr said, "We have some pig fat in our drekar. We put that on the gates and they will burn quicker."

I smiled at Ragnar's surprised expression. His son had spent more time with me of late and I knew him better than he did. "A good idea. When the gates burn we sound the horn and begin our attack. Aðils Shape Shifter can use our archers to deter them from dousing the flames."

"They are running short of arrows, Dragonheart."

Aiden was clever. He was not just a galdramenn, he used his mind as a weapon. "Then they use them judiciously. We attack the walls along their length. We have shields we can use to scale them. With Conan and Mánagarmr attacking the other side we will confuse them and split their defences. Ragnar, divide the men into groups of ten. Allocate them a section of the wall to attack."

The defenders must have known something was going on for the field before their walls began to fill with men. The pots were prepared at our camp but our warriors went to view the section of wall they would attack. We were not mindless barbarians. They did not want a glorious death trying to climb a wall. If they were to die then they would do killing an enemy! My men looked for dangers and looked for that which they could use to scale the walls. The wood which would be placed under pots and the kindling we would use were placed together. All that we awaited were the pots. There was a great deal of activity on the walls. They knew we were up to something and they were watching us.

As darkness fell the pots were brought and Aðils and his archers closed with the walls. The pots were carried towards the walls. The time it took for us to get into position and prepare the fire would allow the drekar the time to get to the river bank and become the bridge. It would be the Ulfheonar who carried the two pots the last two hundred paces to the walls. They also carried the coils of rope they would use. Ragnar said, "You will not go, grandfather. We will not risk you. Give me your cloak and I will go. I will carry the kindling!"

I tried to argue but there was a mutiny. My captains and family refused to allow me to risk myself. It was Aiden who convinced me. "Hiding on the ground while you waited for an enemy was one thing but this needs men who can move swiftly over the open ground. Your leg is healed but you still limp. Would you allow Cnut Cnutson with his bad leg to go?"

He was right. This needed warriors who were perfect. The five of them slipped away in the darkness. Haaken and Rollo had ropes around the neck of one covered pot and Olaf and Rolf the other. They picked their way across the corpse-littered ground. There was noise. It was the sound of rats scurrying among the feast we had made for them. I could barely see them when they were twenty paces from us and then they disappeared. All the rest of our men were in position and we moved slowly forward. I heard no twang of a bowstring. Aðils and his archers had no need to send an arrow for the Ulfheonar were invisible wraiths.

We moved closer. Still, there was no sign of the five men. I could not stand the tension. I would rather be the one in danger than risk my grandson. Sámr, Baldr and Germund were close behind me as was Cnut Cnutson. We had the men who would attack our section of wall with us: Haraldr Leifsson, Haldi Haldisson, Snorri Gunnarson, Ulf Galmrson, Sweyn Olafsson and Harald Jorgenson.

Ragnar ghosted from the dark. He slipped my wolf skin from his shoulders and gave it to me. He smiled. Putting his mouth to my ear he said, "I was Ulfheonar but briefly. Now I feel like a real warrior."

Olaf and Haaken held the two ropes. I turned to Cnut and nodded. He put the cow's horn to his lips. I said quietly, "When you are ready, Haaken and Olaf!"

They both pulled their ropes hard. There was a double crash. Suddenly a flame flared up.

"Now, Cnut!"

The horn sounded three times and, with shields held before us, we advanced the one hundred paces to the walls. The flames rapidly leapt up the dry gates and began to devour the wood. Men were highlighted by the inferno and our archers began to pick off the ones they saw. We picked our way over the bodies and closed with the walls. We all kept away from the gates. Aðils Shape Shifter, the Ulfheonar and the archers would charge through them when the time was right.

When we reached the wall, I turned my back and leaned it against the wall. There would have been a time when I would have been the one to climb. Now I was the ladder. I was taller than most of the others and while they paired up and held shields I cupped my hands. Snorri Gunnarson ran at me and when he placed his foot in my hands I threw him up the walls. Baldr came next and he soared like a bird. Germund did the same for Sámr. I turned as ropes were dropped. I could hear the sound of battle on the walls. Luck determined who had a fight and who did not. We had none above us and I walked up the walls like a human spider. Once on the fighting platform, I saw that there was a battle to the west of us. I swung my shield around and raised Ragnar's Spirit. I might have been too old and slow to carry the pots but I could do this. I led my ten men towards Bergil Hafþórrsson and his brothers as they fought off a knot of Hibernians who had been guarding the walls.

My blackened mail hid me from sight and when my sword rammed through the unprotected back of the Hibernian who was trying to get at Beorn our surprise was complete. A night battle was a confused affair.

The Hibernians we fought were easier to kill for they did not wear mail but once we faced Vikings we would be facing our own kind. As the last of those fighting Bergil Hafþórrsson and his brothers were slain I turned to Sámr, "Keep close behind me. You, Baldr and Germund watch my back."

The walls did not have steps they had ladders. Bergil led his brothers down them and with their knot of men cleared a space to allow us down. The defenders were rushing to the walls. They came at us piecemeal. Bergil's improvised shield wall afforded us the time to join him. We now had twenty-one men. There were houses built close together but I saw that they were wide enough for six men.

"Bergil, form a wedge!"

I joined the five men at the rear and my men behind me. I put my shield in the back of Hrolf Bennison and we began to march. We chanted as we moved, "Clan of the Wolf! Clan of the Wolf!" It helped us to keep in step and I knew that enemies would be intimidated by it. As Vikings and Hibernians ran between the houses to get at us they found themselves facing swords and shields. We ploughed through them like ploughshare through soft earth. The sounds of battle filled the air. Men were dying. Behind us, I knew that the walls were burning for it looked like a sunrise. The light from the flames lit the faces of those before us. Some stood to face us, knowing that they would die while others just ran. I hoped that our allies were now attacking the other walls.

We fought our way to the centre of the town and the jarl's hall. I knew it well for I had stayed there with Thorghest and Erika. The last of the Vikings of Garðketill the Sly were in a shield wall. He was in the third rank. I did not see the Hibernian King but I could hear fighting by the river gate. Perhaps they had divided their forces. I saw some of our younger warriors throw themselves at the shield wall. They were butchered. The ones who remained with Garðketill the Sly were the best of warriors. They wore mail. They would not die easily.

"Hold! Form a shield wall! Ulfheonar!"

The reckless young warriors heeded my shout. The enemy cheered as they fell back. To them, this was a victory. The fire had taken hold to such an extent that it looked as though dawn had come early. The houses and huts which lay close to the gates were now ablaze. We had to end this quickly or else we would all have a fiery death.

My Ulfheonar, Ragnar and Raibeart joined me. I pointed at Garðketill the Sly and his men. "We need to destroy them quickly."

Aðils Shape Shifter said, "We do not have enough arrows to use that weapon. This will have to be blade to blade."

Aiden had not advanced with us and I needed his wisdom. Ragnar said, "They are three ranks deep. I think there are less than a hundred of them left. We outnumber them."

Olaf snorted, "That just guarantees that they will not surrender and will try to take as many of our men as they can. We have fewer men with mail. This will be finely balanced, Jarl Dragonheart."

There was just one way. Shield wall to shield wall would see us lose too many men. We had to use the best that we had. "Wedge. Ulfheonar at the fore!"

Olaf nodded, "And I will be the point. Jarl, you will be behind Rolf and Rollo!"

They began to form the wedge and I had no opportunity to object. Aðils Shape Shifter stood on one side of me and Haaken One Eye on the other. Haraldr stood behind me with Cnut Cnutson and my standard. Bergil and Benni Hafþórrsson flanked them. We had hardened steel at our fore. Haaken began to bang his shield and chant. We had done this before and knew that our chants put iron in our men and shook the resolve of defenders. It allowed the wedge to form. We sang the sword song. I gripped Ragnar's Spirit and felt its power surge through me as the story of the fateful night on Man was sung.

The storm was wild and the gods did roam
The enemy closed on the Prince's home
Two warriors stood on a lonely tower
Watching, waiting for hour on hour.
The storm came hard and Odin spoke
With a lightning bolt the sword he smote
Ragnar's Spirit burned hot that night
It glowed, a beacon shiny and bright
The two they stood against the foe
They were alone, nowhere to go
They fought in blood on a darkened hill
Dragon Heart and Cnut will save us still
Dragon Heart, Cnut and the Ulfheonar
Dragon Heart, Cnut and the Ulfheonar

The storm was wild and the Gods did roam
The enemy closed on the Prince's home
Two warriors stood on a lonely tower
Watching, waiting for hour on hour.
The storm came hard and Odin spoke
With a lightning bolt the sword he smote
Ragnar's Spirit burned hot that night
It glowed, a beacon shiny and bright
The two they stood against the foe
They were alone, nowhere to go
They fought in blood on a darkened hill
Dragon Heart and Cnut will save us still
Dragon Heart, Cnut and the Ulfheonar
Dragon Heart, Cnut and the Ulfheonar

When we finished it, we began banging our shields. We stopped as one and I shouted, "Forward the Clan of the Wolf; we have vengeance this day!"

The men who faced us had a mixture of shields and swords. Our formation was aimed at the centre of the line where their jarl stood. Olaf, Rolf and Rollo would strike at the two men in the centre. They would both be good warriors but they would find it hard to defeat three Ulfheonar. The discipline of the rest would be tested for there would be a temptation for the wings to lap around the side of our wedge. If they did so then they would have lost for, like an arrow, in mail, our tip would break the stretched steel skin of the enemy snake. There was a mighty clash as the axes of Rolf and Olaf smashed into the two warriors. Rollo's sword darted forward and the two men fell. I pushed my shield in Rolf's back as we surged through their first rank. Haaken slashed his sword sideways and it bit into the side of a warrior's helmet. Benni Hafþórrsson's sword finished the job. Rolf's axe swung and took the head of a warrior in the second row and then disaster struck. A spear darted from the third rank and I saw the head erupt from the back of Rolf's skull. Rolf Horse Killer died. It was as quick as that. Haaken stepped forward to take his place and Benni Hafþórrsson joined me. Ragnar moved into the rank behind us.

Rollo and Rolf had joined my band together and had always fought side by side. They had adjacent farms. Rollo Thin Skin could not contain himself. He turned to hack and slash at those to his left and Aðils Shape Shifter was forced to turn to protect him. The wedge began to crumble. Olaf was forced to turn to his right and help Haaken fight off the warriors there.

I was left to face Garðketill the Sly. "I am pleased that I will be the one to kill the killer of my child."

Garðketill the Sly wore an open-face helmet. I saw that he filed his teeth and blackened tombstones greeted me as he spoke, "I may die this day but I will kill an old man first and I will die with Ragnar's Spirit in my hand. You should have stayed at home. This is a day for warriors and not old men with old wounds!"

Even as he spoke he tried to back slash his sword at my weakened leg. When he had said, *'old wounds'* I had known what he intended and my shield was already sliding down to block the blow. I then brought up the edge of my shield and rammed it under his nose. I heard it break. Cartlidge and blood-spattered. His vision would be impaired. Haaken had his back to me and I could not swing my sword. I brought back my head and butted him hard. The new blue stone struck him in the middle of his forehead. I saw the mark it left. He reeled backwards and, stepping forward, I was able to swing Ragnar's Spirit. As he fell backwards instinct took over and he raised his shield. My sword struck the wood and he fell backwards against the wattle and daub of the hall. He could not see me for his eyes were streaming but he quickly stood and pulled his sword and shield before him. I held my sword above my shield and I ran at him. Two things happened. My sword slid along the side of his skull. It sliced off his left ear and knocked his helmet from his head. Secondly, our combined weight was such that we broke through the wattle and daub. I landed on him heavily. We were inside the hall. Blood oozed from his ear and skull. I used my shield to push myself to my feet and, throwing away my shield I held Ragnar's Spirit in both hands and plunged it through his neck and into the ground.

Outside I could hear the battle raging. Men were dying. I took my sword and hacked off the head of Garðketill the Sly. Holding it by the hair I walked out of the door and held it high, "Garðketill the Sly is dead! Surrender and you shall live! You have the word of Jarl Dragonheart of the Clan of the Wolf!"

There was a momentary pause and men turned to stare at me.

"This is the sword which was touched by the gods and I am never foresworn! Surrender or die and your death will be useless for your leader is dead!"

Swords and spears were lowered. One pigtailed warrior with battle bracelets took off his helmet. "And what happens to us?"

"Who are you?"

"I am Sven the Boneless."

"Then, Sven the Boneless, you take one drekar and leave. If we see you again in this land or the Land of the Wolf then you die."

He nodded. "We will take the drekar and we will quit this land. We will go to the land of the Angles and the Saxons."

And with that our battle was over. As dawn broke we collected our dead. We had lost an Ulfheonar and this was no victory. Olaf, Rollo and the others carried Rolf Horse Killer's body. He would be buried on Hǫfuð. That would be when the battle for Dyflin was over.

Leaving Ragnar and Raibeart to watch the captured Vikings I went with the rest of my men to the river gate. I arrived as Conan took the head of the Hibernian King. He held it aloft. Here there was no talk of surrender. Ever warrior who had fought us was put to the sword. Dyflin was ours and Thorghest, Erika and Moon Child had been avenged.

I turned, "Sámr, go and fetch the captured Vikings. I would have them leave now. Some may be regretting their decision to surrender."

I clasped Conan's arm, "You have won. What now?"

"Now? We go to Tara and claim the crown."

"You have royal blood?"

He laughed, "You should know better than any, Jarl, every Hibernian has royal blood."

"And what of Dyflin?"

"As long as I have been alive this has been a Viking port. I have no desire to rule this port. So long as the Vikings do not try to take my people or my land then there will be peace."

I turned to Mánagarmr Long Stride, "And would you rule Dyflin?"

He shook his head, "I am happy with my fjord. I wanted vengeance for my shield brothers. This is yours, Jarl. You appoint one to run it for you."

Just then the defeated Vikings trudged towards us.

"I have promised these one drekar. They will leave and never return."

Mánagarmr Long Stride pointed his sword at them, "The Jarl Dragonheart has just saved your lives. Take a drekar but if it is seen in these waters again then all of you will be given the blood eagle. That I swear."

They parted and the fifty-odd survivors, some of them wounded, walked with hung heads through the charred river gates of Dyflin. We watched as they chose a larger drekar. It was the one on the sea side of our drekar bridge and as such the easiest to take. It would be interesting to see if they had enough skill to sail through the narrow gap between the sunken ships and the river bank. They had skill and we watched the sail of the drekar as it was unfurled and sailed south.

I took off my helmet and handed it to Germund, "Come, Clan of the Wolf, we have a shield brother to bury."

We had lost many men but the greatest grief was for the Ulfheonar, Rolf Horse Killer. Olaf had given Rolf his first axe when, as a young warrior, Rolf had saved us from disaster. He had died well but he left a hole which could not be filled. I had but four Ulfheonar left now. How long could Haaken and Olaf fight? I saw Olaf Leather Neck's shoulders droop as we laid the last piece of turf on Rolf's grave. Long after we had gone, he remained silently staring at the earth. That day Olaf changed.

We had little time to mourn for we had a fire to douse. The wind had turned and it was not spreading any further towards the river but we had to put out the flames. It took all day. Our dead were buried and we collected the enemy dead. We carried them well to the north of the port and made a pyre of them. Aiden set it alight. The wind blew the smell out to sea but, as we ate that night we could see the glow of the fire as the dead were burned.

Haaken had been silent since the funeral and, as we sat drinking the last of the ale he began a song. He had a beautiful singing voice and his words were both melancholic and poignant.

The wind that blows across the sea
Carries the song of the dead to me
Sea birds cry and soar on high
When skies are grey and storms grow near
When women at home shed a lonely tear
When I raise a horn of ale
Then I will sing the Ulfheonar tale
When darkness comes that is your world
A wolf cloak, axe and a banner unfurled

When darkness come you howl and kill
No man is safe from Ulfheonar skill
We now are few where once were more
Our dead wait now beyond Valhalla's door
Wait for us brothers for we will come
Odin's table will be our welcome
We fight the fight for the land of the Wolf,
Farewell my friend, farewell Rolf
When darkness comes that is your world
A wolf cloak, axe and a banner unfurled
When darkness come you howl and kill
No man is safe from Ulfheonar skill
The knot and the web twist and turn
They cannot be cut and will not burn
They tie the past and the glorious dead
Old faces flash and speak inside my head
When darkness comes that is your world
A wolf cloak, axe and a banner unfurled
When darkness come you howl and kill
No man is safe from Ulfheonar skill

When it was finished I saw that Olaf was wiping what might have been a tear from his eye. He said nothing but put his arm around Haaken's shoulders. No words were needed and we slept in silence; each wrapped in our own thoughts.

The next morning, I gathered all of the jarls and captains around me. Mánagarmr Long Stride took two of the captured drekar to sail back home. Before they did so they cleared the channel of the wrecked drekar. The blackened skeletons were dragged well out to sea. There were two drekar left.

I addressed my men, "Jarl Mánagarmr Long Stride and Conan mac Finbarr have left this empty shell of a town to us. The women and the children who were here are fled or dead. This is my town but I do not wish to live here. There are too many sad memories. I am happy with the Land of the Wolf. If any men wish to stay here then there are two drekar for them. I promised that whoever rules here would not make war on

Mánagarmr Long Stride or King Conan. Are there any who would stay here and keep the word and law of the Dragonheart?"

I saw men looking at each other. Ragnar and Raibeart would not wish to live here but I saw others showing an interest. Eventually, Bergil Hafþórrsson stood, "Jarl Dragonheart, we have families and we would bring them here but I feel like a traitor deserting the warrior who has given me so much."

Aiden stood, "Bergil, do not think those thoughts. This is the work of the Norns. When you came to us you had a sword and a shield. Now you are a mailed warrior. You are a warrior who has served his jarl well. You owe the Dragonheart nothing but if you would continue to serve him then do as he has promised and keep this as a free port."

He nodded, "That I swear. Are there any who would follow me?"

Fifty of my men, mainly those without families stood and swore an oath. It was not a large warband but it was a start. Others would come and join Bergil and they would take women so that they would grow. The threads of the sisters now bound us across oceans and clans. It was *wyrd*.

**Part four
The lost son**

Chapter 12

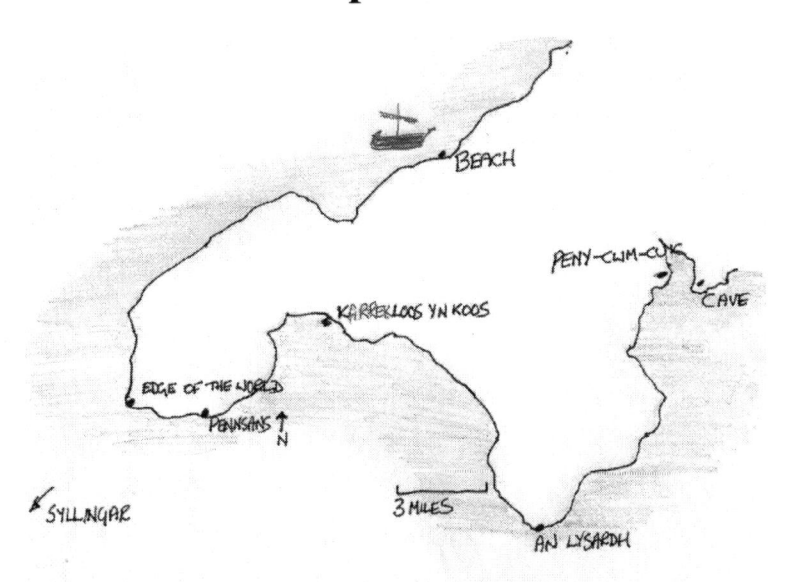

We had been at home for more than a month and there was still neither word of Gruffyd nor news of his fate. Ebrel and Bronnen were distressed. They rode to my hall, "Jarl Dragonheart, when Sámr married you promised that you would find our husbands and my son. It has now been almost three moons since then."

It had been on my mind and I nodded, "I had hoped that winds kept them from us. You are right to chastise me."

Atticus shook his head, "No they are not, Jarl! You have done nothing but fight and sail the seas. This is the task of another."

"Peace, Atticus of Syracuse. My work will be done when I lie beneath the ground." I turned to them. "I will ask for men to follow me and we will seek your husbands but first I must speak with Kara and Aiden. They may have dreamed."

Ebrel grabbed my hand, "I am sorry that I have to ask you. Atticus is right you have done too much for us already but it is my husband and my son. They are my world"

"And he is my son and grandson."

"You will go?"

"Where was he headed? I know that you said Om Walum but that is a large place and I know my son. He would have had a target in mind."

She nodded, "He said he would raid Karrek Loos yn Koos and the lands around there. We had told him that Peny-cwm-cuic had a deep anchorage. He thought to use that."

I frowned. "We sailed those waters when we fled the Danes. We saw neither drekar nor wreckage."

Bronnen shook her head, "You would not for Peny-cwm-cuic has an anchorage hidden from the sea."

"Then why has he not returned?" Even as I asked the question I knew I was being foolish. The women were not sailors. This was the work of the Norns. I knew that I had procrastinated. I kept expecting my son to return home and now, probably two moons too late I was doing something about it. The Norns had sent the Hibernians and Æthelflæd into my path and I had been ensnared by their threads. I had passed Karrek Loos yn Koos twice. Had I taken Aiden then he might have sensed that my son was in danger. I saw the web and felt the threads tightening about me.

We went to my daughter's hall.

"Do you know if my son lives or is he in the Otherworld?"

They looked at each other and then at Ylva. Ylva and my son were close in age. Ylva said, "He is not dead but he is hidden from me. Not long after you returned with Æthelflæd I was disturbed by a dream. I have wrestled with it ever since. I saw water, an island and a cave. There were monks."

I nodded, "Karrek Loos yn Koos but you did not mention this. Why not?"

"For it was not Gruffyd whom I saw there. It was you. You fought a dragon and the dragon had teeth. It tore your throat from you. I feared I had dreamed your death. Since then we have been to the spirit world but there is a power which fights us and casts a veil over what we can see."

"The witch of Syllingar."

For the first time in many years, Ylva looked less than confident. She had been taken by the witch. She was her nemesis. I looked at Aiden, "Is this my death?"

"We know not."

Ebrel looked frightened, "Then go not. Send another. Ragnar can go or Raibeart."

"I cannot send another to fetch my son. If this is the Norns then there is only one they wish in exchange for my son and grandson and that is the Dragonheart. I will go. If this is to be my death then it will serve a purpose. My legacy is my blood. I cannot leave Gruffyd and Mordaf to die alone."

"But, father, this may be a trick of the witch to trap you."

"It most certainly is, Kara, but that does not mean I will not go."

"We will come with you."

I shook my head, "You need to protect my land. I have wrestled with this witch before. My sword will protect me."

None could dissuade me. I had Ebrel and Bronnen escorted back to their home and sent orders for Erik to prepare a drekar. I then put my affairs in order. Part of that was to visit with Sámr and Æthelflæd. They now lived in my old hall. It was not yet finished but they were happy there.

I told them what I would be doing. Sámr said, "I will come with you."

"You cannot. When I am away this will be your stad to rule and protect. The Danes have yet to have their vengeance but it will come and you and the others who live in my land need to be vigilant. You said you were not yet ready to be. Now you can practise knowing that I will return." Even as I said the words I did not believe them. "This is a task appointed to me. You have come of age. The battles you have fought have shown me that you are a man and a leader. If I do not return I will sleep in the Otherworld knowing that my land is safe. You will guard it."

They also tried to dissuade me but I knew that this was the witch's ultimate revenge. They had lured my son south knowing that it would be a trap I could not ignore. I was dealing with the most cunning of enemies: the Norns. I returned to my home and ate alone. Alone this is save for Uhtric and Atticus. I was silent and I was morose. The two had become accustomed to eating with me and normally they were pleasant meals for we all had much to say. This evening even some of the wine we had brought back from Miklagård did nothing to raise my spirits.

Atticus rose and went to the box with the chess pieces. I said nothing as he laid the pieces out. "Black or white?" Then he smiled, "With your humour, it has to be black and I get to move first!"

He moved a pawn and then leaned forward to study the pieces. "This will not work, you know."

"What?" He asked innocently.

"Trying to lift my spirits with this game. It is for children!" I made a foolish move.

He shook his head, "And that is where you are wrong, Jarl. This is a game for," he sighed, "I was going to say kings and emperors but that means nothing to you." He gave me a sly smile, "Perhaps if I say a game for gods and Norns!" He shook his head, "I cannot believe that I just said that nonsense." He moved another pawn.

I made a sensible move and asked, for I was intrigued, "What do you mean a game for gods and Norns?"

"These witches play a game with you. They wish to entrap you. You have played a clever game. You avoided Syllingar and they could not trap you. They chose another tempting target: Karrek Loos yn Koos. You were clever and avoided it and so they made a sacrifice. They planted the thought in your head and you came for me. Then they tricked your son and you went off to save the Saxon princess' father." He made another move and I responded. "They led you a merry dance to Hibernia and then home. They even let us pass the place they had your son and we beached within shouting distance of him. Each time they have made the moves." He moved another and I responded. "You reacted to what they did and you are doing it now."

"You are talking nonsense. You know nothing of the Norns." He made another move and I moved a rook.

"I need know nothing of the Norns. The witch has your son and now you will follow him." He made another move. "They snap their fingers and you react," I responded.

"Check mate!" I looked and saw that he had won. He had trapped me. He leaned back and put his hands behind his head. "And that is why it is not a child's game. You need to plan moves ahead and see where you are being led. Do you think that the witch is cleverer than you?"

I shook my head, "She is cunning and she has the help of her sisters."

"And you have rejected the help of your own witches and wizards."

"I cannot risk them too."

"In that case let us work out how we defeat them and get your son back."

"You would come with me?"

He laughed, "I do not believe in witches and magic. There is an explanation for all that they do. Warriors with swords frighten me but not women who are unwashed and cannot get a man."

The three of us talked through the problem. Freed from the depression which had weighed me down and with the advice of Atticus and Uhtric I began to see a way to save Gruffyd.

The key came when Atticus made me question the place they were holding Gruffyd. We had worked out that if he was not dead then he must be a prisoner somewhere. I had thought of an island and a cave as being Karrek Loos yn Koos. Atticus pointed out that it was highly unlikely to be there. "Priests have little time for witches and there would be too many people there. Your witch has your son and his friend secured somewhere but it is not in a Christian church. The monastery is a trap. Vikings have raided it before and there will be warriors watching. If you go there then you will lose men. I would begin at this place called Peny-cwm-cuic."

"Why there?"

"Your son is clever. Not as clever as you but he uses his head. He would go there first to give himself a base. We go there and see if there are signs of him. However, I would not travel there by sea."

"We fly?"

He gave me a dismissive wave of his hand. "God will never allow man to fly for that would be against his laws of nature." He took a map from the table and unrolled it. "Your galdramenn has fine maps. They need refining but I can do that. See here," he jabbed a finger at a spot to the north of Peny-cwm-cuic. "This is but twelve miles from Peny-cwm-cuic. It saves you sailing around An Lysardh. You leave your ship there and head across land. Your enemies will look for a drekar."

"I can see how we can get to Peny-cwm-cuic but how do we find my son?"

"Simple. A drekar and its crew cannot simply disappear. Two? Impossible. If they were sunk then there will be wreckage. If the men drowned their bodies would have been washed ashore. That is why you need me. I can go into settlements and ask questions without suspicion."

"And if we find nothing?"

He said flatly, "Then your daughter, her husband and your granddaughter are wrong and your son is dead already."

"That is what you believe?"

He said, sadly, "I believe that if he could he would have returned. Unlike the others, I do not believe in magic. If he is not yet returned he is a slave or he is dead."

"Then tonight I will dream and discover for myself."

Aiden had once given me a draught to make me dream. I had not taken it all and that night, before I retired, I drank more wine and the draught. I dreamed. It was a bizarre dream.

I saw Gruffyd's face and he was screaming but I heard no words. He seemed to be at the end of a long tunnel. I saw the witch and, as she had before, she turned into a dragon. I cut her again and again but no matter how many times I did so I could not hurt her. When I chopped off a limb then another grew. I became weary. Then I saw the blue pool where I had found the sword which hung on my wall. I reached down and took out the sword. This time, when I struck at the dragon I took its head and she disappeared. I awoke.

It was dawn. I climbed down from my sleeping chamber. Atticus and Uhtric were already awake. Atticus looked concerned. "We heard you screaming, lord. Is aught amiss?"

"I dreamed." I reached up and took down the rusted sword. When we had brought it back we had used sand to clean it. There was one blue stone still in the pommel and one of the green ones. The rest had all gone.

"That's an heirloom, lord. What is its significance?" I told him how we had found it and about my dream. "Then you are meant to take it... if you believe dreams, which I do not."

I laughed, "Uhtric, find me a spare scabbard for it." When he hurried off I said, "Atticus, find the best four blue stones we have left."

"The beryl?"

"Aye, the dream pointed me in their direction. While we sail south you can make them into a necklet for me." Although he did not believe Atticus was pleased to be doing something to help. "And as Aiden will not be with us then you will need to take medicines in case we need a healer."

We spent the morning preparing and gathering the men. We left at noon. Only Olaf and Haaken would be coming with me from the Ulfheonar. Rolf's death had shown the other two of the frailties of the flesh. They both had families. I think the thought of bearding a witch made them think twice. We were just about to leave and I had said farewell to my family when Sámr and Baldr rode in.

"I said I would not take you, Sámr."

"And I know your reasons but hear me out. Baldr Witch Saviour wishes to come. That will not change the future, will it? Germund can watch over you and Baldr is unafraid of witches."

I smiled, "Then come and welcome."

Ylva took the jet necklace from around her neck, "Here, Baldr Witch Saviour, this will give you a little more protection and I will be able to read your thoughts a little clearer."

"Thank you, Ylva, I am honoured."

As we headed south I said, "Are you sure about this?" He nodded. "And Nanna?"

"She will be waiting for me. Jarl Dragonheart, she and my lady understand better than any. They were kept captive and you came for them. When I return then we will be wed and I will have my own hall on the ground beneath Old Olaf. There I can breed horses."

Wyrd.

"When will you wed?"

"As soon as we can."

I nodded, "Then if this goes well I shall marry you at Samhain. Your bride will not care about the date but it is an auspicious one and will help you to father many children."

We rode hard and reached Whale Island by dark. **'Heart of the Dragon'** had needed too many repairs and so we took **'Wolf'**. That suited us for she was a smaller, faster ship than **'Heart of the Dragon'**. Knut Eriksson would be her captain. I had fifty warriors and they were led by Haraldr Leifsson and Sweyn Alfsson. Like Nanna, they felt they had a debt to pay.

Our send-off was both dramatic and poignant. Ragnar and Astrid were not happy that I was going and Ulla War Cry wished to come with me. He had fought well in Dyflin but I would not risk a family member. Ebrel and Bronnen, in contrast, were joyous that I was going to try to save their men but fearful that I might fail or that they would be dead. If it were not for Kara's family then we would all believe that they were dead. Had my daughter been fooled? Were they dead already?

It was dark when we rounded the island and laid in a course south. We had four days of hard sailing ahead of us. If the winds turned then it would be even longer. I sat with Knut and Atticus at the steerboard while Olaf and Haaken arranged the rowers. This was a new crew and they had to be balanced. Baldr would be rowing and it would be his first time without Sámr by his side. He was excited and nervous in equal measure.

Aiden had given him some of his salve to ease the pain his hands would inevitably suffer once he began to row.

The darkness enfolded us. Knut kept us well out to sea. There was nothing before us until we reached the island of Ynys Môn. We would not even be close until the middle of the next morning. Atticus fussed with his bed. He had asked for a barrel but Knut was not his father. He did not want the lines of his ship to be spoiled by an ale barrel. Atticus had to make do with a piece of old sail. He was not happy and glared at the captain.

Once the chests had been organised Haraldr came to the stern with Olaf and Haaken. "You are happy with the crew, Olaf?"

"They will do."

He looked astern and then headed to the main mast.

"What is wrong with him?"

Haaken shook his head, "It is the death of Rolf. It plays on his mind. Rolf leaves a widow and four children. Olaf has neither a wife nor children. He is a lonely man who does not make many friends. Rolf and Rollo were his only two save us two."

"Haaken, go and speak with him. You have a way with words."

"I fear it will be a waste of time but when has that ever stopped me talking?"

Left with just Knut and Haraldr I went to the larboard side, "You know you need not have come with us. You have still to fully recover from your ordeal."

"If your son is in trouble then Sweyn and I know it better than any. When we were taken on the Blue River I felt guilt for the loss of our oar brothers. I thought I had let everyone down. The work in the mines was just a punishment from the gods. I know Gruffyd. We are of an age. When my father carried your banner, we used to practise together. I will feel better about the men we lost if I can bring him, your grandson and Einar back."

"Then you believe they are alive?"

He rubbed his beard, "I think I do. When we were prisoners and toiling in the copper mines I never gave up believing that we would escape or be rescued. Of course, I did not know how we would escape with old Atticus but I believed. Each night I prayed to the Allfather and to my father's spirit. I never gave up hope."

"I do not want any of the crew to die because of my quest. Haaken, Olaf and I will be the ones to put our lives at risk. You and the crew need to keep the ship safe so that if we do find them we can get home."

"The crew will not thank you for that. Do not worry, Jarl Dragonheart. This crew is made up of those who owe you much. You have led this clan for so long that there is not a family in the Land of the Wolf which is not indebted to you. They are just paying you back." He stretched "And now I will get some rest. I know that we will have to row before we reach Om Walum."

He was right and I curled up by the steering board. When I woke it was not quite dawn and the skies had darkened. It felt like a late summer storm was brewing. It was Knut's son, Erik who was steering. "My father needed a little rest. He thinks he will have to be at the steering board soon. He did not want to have me steering. I have not done so very often."

"I remember your father sailing with your grandfather when he was your age. I will watch with you." I looked at the masthead pennant and the billowing sail. "You are doing well. I will just make water."

When I returned I pointed to the backstay. "If I were you I would have Snorri tighten that backstay. It will make it easier for you to steer."

"Snorri, backstay!"

"Aye, captain!"

He shook his head, "I still cannot get used to that!"

"While you hold the steering board, you are the captain. Do not worry you will become used to it." I remembered his father when I asked him to take over from Josephus. He had had the same trepidation.

"My father says you were born to lead."

I laughed, "Then I wish someone had told me that when I was ship's boy. No, Erik, I worked hard and I watched. I saw how Old Olaf and Prince Butar did things and tried to copy them. I made mistakes but they were kind and did not punish me too much."

"If I make a mistake, Jarl, I could lose the ship."

"But you will not. She is a sound vessel and so far you have not made a mistake. You have the blood of mariners coursing through your veins. They have made you what you are. It is the same with my family. They have my blood and when I am gone they will do as I have done and watch over the clan."

I had just eaten when the wind picked up and the seas became a little rougher. Olaf had already roused the crew but an exhausted Knut slept on. "I shall go and wake your father. This storm is about to become worse. He will not thank you for letting him sleep longer!"

As soon as Knut woke he had the sail reefed and the oars run out. He needed to keep the ship heading into the waves. If they struck us side on then we could broach. We fought the seas for the rest of the day and into the night. It seemed to me that we were being tested. On the second day, when we woke, we were south of Ynys Môn. I smiled at Knut. His face was salt rimed and he looked exhausted, "Well the gods took us south of danger! You need rest. Your son can take it from here. There is nothing now until Om Walum."

"You are right, Jarl. I need the sleep for tired men make mistakes."

After I had made water I went around the drekar. We had been lucky. *'Wolf'* was a newer ship. Had this been *'Heart'* then there might have been more damage. I saw ship's boys replacing ropes which had sheared. We always had plenty of new rope aboard. The sail would need stitching but it would hold unless we had another blow. I glanced south and east. There was an estuary where we could lay up and effect complete repairs but that would be the river which led to the mine. That would not be a good idea. We had two days of sailing and then Knut could repair the ship while we hunted for my son.

I reached the prow. Atticus slept beneath his canvas sheet. One thing about a strong sea it rocked you to sleep. I saw that one of the knots had loosened. I guessed it had been tied by the Greek. Ship's boys would not make such a basic error. I retied it. Baldr joined me as I headed back down between the sleeping warriors.

"A fierce storm, Jarl, I thought we were doomed."

"It was a warning from the gods. If that is the worst ordeal on this voyage then I will be content." I pointed towards the coast, "That is where your Nanna was held before we rescued her."

He leaned on the gunwale. "Those mountains look like dragon's teeth."

"They were in one of the valleys but you are right for the mountains guarded the stronghold."

"Will there be mountains where we go?"

"No, but there will be walls guarded by men with shields. We will be alone and our march will take us through the heart of their land. If you wish to stay on the drekar…"

He shook his head, "Sámr asked me to guard your back. I am a warrior, Jarl. If I had stayed in my own land I would have been leading a hundred. We would have raided the trade routes and my sword would have been red with the blood of foes."

"Were your swords the same as ours?"

"No, Jarl, they are shorter and curved. We never use the point."

"Few of my men do."

He nodded, "We used bows too. They are like the bows used by Sámr. I was taken when I was too young. I never trained to use one." He tapped his chest, "The warriors in my clan all have broad chests and arms like young oak saplings. The slavers took that away from me."

"That is where I was lucky, Baldr, when I was taken as a slave, I was young and I trained for war."

He smiled, "The rowing will make up for the undone years when I was a slave. I will catch up and then I will get one of those bows and you will see a better warrior."

The crew began to wake and our conversation ended. We had both been slaves and yet we had both ended up with Vikings. The threads of the Norns went all the way from the heart of lands so far to the east that it was almost a different world to the Land of the Wolf. I was daring to face them once more. Was I a weapon of the gods? Were they using me to keep the Norns in check? Time would tell. My family had been taken from me four times. Perhaps I was cursed. The sword I bore protected me but there was a price to pay.

The ship was tidied and temporary repairs were made. We saw the wreckage on the sea. This was too far north to be my son's ship but it reminded me of the dangers of the sea and that the two drekar could be with Ran. The only hope was that Kara, Aiden and Ylva were correct and that Gruffyd lived. What if he was the only one to have survived? That would make him even harder to find. Where would the Norns have taken him?

Two days later we saw the coast of Om Walum. Atticus had spent an increasing amount of time with Knut as we had neared our destination. Atticus knew maps and Knut the sea. The beach we chose was one which was deserted. Two arms of rocks came around the small bay to make breakwaters. Even better were the cliffs which rose vertically from the beach. We had passed other beaches which were also deserted but all had easier access from the land. This one had a narrow path which zig-zagged up the rock. It seemed to me that it had been made by animals.

We pulled in at dusk and landed to make a camp. It was high tide and we had a small beach of perhaps forty paces deep and two hundred paces long. It was small. I went with Olaf, Haaken, Baldr and Haraldr. We climbed the path. It would be too much of a risk to attempt this at night but the west-facing bay would have enough light for us to reach the top and see what lay to the east. I took a spear with me. I used it as a staff. It made the ascent easier. Stones and rocks skittered to the beach as we climbed. The animal droppings confirmed that this was used by animals. I did not see any sign of man.

Haraldr was first up and he crawled the last few paces. It was only when he waved us forward that we rose and walked the last few steps. The land rolled away to the east. There were trees but no sign of a dwelling. The others spread out to look for a path and I rested on the spear. Atticus had determined that Peny-cwm-cuic lay to the south-east of us. When daylight came and we headed there we would stand out on the skyline. This was not the Land of the Wolf. There were no valleys and gullies to use. The others returned.

Olaf pointed to the south. "This path goes along the cliff. I fear it follows the coast. It does not take us where we wish to go."

I had already worked that out. "Then we will use this open land as the sea and navigate across it. We use the sun as our guide. We will plot a course which uses those trees that we see. This will not be easy but then the Norns rarely make our lives obstacle free. Come, we will descend while we can still see."

The last few hundred paces were almost in complete darkness. I led and my spear guided us to safety. Knut, Atticus and the others awaited us, "We can light fires. There is none to see them." We had our camp.

Chapter 13

When the tide went out, we found that we had a smaller beach than we might have hoped but it would have to do. It was, perhaps half a mile long and we saw a rock shelf leading to the next, wider bay. I gathered my men and told them who would be staying at the camp. Atticus wished to come with us but I knew that he would struggle with the journey. "If I am not to come with you then why did you fetch me here, Jarl?"

"Because you demanded to come. Stay here and organize the camp. When we return we may be in a hurry. We might have wounded men with us. You can be ready to help heal the men."

He was not happy but he accepted my decision. Choosing the men was equally hard for all wished to come with us. There were twenty of us who left. I chose them all carefully. They had to be the best that we had. Once we reached the top of the cliff we headed not to the south and east directly but to the nearest cover. We moved from cover to cover. The ground rose to a ridge. We headed for it. After a mile or so Haraldr held up his hand. He was at the front and he tapped his nose. He could smell something. We squatted on our haunches while he and Sweyn crawled through the overgrown scrub. When he returned he said, "There is a settlement ahead. It is just five or six houses. I think there is a mine. I can see what looks like a wooden tower. They had one at the Blue River and used it to haul up the ore. There is a road which runs through the place. It does not go where we wish."

"Can we avoid it?"

"We can go south and cross the road there. The ground looks to dip."

We followed the two men. Had Haraldr and Sweyn not been taken prisoner then we might not have known the purpose of the tower. *Wyrd*!

We soon disappeared in some scrubby bracken. It was uncomfortable walking hunched but we passed into a piece of dead ground and Haraldr led us towards the road. We were able to stand and move more quickly. We sprinted across the road. The ground fell away and we saw, in the distance the sea again. This neck of land was narrow. As we were so close to the sea we did not risk a road. We could see in the distance the smoke which marked Peny-cwm-cuic. Haraldr led us along a beck which meandered south and east. It had to lead to a river and thence to the sea. We had passed the higher ground. Rivers and streams do not run uphill. We only had twelve or so miles to cover but keeping to the twisting streams and rivers meant it took most of the morning. When we reached a piece of water which had to be forded we stopped. There was shelter and shade. We could hide in the undergrowth by the river. Now was the time for the Ulfheonar to use our skills. We left Haraldr in charge of the camp. The three of us forded the river and headed north and east. The smoke had remained to the north of us. Gradually we turned until we were travelling due east. We followed the contours of the land and the smoke we could see in the distance. We heard voices less than a mile from where we had left our men. We dropped to all fours and crawled to the line of elder and blackberry.

We wore no helmets and our shields were around our backs. We rose so slowly that barely a blade of grass was disturbed. We saw Peny-cwm-cuic. It was five hundred paces from us, or at least, the grazing animals from the town were. There were also men working. They were building a wall and they were slaves. We spied the yokes and saw the whips raised and cracked to make them work harder. As we stared I saw that some wore sealskin boots. When I looked more closely I recognised them. They were warriors. They were the Clan of the Wolf. We had found Gruffyd's men. The intake of breath from Haaken told me that he had seen them too. I counted them. There were fourteen. There had been sixty men with Gruffyd and Einar Fair Face. Where were the two leaders and where were the rest? I saw that there were ten guards watching them. Four had bows and the leader wore mail. It was a Viking byrnie. Beyond the wall they were building I saw the houses of Peny-cwm-cuic. There was a hall. I could only see the roof and upper walls but it was made of stone. The sea lay below the town.

We watched for an hour until I had the layout etched into my memory. During that time, we had seen four riders appear. All wore Viking byrnies. One looked to be Gruffyd's. I had seen enough and I tapped the other two on the shoulder. We said nothing until we approached the river. "They are our men. We will return this afternoon and see where they take our men. We will rescue them."

"But where are the others, Jarl Dragonheart? Where is your son, grandson and Einar Fair Face?"

"I cannot answer that, Haaken One Eye. We take one step at a time. We rescue our men and ask them."

"But that might mean we are discovered and have to head back to our ship!" Olaf Leather Neck was ever practical.

"Then so be it. If we procrastinate then we risk discovery anyway."

When we reached our men, I explained the situation. "We will rest until late afternoon and then head back to the settlement. We need to see where they take our men. As we can only see less than fifteen of them we have to extract them silently and find out where the rest are. It is highly likely that we will have to fight our way back to the drekar. As we saw no strongholds on the way here I am hoping that means there are few warriors living hereabouts. The ones we saw wore our men's byrnies. If they took the crews of two drekar then these are warriors. This will not be easy."

I was gratified that none of them seemed overly worried. I was. Once we took our men then there would be a hue and cry. The country would be raised. We might be able to take the captives but what of the rest? What of my son and grandson? The Norns had woven not just a spell but a mighty trap. We ate. We drank. We waited. Summer had waned and the days were slightly shorter. I watched the sun as it moved towards the west. When I deemed it time I stood and donned my red cochineal and my helmet. The old sword hung across my back. It was not there to be used as a sword. It was there to protect me. I slung my shield over my back and draped my cloak over it.

"It is time."

I led.

We had, the first time we had travelled this way, managed to find the safest route. Part of that was instinct and much of it was luck. We reached the low rise and the hedgerow about the place they were building the stone wall. Even as we hunkered down to wait I heard a cry as a whip was lashed across the naked back of Siggi Arneson. I heard the hiss from Olaf. We never whipped slaves. I fingered the new necklet around my neck. Would I need the power of the stones? I would not need it to rescue these poor captives but my son?

It seemed like an age we waited but it could not have been long for the sun was sinking quickly in the west. The guards shouted something and our men picked up their tools and began to trudge wearily east. I tapped Haraldr on the shoulder and after handing his helmet to me, he scurried ahead, keeping below the skyline. We rose and followed too. The captives disappeared from sight but the man on the horse could still be seen and we followed him. The east was much darker now and we relied as much on our ears and our noses as our eyes. We heard the clip-clop of the horse as it walked along a stone track. We found that we descended too. Suddenly the trees and shrubs ended and we could see, below us, the fjord. It was not as rocky nor as steep as a Norse one but we could not move for such a large number of men would be seen. I saw boats in the water heading for the jetties and quays which were hidden by the folds in the land. There was no sign of Haraldr and we waited.

As we waited I looked across the fjord. There were cliffs on the other side and I spied a couple of caves. What I did not see was any sign of houses or halls. Our men had to be in Peny-cwm-cuic or they were already dead. It was pitch dark when Haraldr appeared. "Jarl, I have found them. Half a mile down the path there is a hall. They were taken inside. The door was barred from the outside and there is a guard. Four men sit around a fire and drink. Two wear our men's mail."

"Are there defences through which we have to pass?"

He shook his head. "The wall we saw them building looks to be the start of their defences. There is also a stone tower which is being built. That is closer to the harbour and the centre of the huts."

"A warrior hall?"

He nodded, "By the tower, they are building."

"And how far is that from the place they hold our men?"

"Four hundred paces and there is nothing between them."

"Then we give them an hour or so to drink more and to become sleepy. Haraldr, you will come with the Ulfhoenar. We will eliminate the guards. Sweyn, you take charge of the rest. When I whistle then bring them forward." I could see Baldr resented being left behind but I needed proven killers. Haraldr was such a one. I handed him his helmet.

Men prepared themselves. Helmets were tightened and shield straps adjusted. We waited.

"Haraldr, is there some cover for the men?"

"Aye, Jarl, now that it is dark."

"Then lead on." I took Wolf's Blood from its sheath. This would be knife work. The path led down the slope and I felt exposed for the trees and shrubs were gone. I could hear noise ahead. It was the guards. That was not good for they were awake. It could not be helped. If we had to fight our way out then we would. We were the Clan of the Wolf. Haraldr held up his hand when we came to a stunted sycamore surrounded by some young trees grown from the sycamore's seedlings. It was little enough cover but it was better than nothing. I signalled to Sweyn and he led the rest of the warband to hide beneath the branches. They lay on the ground.

The four of us dropped to our hands and knees. We crawled. I did not need to tell them to spread out. We would approach the guards from four different directions. I saw that one was lying down and was asleep already. One had a head which lolled but the other two were talking. They were opposite each other and that meant they were facing the fire. They would have no night vision. So long as we moved slowly and without sudden movements then we were relatively safe. I saw that my path would take me behind the one who was awake. The problem would be Haraldr. Olaf, Haaken and I had done this before. We knew when the other would move. I saw that Haraldr was heading towards the sleeping form. He could afford to delay until we had struck and then eliminate his target.

I could hear them speaking. I understood some of their words.

"I hate this duty."

"It will not be for much longer. When the tower is finished then they can all be put to work on the wall. There are but ten days of work left. Then they can be killed and we will be safe from another Viking raid!"

"I am surprised that Lord Arfael allowed them to live this long. They killed his brother and his son. I would have crucified them!"

"I think he would but for the witch."

The other, who was facing me, made the sign of the cross, "Do not mention her. She terrifies me."

The one before me stood and stretched, "Now I must make water! You are in command!"

He stood and scratched himself. Our plans were almost thrown into disarray. I rose with him knowing that my body was hidden from the other guard. He would see my hand when it came around his companion's throat but that could not be helped. My left hand wrapped around his mouth as my dagger sliced across his throat. The blood spurted and hissed in the fire. As I lowered him, I saw that the other three had slain their victims. We had not yet been discovered.

I whistled and, picking up brands from the fire, we headed to the hall. I heard the slight skittering of feet on grass as my men hurried towards the hall. I lifted the bar. I nodded and Haraldr lifted the bar. I put the brand in the entrance and said, quietly, "It is Jarl Dragonheart."

It was fortunate that I did for Siggi Arneson and his brother Leif were poised with a rock to crush my skull. I stepped inside and my brand lit up the interior. I saw that there were more than twenty of our men but no sign of Einar or my son.

"I am sorry, Jarl, we …"

"There is no time to talk." I waved some of my men in, "Get these yokes from their necks. Arne, where is my son?"

"When we were attacked…"

I waved a hand, "There will be time for that later. Is he alive? If so where is he?"

"I do not know, Jarl Dragonheart. We were brought here and he was taken in a boat. They headed across the fjord."

"Around the headland?"

"I know not save the men who took them have crossed back more than once. It cannot be far."

"But he is alive?"

"They both are but they were wounded in the battle." He turned and gestured towards the back wall, "But we have Mordaf. He has been ill. He was whipped."

I ran to my grandson. He gave me a wan smile, "I knew you would come, grandfather." He threw his arms around my neck and wept. I felt his sobbing body and I felt cold anger that he had been whipped and forced to endure this. Those who did it, man and witch would pay.

I waited until his sobs subsided and then held him away from me, "You must be strong. I will find your father and Olaf Leather Neck will see you safe."

Olaf nodded, "I will, I swear."

I saw that the yokes had been removed. I made a decision. "Olaf, lead the men back to the drekar. I will take Baldr and Haaken with me."

He nodded, "What will you do?"

"Find him. We will try to get to you. If we are not in the bay in seven days' time then we are dead and you should sail home."

"Jarl, this does not sit well with me."

"I care not. I have given commands. Make it so. You can save my grandson. Until I reach the ship he is yours to guard."

"Then I will give my life for him!"

Haraldr said, "Let me come, Jarl."

"You have done enough. This is a task for a small number of men. We may need to use horses. Baldr is the horseman."

Olaf nodded, "Do not make me come to get you, Jarl Dragonheart!" He waved to Siggi, "There are four dead men outside, take their weapons. Haraldr, lead off and I will bring up the rear!" He picked up Mordaf as though he was a feather and slung him over his shoulder.

I turned to Haaken, "We put the bodies in here and bar it. It will slow the pursuit by a short time but any delay will help Olaf and the others. The men of Om Walum have horses." We carried the corpses into the building and barred it.

As we slipped the bar into place Haaken asked, "And what do we do?"

"We explore the opposite headland. We head down to the harbour and we steal a boat. I spied some caves close to the waterline on the other side of the Fjord. We will hide in one. I care not which one, Haaken, just so long as we are hidden from sight."

He nodded and then smiled at Baldr, "I hope you can think quickly for Jarl Dragonheart does and we have to read his mind!"

We sheathed our weapons and headed down the path towards the tower, warrior hall and harbour. I led and kept us close to the buildings. The tower was unfinished but that did not mean that it would be unguarded. Hours had passed since dusk and most people were abed. All would be indoors save for the shadows we could see moving along the quay. It was a wooden quay. I could hear the sound of their boots on the wood. When we neared the open area before the hall we darted across the gap between two buildings. From the smell one appeared to be somewhere they sold or prepared fish. When we were in the dark between two buildings then we stopped and I listened. There were two guards and they were together while they talked. They did not speak loudly and their words were indistinct but they helped to locate the two of them. I pointed to the corner of the building and tapped Haaken and Baldr on the shoulder. I walked back a few paces and found another passage between the fish house and what looked like a storehouse. I hoped it would bring me out further down the quay. I hurried silently down it. I found that it did indeed come out on the quay.

The two guards passed me. I was in the shadows with my wolf cloak about me. They did not see me. I waited for them to return. I slipped my dagger into my hand. I kept my face in the shadows but their attention was on each other and the river. When they had passed I stepped out. This was the risky part. Even as I stepped on to the wood I was aware of the masts of small fishing boats. There was a way to get across the fjord. We were two hundred paces from the warrior hall and tower. Even if the alarm was given then we could board a boat and be halfway across the river before they knew. It was dark and there was a chance we could escape. I had to time this right. I knew where Haaken waited. He would need no command from me. He was my shield-brother and had been so for almost my whole life. He would know what I intended. I saw the gap where he and Baldr waited and I stepped forward, grabbing the guard who was at the water's side. With my hand across his mouth, I pulled him back. His companion stopped and turned. Even as my blade tore through flesh Haaken had clamped his hand across the mouth of the other and slit his throat too. I lowered my body to the quay and then let it roll into the water. The sound was like that of the tide against the wooden wharf. Haaken disposed of his body the same way.

I chose a fishing boat which I felt I could sail. It was the type which had a crew of four or five. "Haaken, untie as many of the other fishing boats as you can. Push them off from the quay. Let us sow confusion and make them think our men escaped by sea." I pointed to the middle and held the boat so that our most inexperienced warrior could climb aboard. Baldr was no sailor and he would be in the way. I only needed him if we found my son and had to escape across the open country. Horses would be the only way we could do that. He climbed in. Haaken had let three boats loose and I waved him back to us. He climbed into the bow. I took off my helmet and shield and dropped into the seat at the steering board. Haaken hoisted the sail. I made sure that they had left the steering board attached and then untied the rope at the stern. The sail hoisted, the boat tugged at the last rope. As soon as it was loosed we leapt across the fjord.

Our path to the river and the dark made it hard for me to estimate where we had to reach to be safe. We were partly in the hands of the wind although I was able to turn either way. The wind was from our rear. I took us across the fjord. The sail and mast meant I could see little ahead of me. I relied on Haaken. Haaken's white hand waved me to larboard and I turned it. He held up a thumb and I stopped turning. The fjord was wider than I had thought. As I had brought us too far to the south we had to tack into the wind. Haaken should have signalled earlier.

I risked speaking for we had to be in the middle of the river. "Baldr, pull on the sheet at the larboard side of you." He had learned enough about sailing to know the terms and he did as I asked.

I was able to move the steering board but we were now moving much slower. I did not want to come about and so we crabbed our way north. The fishing boat sailed well and close to the wind. It was good that she did. Haaken had realised what I was doing and he gave no more signals for a while. Then he pointed to steerboard. I could now see the black cliffs as they loomed above me. As soon as I turned we moved much more quickly.

"Baldr, take in the sail a little. We need to slow." I saw that Haaken had realised the problem and joined Baldr. With the sail taken in a little, we slowed and, more importantly, I could see the cave or the one which Haaken had chosen, at least. As we turned I saw that the sky was becoming lighter. We were still hidden but we needed to get inside the cave and hide until dark. Then I would risk sailing around the headland and searching for my son. Now I knew that he was alive.

"Steady, Jarl, there are rocks."

"Dawn is coming."

In answer, Haaken made the sail as small as it could be and I saw the cave. It was forty paces ahead of us. It looked barely big enough for us. I headed towards it. The closer we came the larger it seemed.

"Baldr, get that fishing net and hang it over the side. It will act as a buffer."

"Aye, Haaken One Eye!"

I saw the white water which marked rocks. They were perilously close to the larboard side of the boat. And then we were engulfed in the dark as we entered the cave. Haaken dragged down the sail and I pushed over the steering board to stop us. The current and the surge lifted us and turned us around. We stopped but we almost broached. I felt the top of the mast scrape the roof. We had made it. I could not see the entrance and the cave was as black as night but we could not be seen.

We spoke quietly. I know not why. There were sheer cliffs above us. There was no one here. "Haaken, can you see the side?"

"I see the water surging. Baldr, there is an oar. Scull us to the larboard side."

"Aye, Haaken."

I used the steering board like an oar. Suddenly we scraped against rock. The fishing net stopped us from being damaged too much. Haaken grabbed hold of something. "Baldr, climb over me and tie us to a rock!" Baldr scrambled like a spider over Haaken's back. He held the rope in his hand. I heard his feet slap on the seaweed-covered rock. It seemed an age but then he said, his voice echoing, "We are secure. You can let go now, Haaken."

"Come to the stern." His white face appeared from the dark and I threw him the other rope. My eyes were now accustomed to the dark or perhaps the sun was coming up for I could see the metal post to which he attached the rope. I frowned. What was a post doing here? I scrambled ashore. Baldr went to fetch his helmet. "Leave them on board. We should not need them."

Haaken pointed to the mouth of the cave. "See, Jarl, dawn."

It illuminated the cave mouth. I walked towards it with Baldr. I gambled that even with daylight the cave would hide us. Keeping to the shadows I looked across the river. The sun, shining from the east suddenly bathed Peny-cwm-cuic in light. I heard a horn and saw men racing from the warrior hall. The escape had been spotted. We had just made it.

Just then Haaken came running to me. His eyes were wide. He pointed to the far recesses of the cave. "Baldr, watch the other side of the fjord. Tell me if there is danger. Jarl, you had better come and see this." I followed Haaken. I saw that the cave went deep under the headland above. It widened and rocks showed where the cave had been enlarged. I saw a shelf which must have been another cavern at one time. There were stones with masonry marks upon them. I was not surprised at that but I was surprised at the wooden post which was driven into the cracks in the carved stone. On top of it was a woven piece of material. This was the cave of the witch. We were trapped!

Chapter 14

I did not dare risk making too much noise. Had we alerted her already? Then I shook my head, she knew we were there. Once again, she would be toying with us. I had been led here. Haaken had headed for the cave the witch had chosen. She was like a giant spider sitting in her web and just waiting for us to come. Just then I saw that there was another channel. Now that there was light coming from the mouth of the cave what had been darkened shadows now took form. I saw that the cave was bigger than I had thought. It went deep under the headland. There was also another channel leading off to the side.

Baldr waved to attract my attention. I hurried back to him. He pointed. A fishing boat had put off from the other bank. Its bow was heading for the cave. Siggi had said that a ship came across the water each day. He had thought it came around the headland. Now I knew better. We had heard from the guards that the witch was in collusion with the lord of this land. This confirmed it. "Stay here and let me know when it is closer."

As I went back I saw that there was sand at the end of the other channel. I had an idea. I whistled to Baldr and waved him towards me. "Untie the fishing boat." When Baldr came I said, "Take off your byrnie. We are going to push you into the other channel. Pull the fishing boat until it is out of sight. Then swim back."

Haaken said, "Jarl, remember the shipwreck!" Baldr had been adrift at sea when we had found him. It would have scarred him.

Baldr said, "I can do this." He pulled off his byrnie. It was slightly too large for him and came off easily. We untied the fishing boat and he clambered aboard. We dragged it back. I saw that the tide was rising.

"Hold the steering board in the centre. The tide and our push will take you to safety."

I pulled on the rope while Haaken pushed and the fishing boat leapt into the dark. I heard it ground on the sand but all that I could see was the steering board. Baldr leapt out and pulled "Haaken, find us somewhere to hide." As Baldr pulled I heard the keel as it scratched and scraped over stones and sand. Then the steering board disappeared. It was as though it had disappeared. There was a splash and Baldr floundered his way back against the incoming tide. He had not taken off his sealskin boots and he was in danger of drowning. I lay down and leaned as far out as I could get. His head went under the water and then he disappeared. I put my hand beneath the water but all that I felt was the swirling current. I had lost him. Then fingers found mine and I grabbed his hand. I tugged him up and he rose like a dolphin from the water. I dragged him up onto the stone quay. "Get to Haaken! Don your mail! You have done well!"

I ran to the entrance. There was no mistake. The fishing boat was heading for the cave. It would be with us soon. I ran back into the cave and looked for the other two. I could not see them. A hand appeared just above my head and waved at me. I scrambled up the rocks. There was a weed-covered shelf and the other two lay there. I found myself an empty place and lay where I could watch the entrance. I still had the red cochineal on my face and I would be hidden, I hoped. When the men came in they would be looking down for the mooring post.

It seemed an age but eventually, I heard the boat as it scraped along the side of the cave.

"Careful you fool! Those Vikings have already taken four ships! We cannot lose this one too!" I risked a peep and saw the warrior who had been on the horse. With him were two other men but neither wore mail. The boat slid along the channel and one of the men jumped out to tie it to the post. "Stay here. We will not be long. She has had long enough with these two. They die today! Then we will sail after them. They will not escape their own drekar!"

The warrior and his servant headed into the cave. I slipped Wolf's Blood from its scabbard. I peered over the top. The last man was securing the boat. His hands were occupied. It was now or never. I rolled over and a rock tumbled into the channel. The man looked up. It was the last thing he saw. My dagger drove into his chest as I fell on him. I had my hand over his mouth and he tried to bite me. When he stopped moving then I knew that he was dead. I slipped his body into the water and stood. Haaken and Baldr joined me.

"Baldr, if you wish to stay here then no one will think badly of you. There is a witch in there and she has powers. She can play tricks with your mind."

"I know, Jarl Dragonheart, Sámr told me. I am oathsworn and my father is watching me. I will go with you."

We drew our swords and I led. Baldr sloshed along in his wet boots. It was too late to change them and, hopefully, he would not be needed.

I know not what I expected. The cave on Syllingar was dry and delved into the depths beneath the island. This one climbed and twisted. It felt like a staircase. There was no light. I could not hear anything from ahead and that worried me. The witch would know we were coming. The sloshing behind me stopped. I turned and saw that Baldr had taken off his boots. He gave me an apologetic shrug. We turned another corner and I banged my head on the roof of the tunnel. I felt blood drip down my face. I used my left hand to waft before me as I kept my head down. I could smell fire. That warned me that the witch was ahead. It was my wafting hand which saved me. The warrior's sword sliced across my palm instead of my face. I struck blindly and my sword entered the ribcage of the second warrior. He screamed as he died. I saw this body had hidden the entrance to the witch's lair. It was to the left and above me. When he died I saw the glow from the fire. I stepped in and saw the witch. This was not the same one I had seen in Syllingar. This one was older. She was naked and sitting on a rock above the fire. Her eyes were closed but I knew that she could see me. The mailed warrior stood between Einar and my son. The two of them were hanging from a wooden beam in the cavern's roof. Both were naked. They were thin and their bodies bore the marks of many cuts. There were scabs, scars and freshly made wounds. I felt a cold anger. This was my son. He was my child and no one did this to my child. He held a dagger to the throat of Einar and his sword was touching Gruffyd's groin. Both appeared to be unconscious.

The warriors shouted, "Drop your weapons. If you do not then I will kill them both. They will die slowly."

Haaken stood on my right and Baldr, still clutching his sealskin boots stood on my left. I was aware that the smoke from the fire was growing thicker. That was the witch. She was conjuring and the smoke would aid her and harm us.

"You are going to kill them anyway. Know that when you do kill them then we will rush you and give you the blood eagle. Have you heard of the blood eagle?" His terrified face told me that he had. "I promise you a quick death if you take your weapons from their bodies."

Just then I heard a voice. It seemed to come from the cave itself, "Have you forgotten me, Dragonheart, for I have not forgotten you? My sisters and I have spun for half a year or more to bring you here. Do you think that you will leave this time?"

I was about to answer when Baldr suddenly threw first one boot and then the second at the warrior. Even as I saw him reel I ran towards him. The boots had briefly unbalanced him but he reacted quickly. His dagger was driving into Einar's side even as my sword rammed up under his chin and into his skull. He fell backwards. I whirled for I heard a scream. Baldr lay screaming on the sandy floor of the cavern. The cave was filling with smoke.

"Haaken, get the boys. Leave and I will deal with the witch!"

I drew my dagger and walked towards her. Suddenly the flames from the fire leapt into the air. It looked like dragon fire. I leapt across the inferno. I felt the flames ignite my hair. I think I was saved by the blood from my wounds. Instead of burning, I smouldered. Whatever the reason I landed beneath her. She leapt upon me with long talons and sharp teeth. She looked scrawny but she landed on top of me. She ripped Wolf's Blood from my bleeding hand and put her weight on my right shoulder. She opened her mouth and I saw that she had sharpened teeth too. Spittle dripped from them. She had a wild look in her eyes.

"Today we have our vengeance. Today I tear the throat from the Dragonheart and eat his heart! My sisters and I have waited many years for this!"

I could not move. I tried to push her from me but I could not. There was magic at work here. I had neither volva nor galdramenn. I began to slide my left hand down to the seax I kept in the boot. It would be too late. I could smell her breath as her gaping mouth drew closer to my throat. It felt hot as fire.

I heard a voice, seemingly from far away, "I have them safe, Jarl! Flee!" It was Haaken. He could not see me for the smoke but at least my son was safe. If I died then Sámr would rule.

I saw her head as she brought her mouth closer to my throat. Her hair appeared to be alive and wriggled. I could smell the foul stench of her breath. Her nails dug deeper into my flesh. My son was safe but I would die. This would be the end of the Dragonheart. Her long fingers and nails worked around my back. There lay the old sword. It had not helped me after all. I felt the sharpened teeth rasp against my throat and then she screamed and her back arched. "The sword that was lost! The Queen has her vengeance!" She put her hands around my neck. Her scream intensified and filled the cavern! "Odin's stones! You have Odin's stones."

I knew I did not have long and I pulled the seax from my boot and rammed it up under her rib cage. I buried my hand in her scrawny body. She screamed and it hurt my ears. The whole cavern shook. Stones fell from the roof. She threw something in my eyes. It made me blink but I held on to the seax. Then the weight went and when I opened my eyes I held the handle of the seax and that was all there was left. The blade had disappeared. I sheathed my sword. I heard a rumble and, even as I moved a stone thudded from the ceiling. It struck where I had lain a moment earlier. I stood and saw that Baldr lay their yet. Haaken had not seen him in the smoke and the darkness. I hoisted him up and slung him over my shoulder. I threw away the seax handle and picked up Wolf's Blood. There were more rocks falling and I heard a terrifying scream which seemed to emanate from the bowels of the earth. It was the witch and she was not dead despite the blackening blood on my hand! As I ran down the tunnel, hunched over so that Baldr would not strike his headstones and rocks fell. It was like an earthquake and if we did not escape we would be buried alive.

By the time I reached the water Haaken had already loaded the two unconscious forms into the bottom of the boat. He looked aghast as he saw that I carried Baldr. "I did not see him. I thought he had fled!"

"No matter he is here. We need to get our shields and helmets from the other boat. Before this ordeal is done we will have to fight again." Just then another rock fell into the space I had just vacated. "And we had better be quick."

Haaken pushed us away and I used my hands to paddle up the other channel. I leapt into the shallow water and grabbed our shields and helmets. I dumped them at the bottom of the fishing boat. It was slightly larger than the one we had stolen but with five of us and our war gear, we would struggle to find a balance. We sculled backwards until we reached the main channel and turned the boat around. We used two oars to paddle. More stones crashed and fell. If one blocked the entrance then we would be stuck there forever. The entrance seemed miles away and we both rowed as hard as we had ever done on a drekar. As we burst into the sunlight I almost cheered.

"I will steer. Raise the sail!"

"Aye aye, captain!"

As we headed south and east towards the mouth of the fjord I heard an almighty rumble. The top of the cliff appeared to slide down. It struck the water and, had we not had our stern to the wave, it would have capsized us. As it was it sped us towards the sea. I glanced back and saw that the cave was sealed forever. The three young warriors were blissfully unaware of our predicament which, as we neared the mouth of the fjord, became worse.

Haaken pointed astern, "Jarl, we are not done yet. It is **'Odin's Breath'**. They intend to use our own ship to catch us!" I saw the drekar. We had been seen and with oars manned it began to row down the fjord towards us.

There was little point in recriminations or cursing our luck. We had escaped with our lives. It was up to Haaken and me to see that we reached safety. I could not yet see how we could possibly do that but we were Vikings and so long as we were alive then we had hope. The drekar could and should catch us. My only chance was to outsail her. I could go in shallower water. I tried to remember Atticus' map. We had about nineteen or twenty miles to reach An Lysardh. There were rocks and shallows there. If I could hold off the drekar until then we had a chance of losing them in the dark. I glanced astern. The other advantage we had was that they were not used to sailing a drekar. We both had the wind but they were using their oars. That was a mistake for their crew would tire. More importantly, when they did use both sail and oars they would discover that the dragon ship was so fast that you have to plan moves and manoeuvres long before you did them. I glanced at the three bodies. We had one skin of water and one of ale. We had perilous little food and it would take three days or more to reach our drekar. The gods were not making my task easy.

When we turned west at the mouth of the river I shouted, "Find us shallow water where they cannot follow!"

"Aye." A few moments later Haaken One Eye shouted, "There is a reef to the south of us and a narrow channel. Should we try it?"

My hand went to what the witch had called, 'Odin's stone'. "We will risk it!"

"Then do not deviate from this line. I see flat water twixt the rocks."

Glancing astern I saw the drekar had come racing from the fjord. Even had she wanted to turn she could not for her speed was too great and she had to take a longer course. We had opened up a huge gap for she now had to beat up into the wind to catch us. We flew through the channel. I could see the sharp teeth of the rocks on either side. Had we been four paces wider we would have fouled our hull on the rocks. There was clear water ahead and we were far enough from the cliffs so that we had the full force of the wind to aid us.

"Shift the three men and our war gear around to balance the boat. Try to put them in a line. We need all the help we can get."

With clear water before us, Haaken had the time to move the three unconscious young men around. I wondered what the witch had done to them. I was aware of my bloody hand and forehead. They would have to wait. I was alive and I had not expected to be. Old Olaf had sent me to those mines for a reason. The blue stones had saved me; of that, I had no doubt. I glanced to larboard and the drekar was now a mile south of us and half a mile behind. We had a lead. How long could we maintain it? I saw white water between us. That meant rocks and shoals. The crew would have known of the danger. They would know where they could catch us too. Would they be patient?

Baldr was the first to recover his senses. The drekar was closing with us. She had now cut our lead to less than a mile. There were still some hours to darkness and An Lysardh lay a long way ahead. Baldr rose and looked around with terror in his eyes, "Are we dead, lord?"

I smiled, "Almost but the Allfather was watching over us. We are now fleeing from one of our own ships which is crewed by the men of Om Walum. Have a drink of water. You will need all your wits about you."

Haaken drank some of the ale while Baldr drank the water, "Baldr, come and sit at the bow. Watch for white water and rocks." They swapped positions and Haaken sat next to me. He handed me the ale skin. "Here let me clean that wound." While I drank he took the skin of vinegar and washed the blood from my brow and then from my hand. "We have no honey but the salt water will dry it. You were lucky."

"Luckier than you can know. When you took Einar and Gruffyd from the cave the witch tried to tear out my throat. The blue stones and the sword stopped her. She called them Odin's stones. The necklet and the old sword saved me. I think the Queen who owned the sword was an adversary of the witch. I knew they were magic but not how powerful."

"And she is not dead?"

"She is not dead. She is a Norn. How do you kill a Norn?"

He finished tidying the wound and said, "You know, Dragonheart, as much as I enjoy sharing these adventures with you I think the gods are telling you to hang up your sword. Your wounds are increasing and you get no younger."

I smiled and clutched at the blue stones, "Yet I am alive. There must be a reason for that." I felt the sword across my back, "She said the Queen would have her vengeance. That had to be the work of the sword but who was the Queen? I thought it came from the Warlord who is buried beneath Wyddfa."

"Jarl, the threads are not only manyfold, but they also reach back in time. Even Aiden would struggle to untangle this knot."

He was right. Kara and her family had not seen any of this. Gruffyd had been hidden from them. It had been Atticus' logic which had helped me to find them and there had been luck involved. If Haaken had not taken us to the right cave we would never have found them for they would have been slain by the angry lord.

Haaken moved back up the boat. "They are catching us. It is a race between them and the night."

I saw that they had the oars out and were rowing hard to cut us off. I saw, ahead, An Lysardh. We would both have to stand off those rocks and when we turned the drekar would simply run us down. *'Odin's Breath'* would crush us to kindling. We would be dragged to the bottom of the sea and Gruffyd and Einar would never wake.

"Give them water. It may help to revive them. I would speak to my son before we go to the Otherworld."

I glanced over my shoulder as Haaken tenderly lifted their heads to give them some water. The drekar was catching us stroke by stroke. Even though they were not oarsmen the ship was so well made that it was almost impossible for her to sail slowly. It was not the gods who saved us nor the Norns. The men of Om Walum were not used to rowing in unison. They must have had the oars single manned. There was no chant. The wind would have carried their voices to me. Each man rowed by himself. They were not oar brothers. They were individuals and they rowed as such. Some tired more than others and I saw three oars clash and entangle. One sheared and there was a cry. Four other oars came into the air and the drekar suddenly slewed around and began to head for the shore.

Haaken raised his head, "They will hit the rocks! The drekar is doomed."

I shook my head, "No for see, they have stopped rowing and are turning but it will take them time and darkness is coming, I will take us a little further from the shore. We might pick up more wind." I headed due south. We could give An Lysardh a wide berth. The sun was setting ahead of us but its light showed the white of the sail of the drekar as they slowly worked her around to continue the chase. They were half a mile from us. I turned to a north east direction. I had a plan and I wanted the men of Om Walum to think that we were going to hug the coast. As we turned around the headland that was An Lysardh the sky behind us darkened as the sun set. I put the steering board over and headed south and west.

"What are you doing, Jarl? There lies Syllingar. That is the one place we do not wish to go."

"Nor will we go there. There is little point sailing around the coast. Karrek Loos yn Koos lies there and that is all. We save many miles by heading into the open sea. We sail by the headland close to Pennsans. We should be there by dawn."

"We have no compass and there are no stars."

I clutched the blue stones around my neck. "I have this necklet and the two most powerful swords in the world. I will trust in the power of the old world."

Ahead I could see the last glow of the sun as it dipped in the west. I made sure that we were heading towards it by aligning Einar's body and the mast and then jammed Wolf's Blood into the gunwale next to the steering board. I leaned against the board and it did not move. Even if I fell asleep we would continue to head west. All that would make us turn would be a shift in the wind. I touched the stones, "Allfather keep this wind with us for we are ever your followers. We are warriors like you and we have faced all adversaries with honour and courage. These three young warriors do not deserve to die. Keep your wind to help us home and if any must die then make it me, take the Dragonheart. Let the others live." The fishing boat seemed to leap as the wind pushed us west. I had been answered.

I was tired but my wounds ached and they kept me awake. My son's head lay close enough for me to see him. His body was thin. All that he wore was the cloak Haaken had wrapped around him. The men who had crewed the boat had left them aboard and Haaken had used them to keep the naked warriors warm. He was breathing. I saw his chest rise and fall. There was a story here. Would he wake to tell me? I looked and saw Baldr watching me, "Thank you for throwing your boots at the warrior."

"It seemed a fair exchange, a pair of boots for the life of the Dragonheart's son."

I laughed, "I will have a new pair made for you. You have a good eye."

"When I was a slave they kept weapons from me. You cannot keep stones and rocks from a young boy's hands. It was a way for me to have my vengeance on those who sought to hurt me."

"And now you are a man and soon to be married."

He nodded and then looked worried, "And I have no home for her yet!"

"Do not worry about that. The Viking way is for the clan to join and build you a Viking house. It will be made of turf and not as grand as my hall but it will be a start. You are a young warrior and when we raid you will become richer. You will be able to buy or steal the horses you need to breed."

"And that is a good dream."

I nodded, "Haaken, Baldr, you sleep. I will watch and steer. I will wake you if I feel sleepy."

"Are you sure, Dragonheart?"

"Aye, Haaken One Eye. My mind is too full of the events in the cave for me to sleep."

Atticus had not believed in witches. Yet it had been his logic which had discovered the cave. Logic and just a little luck. Perhaps that was the way to defeat the witches and thwart the Norns. When I had been in Miklagård I had spoken with the doctor. He had approached the operation with cold detachment. He had analysed the problem and sought a logical solution. I was the Dragonheart. That heart was full of courage. Haaken was right. I was getting older. I had to use my mind to solve problems rather than my sword. Age brought with it the wisdom of past errors. I had made mistakes with Wolf Killer. I had made fewer with Gruffyd but I was still guilty of making them. Sámr was my future and, thus far, I had made few errors with him. In the time I had left I would make him the lord of the Land of the Wolf. I leaned against the steering board and began to plan. I needed no sleep for sleep would come in the Otherworld.

The sea was empty but the waves were a little bigger than I would have liked. They came from the north east which meant that although we travelled quickly it was an uncomfortable motion. I kept checking to see that the knife had not moved and that the sail was still taut. Syllingar lay to the south but I would worry about that only when we saw it. The drekar was a bigger threat. Their captain could have anticipated my move and be looming up out of the dark. He could have sailed ahead and we waiting for us on the north coast of Om Walum. Until the sun came up behind us there was little point in worrying about what might happen. The night passed and the wind stayed. I had no idea where we were.

Haaken stirred first. He went to Einar and to Gruffyd first. He used the water skin to moisten their lips. "They are under a spell, Dragonheart."

I nodded, "I know and we have no wizard to help us. We keep them alive until we reach home."

He laughed as he handed the skin to me and took over at the steering board, "You are an optimist! We have yet to find the drekar."

"The sun is rising and we shall see if the ocean is empty. Let us take this one disaster at a time."

Our voices had woken Baldr. He stretched and took the water skin from me. Have we enough food, Haaken?"

"A little." He turned to Baldr, "When you have eaten then drape the fishing lines over the stern. We will catch fish."

"How will we cook it?"

Haaken laughed, "We are Vikings. We eat it raw. There is nothing finer than eating fish fresh caught from the sea."

"Steer for a while."

I moved out of the way so that Baldr could get at the food and the fishing lines. I went to Gruffyd. He was my son. The two of them had been placed on either side of the mast so that their heads almost touched. I would look at Einar but first I needed to see to Gruffyd. He looked so pale and thin. I touched his scars and scabs. Some were weeks old and others fresh. He had been tortured. We were a hard race but we did not torture. I put my ear to his mouth. He breathed. I unfastened the necklet from around my neck and placed it around Gruffyd's neck. Perhaps Odin's stones might help. As I placed them around his neck a shaft of sunlight appeared over my shoulder and lit his face. He looked golden in its light. There was hope. Einar was equally scarred. I took my helmet and placed it on his head. I hoped that the stone I had there would have healing power for Einar. Their heads were close and that was all that I could do.

I stood and watched the sun appear in the east. It bathed the seas in a cold blue light. The waves were not as high as they had been and our motion was easier. I looed astern and to the north. There was no sail. I stepped around our sail to look west. It still appeared a little dark until the sun rose and I saw, to the south west of us, Syllingar! We had been pushed there during the night.

I ran back to the steering board and pulled my dagger from the wood.

"Syllingar! Steer north, north east and let us hope that the Norns are sleeping!" Had I been careless during my long night watch or had this been beyond my control? There was little point in speculating. We now had two enemies and we were between them.

I adjusted the sail to compensate for our new direction. We were sailing across the wind now and we would be travelling slower. As much as I wanted to sit by my son and tend to his hurts I had to concentrate upon the fishing boat. One hope was that the drekar might not spot us. We had good lookouts on our ships. Did they? Would they be looking in the right direction? The sky remained clear and that was a good thing. When the Norns wished to cast their net and web around you they sent a fog. So long as we had good visibility then the Norns might just be sleeping or perhaps recovering from the wounds I had inflicted. I had not killed the witch but I had hurt her.

I turned as something flopped on the deck. Baldr had managed to catch one of the shiny fish we called magpie fish for they loved anything shiny. Haaken took the hilt of his dagger and struck it on the head. "Gut it and throw the head over. You can eat this one. There will be many more."

Baldr gutted the fish and when he threw the head and guts overboard a single gull swooped down to eat it. Baldr looked dubiously at the fish. Haaken laughed and took it from him. He tore a chunk from the flank of the fish. Its bloody flesh hung from his beard. Baldr put the lines back over the side. If he was hungry enough then he would try it and he would enjoy the taste.

I kept glancing south and west as Haaken steered us to what I hoped would be safety. By the time it was almost noon we had lost sight of Syllingar and I could see the coast of the mainland ahead. Baldr had caught six fish and even tried one. Now that one danger had lessened I went aft and took one of the gutted fish. I returned to the mast where I could see both the sea as well as the two unconscious warriors. I sat and ate the fish. I had just finished it when I heard a noise from Gruffyd. I grabbed the ale skin and, cradling his head in my arm I poured some down his throat. In my excitement I must have poured too hard for he began to cough and splutter.

His eyes opened and he stared at me. "You are here." He looked around, "Wherever here is. I dreamed and you came." He grabbed my arm and said, in a very quiet almost hushed voice, "The witch, is she gone?"

I held his head tightly to my chest and said, huskily, "We are at sea and the cave is destroyed. As for the witch? I know not."

"Einar?"

"He still lies in the dream world." I took the necklet of stones from around his neck and fastened it around Einar. "This may help. I believe it protected you and countered the spell of the witch."

His eyes narrowed, "She made us drink a liquid. We fought her but the warrior who helped her jabbed his dagger into us and when we screamed we were forced to drink. We learned not to scream."

"What happened when you drank the liquid?"

He shuddered, "I would rather not speak of that. It brings back memories."

"When you talk it will help to expunge those memories."

He nodded, "We entered her world. It was a dark world filled with huge spiders. They had the faces of women. There were snakes which coiled and hissed around our bodies and all the time they asked questions. They wished to know why I hated you so much." He shook his head, "How can I hate you?"

A sudden shudder raced down my spine, "They were trying to turn you into a weapon to use against me. You fought her."

He said, "Aye we did. That was when we spat some of the potion back into her face. Then we were beaten but that was better than when she entered our heads. And then you came. I think I saw Haaken but I am not certain. I saw Wolf's Blood and Ragnar's Spirit. I feared for you. The witch has great powers. She could become a dragon. I saw her drink the blood of slaves." He shuddered. "She tore out their hearts and ate them too. I saw her and knew that she wished to do that to you. I could not stop her, even though I was in her world! I am sorry."

He began to weep and I stroked his head, "You have nothing to apologise for. This cannot be helped. So long as I am Jarl Dragonheart and lead the Clan of the Wolf then I will have enemies."

He looked at me and said, quietly, "I would not wish this on Mordaf. I do not wish to lead the clan. I would be a warrior like Einar. I would live with a family and amongst oathsworn. I would not risk the enmity of the Norns."

Just then Einar Fair Face stirred, "It seems the stones do have power. They can bring men back from the dreamworld." I lifted Einar's head and poured ale down his throat too. I took the necklet from his neck and my helmet from his chest. I had a feeling that I needed the necklet more than they did.

"Gruffyd, Einar, we are not out of trouble yet. Your drekar is pursuing us. We are west of An Lysardh and our drekar lies…"

Just then Haaken shouted, "Jarl, I see the rock they call the edge of the world!"

I looked up and saw that we could soon turn north, "My drekar lies more than forty miles north of here. If we are to reach it then we need luck and you two will need courage."

Einar was suddenly aware that, beneath the cloak, he was naked. "Clothes! We need clothes!"

"Clothes are the least that we need." I pointed to the masthead pennant. We were now sailing so close to the wind that we would have to tack back and forth. Progress would be slow. "We need a wind and a miracle. Baldr give them some fish while I take over from Haaken. We need to tack."

It was hard work for Baldr and Haaken had to keep ducking beneath the sail as we twisted and turned to take advantage of every puff of wind. The edge of the world still lay to the north east of us. It had taken us hours just to cover the five miles. I began to hope that we might just escape our pursuers. I had taken us further south than I intended and I wondered if I had fooled the men of Om Walum.

Gruffyd stood, somewhat unsteadily. He peered north. "Grandfather, I see a drekar! Is it yours?"

I shook my head, "I doubt it but it may be. If it is coming in this direction then it may be a friend."

I did not believe it but the alternative was too worrying to consider.

We had just cleared the edge of the world when Gruffyd shouted, "It is *'Odin's Breath'* and they have seen us. We are doomed!"

Chapter 15

I saw that the drekar was indeed *'Odin's Breath'*. The men of Om Walum had credited us with either more skill or more luck than we actually had. They must have sailed, and rowed, during the night to try to catch us. They thought they had failed and were returning home but now, with the wind from their quarter, they were bearing down on us. We were fighting the wind. I did not want to believe that we had lost and so I looked for the advantages which we had over the drekar. It seemed to me that our best weapons were our size and the fact that we could tack inside them. We could go inshore and they could not. So long as they had no bows we could try to dodge them in the shallows.

"Prepare to come about!"

Haaken looked at me. "You sail east or west?"

"East we are doomed. We sail west and try to trick them. I want them to think we are heading away from land. When I give the command then I want us to turn around completely." I pointed to the three young warriors. "You three don the helmets. It is little enough protection but with this spar whipping back and forth the last thing I need is for you to have a cracked skull. Haaken and I have thick skulls!"

The three of them grinned as they donned our helmets. I saw that Gruffyd chose mine. There was extra protection with that one. It was only when we made our turn that they saw us. It confirmed what I thought; they had poor lookouts although, to be fair, head on we were a tiny target. I saw the oars come out. It was not a full set for some had been shattered. The sail was adjusted and Gruffyd's drekar began to turn. We whipped across her bows. There were barely five lengths in it. By the time they had made their turn they were twelve lengths astern. Like a fisherman pulling on a line they gradually pulled us closer as the oars and the wind drew them closer to us. I knew that they were unused to rowing. They would tire and once they did then I would make my move.

I kept glancing astern as they came ever closer: seven lengths, five lengths, three lengths. When they were two lengths away I saw that the oars were a little more ragged. Now was the time.

"Come about!"

I put the steering board hard over to face us into the wind. Luck was with us. We were so close that they could not see us below the dragon prow and it was only as they passed, seeming dead in the water, that they did. They had to turn but unlike us they were enormous. As I turned north to take advantage of the little wind we had from the east I saw the oars as they tried to back water and to turn. I tacked to the north west and went a little faster. After a few hundred paces we resumed our northerly course. We would miss our landing site this way but it could not be helped. I turned to look at the drekar. We had left them for dead. They could row and that would tire them.

"Baldr watch the drekar! I need to know when she is on course again."

"Aye jarl." The advantage I had was that I knew what I was going to do and they did not. They would be reacting to what we did and that might just save us. "She is almost turned. She is a long way behind us."

"How many lengths?"

"What is a length?"

"The length of a ship."

Before he could answer Haaken shouted, "More than twenty and she has her oars out again."

I began to estimate our speed, "We were travelling at a slow but steady speed. We would rely on the wind. If the wind changed direction then it would suit the drekar for she had a greater area of sail. It would take all day and part of the night to get close to the landing place and without a compass this would be guess work. My head pounded. It was a sure sign that I was tired.

"Haaken, come aft."

When Haaken sat next to me I gave him my ideas for our escape. He smiled, "Not only will that succeed I will have a great tale to tell when we reach home. You rest. I will wake you before darkness falls or if I make such a mistake that we are about to be taken."

I patted his back, "And that will not happen."

I went to the middle of the boat and curled up around the mainmast. I soon fell asleep. The hand that woke me belonged to Gruffyd, "Grandfather, they are closing. They are now ten lengths from us."

"Ale skin."

My mouth was parched. As I picked it up I realised that it was almost empty. I took a single mouthful and returned the stopper. I rinsed it around in my mouth. I allowed it to seep down my throat. My lips and mouth were rimed with salt. I could have drunk a boatful of ale and not been satisfied. I made my way down to the stern. "How long until nightfall?"

Haaken had been watching their progress and knew their speed. "When they are two lengths away it will be dark."

"And the coast?"

"I have not seen it for some time. We could be anywhere off Om Walum."

"I will take over."

"You have a plan?"

"When they are four lengths away I turn north and west but this time we do not turn back. There is an ocean between us and Hibernia. I let them think we go there. When it is dark we turn and head south and east. We lose them in the dark or find the coast. If we have to we can land and walk to our ship."

"Then I will have a little grandfather sleep. I am getting too old for this."

When Haaken left Gruffyd came next to me, "All of this is my fault. I am sorry."

"You raided. When is that a problem?"

"No, for I wished to show you that I was the one to lead the clan and not Sámr." He smiled, "I know he is your favourite and your heir. I was angry once but the witch has sucked the anger from me. I went with just two ships to steal the great treasure from Karrek Loos yn Koos. When I returned it would be to accolades from everyone in the Land of the Wolf. Haaken would write a saga about me." He shook his head, "How foolish that seems now."

"What went wrong?"

"Everything. We must have been seen when we sailed down the north coast of Om Walum. We did not keep well out to sea as you do. That was my fault. I wanted to see where we rescued Ebrel. I thought I was so clever. We approached Peny-cwm-cuic at night. All seemed quiet. Ebrel and Bronnen had told us of a channel where we could hide. My plan was simple. Take Peny-cwm-cuic and then sail to Karrek Loos yn Koos knowing that there would be no one to stop us. As we sailed up the fjord I saw their ships tied at the wharves and quays. I was almost counting the treasure. We tied up and made our way to the other channel. I left twenty men to watch the drekar."

"They were waiting for you."

He nodded, "I did not question why the gates were open. They were not Vikings and I assumed they were poor warriors. As soon as we were all inside they slammed them shut and then began the slaughter. We were surrounded. Einar and I fought hard as did our oathsworn. Then they were killed we were knocked unconscious and when I woke I was in the hall of the lord of Peny-cm-cuic."

"Why did he hate you so much?"

"We killed his kin when they attacked us. He had us whipped and then… I do not understand this, we were taken away. We were placed in a boat with a hood over our heads and we sailed. I think we went to a cave. The cave where you found us." He shook his head, "I am not certain. I do not even know how long ago this was. When our hoods were moved we were in the place I think you found us. At first the witch was almost kind. She looked beautiful. She wore long black flowing garments. Her lips were ready and she smelled sweetly. She said that the lord was angry but she would help us. All that she needed was my help. I asked her how I could help her but she would not tell me. We were fed and bathed. Our hurts were attended to."

"You did not escape?"

He shook his head, "We were tied up at night and there were guards but, in truth, I felt safe there. Her words were sweet and I enjoyed her touch."

"You were naked?"

"Aye, how did you know?"

"That is how we found you and a naked warrior is less likely to run. When did she change?"

"The lord came back one day and said he had had enough and wanted us dead. He said he had fulfilled his part of the bargain, he had trapped the Dragonheart's men and it was time for her to deliver the sword."

I touched Ragnar's Spirit, "How could you get it?"

"It was then that she told me. She said that if I could lure you down to Peny-cum-cuic so that the lord could have your sword then I would be given great treasure and allowed to go free. I said no and they brought in five of my men. Their tongues had been taken. I was asked again and then one by one they were killed before my eyes. She said they were the last of my crew. Still I refused."

"And then she began to use the potion. She lied. We rescued twenty of your men."

His eyes widened, "Mordaf?"

"Your son lives. He was injured but Olaf Leather Neck was guarding him. Your son is alive. Your men cared for him."

He sobbed and shook his head, "I could never be you. You would not have done as I did. I made too many mistakes. I thought I had killed my son!"

"Sadly, when men like us make mistakes then others die. If we can escape this drekar then you can begin again. You did not do badly but you made mistakes. You cannot allow that which eats inside you to drive you on. You have your family and you have the clan. They should be what gives you reason to raid!"

"The lesson is learned and my men have paid the price."

"Who do you think follows us? He is persistent."

"I think it is Fferferdyn, the new King of Om Walum. He came just before they tried the potions. He said he knew that I had married the daughter of King Mordaf. In return for delivering the sword he would allow me to return to Ebrel. He made me promise that she would never claim the throne." He shook his head, "She wants nothing more to do with Om Walum after the way her people treated her father. King Fferferdyn hated us all but especially you. The West Saxons rule Om Walum through him and he is not happy about it. He believes that the sword could be used to bargain him more power."

"Then he is a fool. The West Saxons would use him and then discard him when the time was right!" I looked astern at the drekar which bore down upon us. "Knowing your enemy is half the battle. Thank you for your honesty. That could not have been easy."

He smiled, "And yet I feel relieved now that it is no longer within me."

I nodded, "Go and wake Haaken."

He moved forward and shook my Ulfheonar awake. Like me he was awake in an instant.

"Right, Haaken, now is the time."

I put the steering board over and headed north west. The drekar moved relatively slowly. We had done this before. They thought that we would return to the same course. We would not. We even made it easy for them as we headed into the sunset. While they were hidden in the dark of the east, we were clearly seen silhouetted against the setting sun. They had long stopped rowing. They were not Vikings. The result was that they closed far more slowly than they had previously. We would be using the same trick we had earlier. The difference would be that we would be invisible for we would be in the dark. I waited a long time and then said, quietly, so that my voice would not carry, "Come about!"

With the steering board hard over Haaken, Gruffyd, Baldr and Einar loosened the sheets and ducked under the spar as it swung around. The wind stalled us until they tightened the sheets once more and we began to move. We were on a reciprocal course. The wind was on our quarter and we moved quickly. I think one of their lookouts may have seen us for there was a cry and someone responded with a shout. I had cast the bones. Now would be a test of both my skill and my luck. Blackness enfolded us. Behind I heard the splash of oars in the water. Once again, we were sailing in the night. There were stars but, all too often clouds scudded by them. Navigation would be difficult. Gradually the splash of oars faded and then stopped. Had we lost them?

Haaken and I took it in turns to stay awake and steer. Neither of us was getting any younger. The other three did not have the skills yet to navigate using the occasional flash of a star or the moon. Each time I saw the stars I had to adjust our course. The currents, tides and winds were making life difficult. When dawn came I saw that we were approaching a wide bay. We had not passed it on our way south and I closed my eyes to picture the map Atticus had with him. The only such large bay was near to the fishing port of Porth Ia. We were too far south but just a few miles from where we wished to be. Even so it was a disaster for the wind had swung to come from the north. I shook Haaken awake.

He looked around, "This is not where we left the drekar."

"No, we are some miles south. We have a choice we can leave the boat and walk but that would mean sailing into the bay and I spy smoke and that means people."

"Your son and Einar cannot fight."

I nodded, "The alternative is to use the four oars and row. We have not passed the headland yet. The row might be six miles."

He smiled, "We need the exercise. I will take down the sail while you turn us around."

Even as I put the steering board over the wind took us another hundred or so paces south. Haaken woke the others. I smiled, "We are almost in touching distance of the drekar but we have to row. You three will have to take it in turns to steer. Just keep us as close to the shore as you can. If the rowing proves too much then we can always land and rest." They nodded, "Gruffyd, you take the first watch."

There were four oars and I sat next to Haaken. Einar and Baldr sat side by side. We began to row. We moved but it was so slowly as to be almost imperceptible. Once we got into the rhythm we moved faster. It was noon when the horsemen appeared. There were cliffs to the east of us and we could not have landed anyway but the horsemen on the cliff top ensured that we kept to the sea. It was when Baldr was steering that hope both appeared and disappeared in an instant. "Jarl! I recognise the headland. We are but a short distance from the drekar. I think I can see the masthead pennant."

Einar said, "Thank the Allfather!"

Then Baldr glanced to the west. He shouted, "It is the drekar which has followed us. She is coming over the horizon!"

I turned and saw that he was right. The drekar was to the north west of us and had full sail. She was making good time and we were labouring. The horsemen on the cliffs ensured that we could not land. We were close enough to almost shout to Olaf and the crew of the drekar.

"We must row as though we were going to war. Haaken, a chant and make it one which will make our backs burn. Gruffyd and Einar, if you wish to see your families again then you must endure such pain as to make you weep."

Gruffyd laughed, "Grandfather, we have endured the attention of the witch. This will not be pain. This will be the joy of life!"

He chose the song of Ylva and the witch. It was good for it celebrated victory over the Norns and that was what this felt like. Even if we fell in battle against the men of Om Walum then it would be in battle and we would die with our swords in our hands.

The Dragonheart sailed with warriors brave
To find the child he was meant to save
With Haaken and Ragnar's Spirit
They dared to delve with true warrior's grit
With Aðils Shape Shifter with scout skills honed
They found the island close by the rocky stones
The Jarl and Haaken will bravely roar
The Jarl and Haaken and the Ulfheonar
Beneath the earth the two they went
With the sword by Odin sent
In the dark the witch grew strong
Even though her deeds were wrong
A dragon's form she took to kill

Dragonheart faced her still
He drew the sword touched by the god
Made by Odin and staunched in blood
The Jarl and Haaken will bravely roar
The Jarl and Haaken and the Ulfheonar
With a mighty blow, he struck the beast
On Dragonheart's flesh he would not feast
The blade struck true and the witch she fled
Ylva lay as though she were dead
The witch's power could not match the blade
The Ulfheonar are not afraid
The Jarl and Haaken will bravely roar
The Jarl and Haaken and the Ulfheonar
And now the sword will strike once more
Using all the Allfather's power
Fear the wrath you Danish lost
You fight the wolf and pay the cost
The Jarl and Haaken will bravely roar
The Jarl and Haaken and the Ulfheonar

We began to move more quickly. As I chanted I could see the land moving quicker and the horsemen who were following us had to begin to canter to keep up with us.

Baldr stopped singing to shout, "I see her, '*Wolf*' is there!"

It was now a race between us, '*Odin's Breath*' and the horsemen.

"They have seen us! I see the sail of our drekar, '*Wolf*'. It is being lowered."

The horsemen on the headland had seen it also and they galloped north. They had a target they could fight. "How far away is the beach and our drekar?" It would be easier for us to board the drekar from the land. If Olaf and Knut had '*Wolf*' stationary then she could be rammed by the men of Om Walum. The men of Om Walum were just ten or twelve miles from home. They did not need a Viking drekar!

"'*Wolf*' is six hundred paces from us!"

I could now see the horsemen as they descended the path down the cliff. It was not an easy path and they had to pick their way down but there were more than fifty of them and I saw, behind them, men on foot. If we headed ashore then Knut might see us. He would have the wind and could pick us up before the horsemen arrived. If we turned east then we could use the wind.

"Baldr, head east. Land us. Haaken, get the sail raised. We will use the wind!" As soon as Baldr put the steering board over and the sail billowed Einar and Gruffyd could stop rowing. They were exhausted. "When we land, Baldr, get Einar and Gruffyd to the drekar. Haaken and I will guard your backs!" I glanced to the north and saw that Knut was bringing the drekar as close to us as he could get. To the west, I saw *'Odin's Breath'* as she raced in for the kill. Knut was already taking in sail to slow our drekar down. I donned my helmet and shield as Baldr took us through the surf to ground on the shingly sand. The first of the horsemen had negotiated the path and were now heading for us. Leaving Baldr to help Einar and Gruffyd from the fishing boat Haaken and I ran towards the horsemen. I found it hard to run for we had been at sea for some days and I had not used my legs. Gruffyd and Einar stumbled like drunks. I saw that Knut had brought *'Wolf'* into the shallows and men were pouring from the side. Olaf Leather Neck led them. His double-handed axe waved forward the twenty warriors he brought with him. We ran up the beach to join them. We had a chance!

Then Einar stumbled. Gruffyd and Baldr helped him to his feet but it allowed the first four horsemen to close with us. Without speaking Haaken and I stopped and locked shields. A horseman liked nothing better than the back of a fleeing warrior. We would deny them that pleasure. They came in a straight line. They held spears. Without straps they would have to strike down. We had helmets, shields and byrnies. We would buy time for Olaf to reach us. I had faced horses many times and these were not large horses. As the riders, eager for victory pulled back their arms, Haaken and I swung our swords from left to right in unison. The middle two horses were so close that Haaken's sword caught the muzzle of one of them. Two spears stuck our shields but they were weak strikes. The horse which had been hit veered to the left to be away from the blade and it brought down one of the riders.

Haaken lunged towards the rider on the left and his sword drove up into the man's chest. I stabbed over my shield and into the groin of a second. I felt a sharp pain in my right shoulder as the dying man managed to spear me. The two men who had fallen tried to rise to their feet. Their companions were less than forty paces from us. Haaken and I ran over and despatched the two stricken men. I saw that Baldr had manhandled Gruffyd and Einar into the shallows and they were being helped aboard the drekar. *'Odin's Breath'* was drawing ever close to *'Wolf'*. My son was safe!

Olaf Leather Neck was as brave a warrior as ever was but he had a wild and reckless streak in him. Even as the men of Om Walum drew closer to our men he threw himself into the heart of their horsemen. Haaken and I ran to aid him for the attackers had switched their attack to the men racing from the drekar. Olaf's axe hacked through horses' heads and legs. It was mayhem. I saw spears rise and fall but it did not stop Olaf. I reached him as a mailed horseman with a plumed helmet raised his sword to hack across Olaf's back. I rammed Ragnar's Spirit up under his arm and into his body. I threw him from the saddle and his dying hands pulled his horse to the ground. I barely staggered out of its way.

Haaken was a fierce warrior. He ducked beneath the spear which was raised and tore his sword across the throat of the warrior's horse. As the horse died the warrior was thrown from the saddle and landed at Haaken's feet. He took the head in one motion and, picking up the head, threw it towards the advancing men on foot.

Olaf's reckless charge had taken him beyond the horsemen and into the heart of the men on foot. He was surrounded and, for the first time in a long time, was not surrounded by Ulfheonar. Haaken and I had a wall of dead horses to surmount to reach him. As I used a dead horse to leap towards him I saw his axe take two heads in one strike. He was roaring and screaming! Then a spear was rammed into his thigh and he staggered. His axe split the spear in twain but a sword hacked into his leg.

I hurled myself towards those men attacking him. He was like a baited bull surrounded by dogs. Another spear skewered his right arm and his swings became weaker. He hurled his axe towards the advancing warriors. The men from my drekar were now closer, Haraldr led them as they fell upon the baying dogs around the dying Ulfheonar. Olaf drew his sword and with his right arm hanging uselessly by his side began to fight left-handed. Haaken killed the man to his left as I stabbed the one to his right. Olaf's sword took the arm of another but a single warrior lurched at Olaf with his spear. He tripped over the body of a dead warrior and I sliced into his back. It was too late. The spear entered Olaf's middle and although he tore it out I knew that it was a mortal wound.

"Haraldr, cover us while we take Olaf back then follow. We have left enough men in this land I have done with it!"

"Aye, jarl!"

Haaken and I sheathed our swords and slipped our shields around our backs. We put our arms under Olaf's. He was a dead weight and I feared he was dead already. His feet trailed in the sand as we dragged him back. He still held his sword in his left hand. Olaf was a warrior to the end; a Viking warrior.

When he spoke I almost jumped. We were approaching the sea, "I came, Jarl Dragonheart. I would be at your side as I have spent my life."

"And none was greater than you." He was dying and you did not lie to a dying man.

"When Rolf died I knew I had lived too long. I had no sons but Rolf was as a son to me. I will see him soon."

Haaken said, "Do not be in a hurry to leave us, Olaf. This will make a great saga!"

He laughed, as we paddled towards the drekar, "My guts lie on the beach. I am dying, Haaken, but I will hear your words when I am in the Otherworld. Now there are but four Ulfheonar."

It was a struggle to get through the water. I heard Haraldr behind. "They have stopped following us, Jarl. I think they leave us to the drekar!"

"As soon as we are aboard have Knut set sail. We will fight and retake *'Odin's Breath'*!"

Olaf became silent and I feared he was dead. We reached the side and I saw Einar, Baldr and Gruffyd leaning over to help to pull Olaf on to the deck. As we boarded I heard Knut shout, "Man the oars!"

We laid Olaf close to the main mast and Atticus hurried up. He looked at the wounds and the blood. He shook his head. I said, quietly, "I know. Tend to the others while we send a warrior to Valhalla."

Olaf opened his eyes. "Jarl, give me your hand. It will help me pass through the door. You have seen it. Soon so will I. Farewell, Dragonheart, it has been an honour…." His eyes glazed over and he was dead.

I closed his eyes and kissed his forehead. "Farewell, old friend. None was braver."

Haaken covered his body with a cloak and then pointed to the north. "Unless we can defeat this King of Om Walum then we will be joining him!"

Chapter 16

I took off my helmet and put it and my shield on the deck. As I stood and looked around the drekar there were fewer men at the oars than I expected. We had been fully crewed and rescued twenty men. I stood next to Knut as we headed for *'Odin's Breath'*. "Where are the rest of the crew?"

"Olaf and the others had to fight a battle to get here. There were men waiting for them on the road and they were ambushed. They slew many but Sweyn Alfsson and nineteen men died. Others were wounded."

"I want to retake Gruffyd's drekar. Their king is aboard. He will be weregeld for Olaf and Sweyn!" He nodded, "Aim for his prow. We will board that way."

I saw that Einar and Gruffyd had clothes now and helmets. They had taken weapons. "Haaken, come with me. You three follow." As we ran down the middle of the drekar I said, "We are going to retake *'Odin's Breath'*! When we strike follow us!"

My men cheered. We had lost warriors but they were in good heart. I turned to Gruffyd and Einar, "If you are not strong enough stay here."

Gruffyd shook his head, "Olaf's spirit is but a little way above our heads. He would be alive had I not tried to be Jarl Dragonheart. Most of my crew are dead. I owe it to them to retake my ship!" he turned to his son, "And you, Mordaf, will stay here! I have lost you once. I will not lose you a second time."

As we neared the prow I knew that although outnumbered we had an advantage. We had fought at sea and they had not. A rolling, pitching deck was not like fighting on the land. You needed a wider stance and you needed to be as one with the ship. *'Odin's Breath'* was our ship. The spirit of Bolli was within her. She would help us. We would show the men of Om Walum that you did not fight Vikings on their own ship!

Knut was a canny sailor. He would not hit the other drekar head on for both would be damaged. He would strike a glancing blow to their steerboard side. The wind would push their stern around. We would stop them and then we would board. We would use the wind, the sea and our ships to help us to win this battle. Two ship's boys waited with grappling hooks. I said, "Sven, Erik, throw the hooks, tie off the ropes and then get out of the way. You are too young for me to take bad news to your mothers!"

They grinned, "Aye, Jarl!" Like all boys, they thought themselves immortal.

Haaken and I pulled ourselves up next to the wolf prow. I patted the head. This was *wyrd*. Úlfarr had protected my family and died doing so now his carved face would retake our drekar.

King Fferferdyn realised too late what we intended. He thought we meant to evade him. I heard a shout and his oars tried to back water. He had too much way on him for the wind was billowing his sail. Ours was furled. Our ship's boys used their bows to send arrows into the men of Om Walum. With one last surge, our drekar struck the steerboard side of the prow. The ropes were thrown and Haaken and I leapt across the gap and landed on the gunwale. I drew Wolf's Blood as I threw myself into the handful of oarsmen who had remained upright. The collision had knocked the rest to the deck.

Between us, Haaken and I had four blades and we used them with skill. None of the men we faced wore mail and our swords hacked through shoulders and stomachs while our daggers ripped out throats. Their blows hit us but they were unbalanced and we wore mail. I had a wound from the beach but it was nothing for I had lost Olaf Leather Neck and there would never be a warrior like him again. Men had to pay. Gruffyd and Baldr appeared on my right. My son had an angry look in his eyes. I prayed that he would not go berserk. The five of us moved down the deck. I was aware of the noise of my men as Haraldr led the rest of our crew aboard. The thud of their feet made the deck shift. The men of Om Walum ran. The only place left to them was the steering board and their king. Few had shields and only the King and his four body guards wore mail.

I raised Ragnar's Spirit and shouted, "King Fferferdyn, today you die. I will slaughter every one of your men! Do not surrender for we wish to kill you. Do not deny us that pleasure!" I shouted it in Saxon. I knew he had understood, as had his men when they flourished their weapons and shouted back at us.

We moved steadily down the deck. We were like a steel wave. The wind had pushed them around so that the two ships were now parallel and our ship's boys began to rain arrows into the men at the steering board. Packed together like a shoal of herring the dead remained standing.

With no shields to protect us, this would be a test of skill with a sword and the will to live. As we approached I saw that some of the men we faced used a two-handed grip on their swords. When you had room to swing then that was a good stance. Here the only blow they could make was from above and we all wore good helmets with padded arming caps beneath. I had not donned cochineal but anger burned in my eyes. They had the fire of the wolf within them. I ran to the battle with a fierce determination to kill. As the sword came down I lifted my sword to block it and rammed Wolf's Blood under the ribs of the grey-bearded warrior. Blood oozed from his mouth as he fell dead at my feet. One of those in the second rank brought his sword down. The end hit my helmet and Bagsecg's well-made helmet held. A second sword came down towards my head and a third. I blocked both with my weapons and then pulled back my head to butt the nearest warrior in the face. As he reeled I brought my knee hard between his legs. His scream was like that of a vixen in the night.

Beside me, Haaken and the others were having success until Baldr called, "Einar is hurt!"

I shouted, "Gruffyd and Baldr, take him clear. Harald and the rest are mailed."

We had to watch our footing for we were fighting on top of the bodies of the men we had slain. Those of my men who were too far away to fight chanted, "Dragonheart, Dragonheart, Dragonheart," over and over. I saw the fear it created in the men before us. Some chose to hurl themselves into the sea and risk a swim to shore. As most did not have mail they might make it, that was, if they could swim. That and our savagely sharp swords began to clear the ranks of the men before us. Haraldr and my other mailed men had joined me now and with a wall of mail we began to slaughter the men of Om Walum.

My eyes were fixed upon King Fferferdyn. He had four oathsworn around him. The five of them had scale armour, shields and a plumed open-faced helmet. The King wore a crown around his helmet. The men before him thinned. I saw the crew who had sailed the ship abandon their posts and leap into the sea. And suddenly we were facing the five men. Around me, there were small battles going on as my men butchered the last of the men who had chased us across the ocean. The four oathsworn stepped forward. I had Haraldr, and Haaken as well as the brothers Siggi and Leif Arneson. The bodies around us meant that only four of us could actually fight. I chose the biggest bodyguard. His sword came down and I blocked it with my sword. He had a shield and my dagger could not pass it. He raised it before his face and so I stabbed blindly down with

Wolf's Blood. I found flesh and he screamed. I had found his knee. As he did so I punched at the side of his head with the pommel of Ragnar's Spirit. He reeled backwards. I swung my sealskin boot and kicked him hard upon the unwounded knee. I must have broken something for he dropped to the deck. I lunged with my dagger. It entered his eye and his brain. He lay dead at my feet and I stepped over him

"King Fferferdyn, you and your cruel Lord Arfael have cost me many men. When you are dead, know that I will return and destroy your monastery at Karrek Loos yn Koos. I will take your people as slaves and your land will be barren and all this because of you, King Fferferdyn. You conspired with a witch."

"I am not afraid of you! I am a Christian King and I will go to heaven!"

"Even though you have used a witch? I think not!"

He lunged at me and it was a clumsy strike. I fended it off with my dagger and hacked into his leg for he wore no mail there. He squealed. His oathsworn were now dead and he was the last man of Om Walum left alive on the drekar. He tried to hit me with his shield. The rolling drekar meant he could not keep his feet and he ended up sprawled on the deck. I stabbed him in his ankle and he began to bleed. "This will not be a quick death, King Fferferdyn. You will die piece by piece. You will beg me to kill you before it is over."

"I beg you now!"

"You have not suffered enough."

He pushed himself to his feet. I feinted with my sword and when he countered with his shield I flicked the crown from his helmet with my dagger. It rattled to the ground and he went to retrieve it. He had scale armour but scale armour had one weakness; it was held together with fine metal wire or leather. The King had wire. I brought the side of my sword around and hacked his left shoulder. Scales fell and blood flowed. He dropped the shield and held his sword in two hands.

Haaken shouted, "Kill him, Dragonheart! I am bored!"

I watched the King's eyes. He was preparing to strike. He lunged at me. It was an awkward and ugly stroke. I used Ragnar's Spirit and Wolf's Blood to flick his sword up and then used my dagger and sword to take his head. It rolled across the deck and then his body fell. As my men cheered I sheathed my weapons and picked up the crown. I saw that Knut had sent his ship's boys up the mast to take in *'**Odin's Breath's**'* sail.

"It is over. Take what we need from their dead and feed them to the fishes." I looked ashore and saw that there were still men on the beach. "We will go ashore and show them the King's head. If they do not flee then we will have another battle."

Atticus said, for he had come on board to tend our wounded, "There has been enough blood."

"There will be enough blood when Olaf and Rolf walk amongst us again. Until then hold your peace, Greek. I am weary!"

He nodded, "You have done too much. You need to rest. You do not mean what you say. When do we sail home?"

"On the morrow. We have two drekar to crew and I have questions which need answers."

When they saw the head of their king the men of Om Walum left. They ran. They would need to choose another. I cared not. I would return to this land and make it a wasteland.

After we had collected the weapons and mail we washed. There were no enemies to harm us and we ate on the beach. We had horses to cook. As the food cooked I asked Siggi, "What happened to the other drekar?"

"She tried to run. We had left men on board both of them. *'Odin's Breath'* was captured but *'Sea Eagle'* managed to make the mouth of the fjord. She ripped her keel out on the rocks and the crew were slaughtered when they tried to scramble ashore."

I pointed to the head of the King. It was on a spear, "And did he visit?"

"He did. He asked what a Viking heart looked like. They killed one of the ship's boys, Lars Longfellow, and opened him up. The King laughed and said he had seen larger pig's hearts."

I had not made his death hard enough.

Gruffyd insisted upon sailing home in his own drekar but Einar had been badly wounded and needed Atticus' attention. Haaken came to me, "I have no sons of my own. Let me be Gruffyd's father for the voyage home. I swear he will not die on my watch."

"Haaken, you are the brother I never had. My son and grandson are as safe as if Odin himself steered the drekar."

We left the bay which was a frenzy of sharks and other fish as they tore the corpses of the men of Om Walum. Our own dead had been burned on the beach. The tide would come in and take their ashes. They would be spread to the seas. When we sailed we would be amongst friends. All had died with swords in their hands. Valhalla had more brave warriors to tell tales of the Clan of the Wolf. With barely thirty-five men able to row on each drekar we had to sail home. We used the winds and we edged our way north until we reached Ynys Môn where the wind switched to come from the south and west. That made the journey swifter and we sped home and passed Man safely.

As usual we were seen well before we landed. We had ***'Odin's Breath'*** and all knew that was my son's ship. By the time we approached the anchorage the wharf and quay were heaving with those eager to see who returned and who they would mourn. People had flocked to see if their husbands, sons and fathers had survived. There would be mothers and wives, sons and daughters who would discover that a loved one had not returned. Olaf Leather Neck would be mourned but that would be by the Ulfheonar, by Ragnar, by Kara and her family. Olaf did not make friends easily. That was the loss of those who found him frightening. He was, to me, the most loyal and resolute of men. He ranked alongside Prince Butar, Old Olaf and Cnut. I had not yet begun to remember him but I had time now. We would not be raiding for some time. All of his coin, and he had much, would go to the family of Rolf Horse Killer. It would not make up for a lost husband and father but Rolf's son would want for nothing.

Atticus appeared at my side as the ones thought dead were welcomed home. I did not mind being ignored. I had done that which I had promised. I was not foresworn. "Jarl Dragonheart, this is your victory yet you do not celebrate your success nor are you applauded."

I shrugged, "I am Dragonheart and the guardian of my people. I need neither applause nor cheers. When I am gone they may remember me fondly but it does not matter. I have sown the seeds of the future. My people will endure."

He shook his head, "So many deaths. And I saw a side of you I did not like."

"There is much about me I do not like but you cannot change who or what you are. I have learned that over the many years I have survived in this harsh world. I have buried too many people that I loved and there are too many that I hate who still live but on the balance of things I am content. Gruffyd will not challenge Sámr and my land will have a good ruler."

"Then you are satisfied and can rest easy in your hall?"

I laughed, "I think not. Now is not the time but I must visit my vengeance on Om Walum. I will make it a wasteland and they will regret ever having challenged the Dragonheart. I have to speak with Ragnar. He must accept my decision about the future but first I need to speak with Kara, Aiden and Ylva. Much of what happened is shrouded in mystery. Before we can move forward I need to know what it all meant."

Ragnar knew that something was amiss. I smiled, "Let me go home and speak with my daughter first. We have security, at least for a while. The Danes will come but not yet. I will speak with you at Samhain. Come to my home. We have plans to make for the future."

He nodded, "I am not Dragonheart nor am I Wolf Killer. I am sorry if that disappoints you, grandfather."

I smiled and embraced him, "You cannot disappoint me for you are of my blood. You cannot change blood. All is well. I am coming to the end of my time here but know that my spirit will always be in the Land of the Wolf."

"Then know that I shall be there."

It was a tiny knot of warriors who headed north along the Water. We were silent for all had lost someone. Haraldr had lost Sweyn. They had endured the mines and the war in Dyflin and now he was gone. Haaken and I had lost Olaf and he cast a long shadow. We had to tell Rollo Thin Skin and Aðils Shape Shifter that we were now but four Ulfheonar. Rolf's wife would also grieve. The coin which Olaf had left would not compensate for the giant of a man who had been like a grandfather to her children. There was neither joy nor glory in our homecoming.

Kara, Aiden and Ylva awaited our arrival. Their faces told me that they knew our news. That did not surprise me. Olaf and Sweyn were now in the Otherworld. They would have spoken. When we entered our gates I said, "Baldr, go and tell Sámr our news. Now is not the time for us to speak. That will come."

"Aye, Jarl."

I clasped his arm, "You are one of the clan now. You are of our people. Men will shed blood for you."

He smiled, "Jarl, this feels like my own clan. We were horsemen but you are warriors of the sea and there is a similarity. You fight as my father did. You do not forgive and you do not forget. I was lost and adrift. Now I have a purpose. I am your man and when you are in the Otherworld I will be Sámr's."

There was silence as they led me into their hall. "We failed you, father. We were deceived. We do not know as much as we thought we did. It was after you sailed that the spirits of our dead men came to us. It was then we saw how the Norns and their acolytes, the witches of Syllingar, had deceived us."

I nodded, "Men died. Olaf is gone."

Ylva came and knelt next to me. She held my hand, "And if we could change that we would but the web which was spun was too complicated for us to entangle. The witch ensnared the King of Om Walum and his men. We did not see that. We failed to understand why Gruffyd left. Now we know. Had we acted then we might have stopped him or told you, at least, we did not."

"So in the last days, it comes down to a sword and the Dragonheart. The spirits are there to guide."

Kara said, "Father, it has ever been thus. This land would not be what it is without the Dragonheart."

"But I am old. I should be dead. How can I keep on?"

Aiden shrugged, "I fear that I shall die before you, Jarl Dragonheart. All I know is that you will outlive me." I looked at him and saw that he was thin and drawn. Death was in his face and his eyes. Aiden was dying.

Kara said, "It is true, father. We have dreamed his death. You have begun to weave your own threads and they are not the ones which the Norns like. That is good for the gods and the spirits like them. Sámr will be your heir but he is not ready yet. Your legacy is prepared but not yet written. We will help you when we can."

Ylva said, "After the wedding and your announcement I shall disappear. You, grandfather, will know where I am. I will live in Myrddyn's cave. There I will harness his power. I cannot save my father but I can save the Land of the Wolf. That will be my fortress."

I squeezed her hand, "Then I am sad. The world is changing."

"And yet, father, for the Land of the Wolf it will stay the same. That is what you leave your people." She kissed my cheek. "You have no applause and you have no cheers for you do not need them. The Dragonheart is the heart of the land. It needs no praise for it is."

I nodded. I was satisfied.

Epilogue

Baldr and Nanna were married in my hall. The warriors of my land built them a hall close to Sámr's. As Æthelflæd was with child that was a practical solution. It was a cold day when they were married. Leaves had fallen and the air had a bite to it. No one minded. When the ceremony was over I stood and looked at those gathered around me. All of my family were there. Aiden looked a little thin but he smiled and Kara and Ylva flanked him.

"Today I announce my heir. When I am gone it will not be my son, Gruffyd, nor my grandson Ragnar who leads the clan. It will be Sámr Ship Killer. Know that this is my decision but all of my family approve."

Each of them stood and banged the table with their knives and chanted, "Sámr Ship Killer, Sámr Ship Killer, Sámr Ship Killer."

I will not leave you yet but when I do my spirit will watch over you and Sámr will lead you. The clan will be safe."

Haaken One Eye stood. He began to sing.

The wind that blows across the sea
Carries the song of the dead to me
Sea birds cry and soar on high
When skies are grey and storms grow near
When women at home shed a lonely tear
When I raise a horn of ale
Then I will sing the Ulfheonar tale
When darkness comes that is your world
A wolf cloak, axe and a banner unfurled
When darkness comes you howl and kill
No man is safe from Ulfheonar skill
We now are few where once were more
Our dead wait now beyond Valhalla's door
Wait for us brothers for we will come
Odin's table will be our welcome
We fight the fight for the land of the Wolf,
Farewell my friend, farewell Rolf
When darkness comes that is your world

A wolf cloak, axe and a banner unfurled
When darkness come you howl and kill
No man is safe from Ulfheonar skill
The wind which blows with the call of the lost
Sweeps the land which bears the cost
The spirits watch from mountains high
It was for the clan they had to die
Do not be sad that they are gone
Remember their light, the way they shone
In every man in this wolf land
Is a warrior with the heart wolf true
And a sword which shines with a stone of blue
A wolf cloak, axe and a banner unfurled
When darkness comes you howl and kill
No man is safe from Ulfheonar skill
The knot and the web twist and turn
They cannot be cut and will not burn
They tie the past and the glorious dead
Old faces flash and speak inside my head
A wolf cloak, axe and a banner unfurled
When darkness comes you howl and kill
No man is safe from Ulfheonar skill

Silence fell when he had finished and I felt tears streaming down my cheeks. There were four Ulfheonar left and soon we would be gone. All that would be left was a sword, a cloak and a song sung by the old. My world was changing and soon all of us would just be a memory.

The End

Norse Calendar

Gormánuður October 14th - November 13th
Ýlir November 14th - December 13th
Mörsugur December 14th - January 12th
Þorri - January 13th - February 11th
Gói - February 12th - March 13th
Einmánuður - March 14th - April 13th
Harpa April 14th - May 13th
Skerpla - May 14th - June 12th
Sólmánuður - June 13th - July 12th
Heyannir - July 13th - August 14th
Tvímánuður - August 15th - September 14th
Haustmánuður September 15th-October 13th

Glossary

Afen- River Avon
Afon Hafron- River Severn in Welsh
Àird Rosain – Ardrossan (On the Clyde Estuary)
Al-buhera -Albufeira, Portugal
Aledhorn- Althorn (Essex)
An Lysardh - Lizard Peninsula Cornwall
Balears- Balearic Islands
Balley Chashtal -Castleton (Isle of Man)
Bardas - Rebel Byzantine General
Beamfleote -Benfleet Essex
Bebbanburgh- Bamburgh Castle, Northumbria also known as Din Guardi in the ancient tongue
Beck- a stream
Beinn na bhFadhla- Benbecula in the Outer Hebrides
Beodericsworth- Bury St Edmunds
Belesduna – Basildon, Essex
Belisima -River Ribble
Blót – a blood sacrifice made by a jarl
Blue Sea- The Mediterranean
Bogeuurde – Forest of Bowland
Bondi- Viking farmers who fight
Bourde- Bordeaux
Bjarnarøy –Great Bernera (Bear Island)
Breguntford – Brentford
Brixges Stane – Brixton (South London)
Bruggas- Bruges
Brycgstow- Bristol
Burntwood- Brentwood Essex
Byrnie- a mail or leather shirt reaching down to the knees
Caerlleon- Welsh for Chester
Caer Ufra -South Shields
Caestir - Chester (old English)
Cantwareburh -Canterbury
Càrdainn Ros -Cardross (Argyll)
Carrum -Carhampton (Somerset)
Cas-gwent -Chepstow Monmouthshire
Casnewydd –Newport, Wales
Cephas- Greek for Simon Peter (St. Peter)

Chatacium -Catanzaro, Calabria
Chape- the tip of a scabbard
Charlemagne- Holy Roman Emperor at the end of the 8th and beginning of the 9th centuries
Celchyth - Chelsea
Cerro da Vila – Vilamoura, Portugal
Cherestanc- Garstang (Lancashire)
Cil-y-coed -Caldicot Monmouthshire
Colneceastre- Colchester
Corn Walum or Om Walum- Cornwall
Cymri- Welsh
Cymru- Wales
Cyninges-tūn – Coniston. It means the estate of the king (Cumbria)
Dùn Èideann –Edinburgh (Gaelic)
Din Guardi- Bamburgh castle
Drekar- a Dragon ship (a Viking warship) pl. drekar
Duboglassio –Douglas, Isle of Man
Dun Holme- Durham
Dún Lethglaise - Downpatrick (Northern Ireland)
Durdle- Durdle dor- the Jurassic coast in Dorset
Dwfr- Dover
Dyrøy –Jura (Inner Hebrides)
Dyflin- Old Norse for Dublin
Ēa Lōn - River Lune
Earhyth -Bexley (Kent)
Ein-mánuðr - middle of March to the middle of April
Eoforwic- Saxon for York
Falgrave- Scarborough (North Yorkshire)
Faro Bregancio- Corunna (Spain)
Ferneberga -Farnborough (Hampshire)
Fey- having second sight
Firkin- a barrel containing eight gallons (usually beer)
Fornibiyum-Formby (near Liverpool)
Fret-a sea mist
Frankia- France and part of Germany
Fyrd-the Saxon levy
Ganda- Ghent (Belgium)
Garth- Dragon Heart
Gaill- Irish for foreigners

Galdramenn- wizard
Gesith- A Saxon nobleman. After 850 AD, they were known as thegns
Gippeswic -Ipswich
Glaesum –amber
Glannoventa -Ravenglass
Gleawecastre- Gloucester
Gói- the end of February to the middle of March
Gormánuður- October to November (Slaughter month- the beginning of winter)
Grendel- the monster slain by Beowulf
Grenewic- Greenwich
Gulle - Goole (Humberside)
Hagustaldes ham -Hexham
Hamwic -Southampton
Hæstingaceaster- Hastings
Haustmánuður - September 16th- October 16th (cutting of the corn)
Haughs- small hills in Norse (As in Tarn Hows)
Hearthweru- The bodyguard or oathsworn of a jarl
Heels- when a ship leans to one side under the pressure of the wind
Hel - Queen of Niflheim, the Norse underworld.
Here Wic- Harwich
Hersey- Isle of Arran
Hersir- a Viking landowner and minor noble. It ranks below a jarl
Hetaereiarch – Byzantine general
Hí- Iona (Gaelic)
Hjáp - Shap- Cumbria (Norse for stone circle)
Hoggs or Hogging- when the pressure of the wind causes the stern or the bow to droop
Hrams-a – Ramsey, Isle of Man
Hrofecester -Rochester (Kent)
Hundred- Saxon military organisation. (One hundred men from an area-led by a thegn or gesith)
Hwitebi - Norse for Whitby, North Yorkshire
Hywel ap Rhodri Molwynog- King of Gwynedd 814-825
Icaunis- British river god
Issicauna- Gaulish for the lower Seine
Itouna- River Eden Cumbria
Jarl- Norse earl or lord

Joro-goddess of the earth
kjerringa - Old Woman- the solid block in which the mast rested
Karrek Loos yn Koos -St Michael's Mount (Cornwall)
Kerkyra- Corfu
Knarr- a merchant ship or a coastal vessel
Kriti- Crete
Kyrtle-woven top
Lambehitha- Lambeth
Leathes Water- Thirlmere
Legacaestir- Anglo-Saxon for Chester
Ljoðhús- Lewis
Lochlannach – Irish for Northerners (Vikings)
Lothuwistoft- Lowestoft
Lough- Irish lake
Louis the Pious- King of the Franks and son of Charlemagne
Lundenburh/Lundenburgh- the walled burh built around the old Roman fort
Lundenwic - London
Maeldun- Maldon Essex
Maeresea- River Mersey
Mammceaster- Manchester
Manau/Mann – The Isle of Man(n) (Saxon)
Marcia Hispanic- Spanish Marches (the land around Barcelona)
Mast fish- two large racks on a ship designed to store the mast when not required
Melita- Malta
Midden- a place where they dumped human waste
Miklagård - Constantinople
Mörsugur - December 13th -January 12th (the fat sucker month!)
Musselmen- the followers of Islam
Njoror- God of the sea
Nithing- A man without honour (Saxon)
Odin - The "All Father" God of war, also associated with wisdom, poetry, and magic (The Ruler of the gods).
Olissipo- Lisbon
Orkneyjar-Orkney
Pecheham- Peckham
Peny-cwm-cuic -Falmouth
Pennryhd – Penrith Cumbria

Pennsans – Penzance (Cornwall)
Poor john- a dried and shrivelled fish (disparaging slang for a male member- Shakespeare)
Þorri -January 13th -February 12th - midwinter
Portesmūða -Portsmouth
Porth Ia- St. Ives
Pillars of Hercules- Straits of Gibraltar
Prittleuuella- Prittwell in Essex. Southend was originally known as the South End of Prittwell
Pyrlweall -Thirwell, Cumbria
Qādis- Cadiz
Ran- Goddess of the sea
Roof rock- slate
Rinaz –The Rhine
Sabrina- Latin and Celtic for the River Severn. Also, the name of a female Celtic deity
Saami- the people who live in what is now Northern Norway/Sweden
Sabatton- Saturday in the Byzantine calendar
Samhain- a Celtic festival of the dead between 31st October and 1st November (Halloween)
St. Cybi- Holyhead
Scree- loose rocks in a glacial valley
Seax – short sword
Sennight- seven nights- a week
Sheerstrake- the uppermost strake in the hull
Sheet- a rope fastened to the lower corner of a sail
Shroud- a rope from the masthead to the hull amidships
Skeggox – an axe with a shorter beard on one side of the blade
Skreið- stock fish (any fish which is preserved)
Skutatos- Byzantine soldier armed with an oval shield, a spear, a sword and a short mail shirt
Seouenaca -Sevenoaks (Kent)
South Folk- Suffolk
Stad- Norse settlement
Stays- ropes running from the mast-head to the bow
Strake- the wood on the side of a drekar
Streanæshalc- Saxon for Whitby, North Yorkshire
Stybbanhype – Stepney (London)

Suthriganaworc - Southwark (London)
Syllingar Insula, Syllingar- Scilly Isles
Tarn- small lake (Norse)
Tella- River Béthune which empties near Dieppe
Temese- River Thames
Theme- Provincial Army Corps
The Norns- The three sisters who weave webs of intrigue for men
Thing-Norse for a parliament or a debate (Tynwald)
Thor's day- Thursday
Threttanessa- a drekar with 13 oars on each side.
Thuni- Tunis
Tinea- Tyne
Tilaburg – Tilbury
Tintaieol- Tintagel (Cornwall)
Thrall- slave
Trenail- a round wooden peg used to secure strakes
Tynwald- the Parliament on the Isle of Man
Tvímánuður -Hay time-August 15th -September 15th
Úlfarrberg- Helvellyn
Úlfarrland- Cumbria
Úlfarr- Wolf Warrior
Úlfarrston- Ulverston
Ullr-Norse God of Hunting
Ulfheonar-an elite Norse warrior who wore a wolf skin over his armour
Vectis- The Isle of Wight
Veisafjǫrðr – Wexford (Ireland)
Volva- a witch or healing woman in Norse culture
Waeclinga Straet- Watling Street (A5)
Walhaz -Norse for the Welsh (foreigners)
Windlesore-Windsor
Waite- a Viking word for farm
Werham -Wareham (Dorset)
Western Sea- the Atlantic
Wintan-ceastre -Winchester
Withy- the mechanism connecting the steering board to the ship
Wihtwara- Isle of White
Woden's day- Wednesday
Wulfhere-Old English for Wolf Army

Wyddfa-Snowdon
Wykinglo- Wicklow (Ireland)
Wyrd- Fate
Wyrme- Norse for Dragon
Yard- a timber from which the sail is suspended
Ynys Enlli- Bardsey Island
Ynys Môn-Anglesey

Maps and drawings

Stad on the Eden - a typical Viking settlement

A wedge formation (each circle represents a warrior)

```
     0
    0 0
   0 0 0
  0 0 0 0
 0 0 0 0 0
0 0 0 0 0 0
```

The boar's snout formation

A boar's snout had two wedges and up to five ranks of men behind.

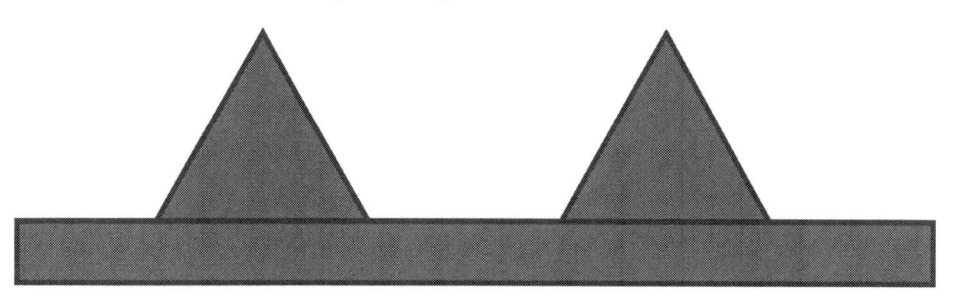

Historical note

My regular readers will notice that this section is much shorter than in previous novels. Some of my readers do not like the lengthy historical note section. You can find it on my website. What I will say is that like them or hate them the Vikings were a unique race. Their descendants were the Normans but they were not the same. The true Vikings were pagans. They sailed further than any man. Columbus made the West Indies. The Vikings landed in New England and Canada! They were an uncompromising people and I hope that I have done them justice.

Some have questioned Jar Dragonheart's longevity. There were examples of Vikings who lived as long. Harald Hadrada was one. They were hard men and their lives were violent. It was war which killed them and not the way they lived when at home.

I used the following books for research:

- Vikings- Life and Legends -British Museum
- Saxon, Norman and Viking by Terence Wise (Osprey)
- The Vikings (Osprey) -Ian Heath
- Byzantine Armies 668-1118 (Osprey)-Ian Heath
- Romano-Byzantine Armies 4th-9th Century (Osprey) -David Nicholle
- The Walls of Constantinople AD 324-1453 (Osprey) - Stephen Turnbull
- Viking Longship (Osprey) - Keith Durham
- The Vikings in England Anglo-Danish Project
- Anglo Saxon Thegn AD 449-1066- Mark Harrison (Osprey)
- Viking Hersir- 793-1066 AD - Mark Harrison (Osprey)
- Hadrian's Wall- David Breeze (English Heritage)
- National Geographic- March 2017
- The Tower of London – Lapper and Parnell (Osprey)

Griff Hosker July 2018

Other books by Griff Hosker

If you enjoyed reading this book, then why not read another one by the author?

Ancient History

The Sword of Cartimandua Series
(Germania and Britannia 50 A.D. – 128 A.D.)
Ulpius Felix- Roman Warrior (prequel)
The Sword of Cartimandua
The Horse Warriors
Invasion Caledonia
Roman Retreat
Revolt of the Red Witch
Druid's Gold
Trajan's Hunters
The Last Frontier
Hero of Rome
Roman Hawk
Roman Treachery
Roman Wall
Roman Courage

The Wolf Warrior series
(Britain in the late 6th Century)
Saxon Dawn
Saxon Revenge
Saxon England
Saxon Blood
Saxon Slayer
Saxon Slaughter
Saxon Bane
Saxon Fall: Rise of the Warlord
Saxon Throne
Saxon Sword

Medieval History

The Dragon Heart Series
Viking Slave
Viking Warrior
Viking Jarl
Viking Kingdom
Viking Wolf
Viking War
Viking Sword
Viking Wrath
Viking Raid
Viking Legend
Viking Vengeance
Viking Dragon
Viking Treasure
Viking Enemy
Viking Witch
Viking Blood
Viking Weregeld
Viking Storm
Viking Warband
Viking Shadow
Viking Legacy
Viking Clan
Viking Bravery

The Norman Genesis Series
Hrolf the Viking
Horseman
The Battle for a Home
Revenge of the Franks
The Land of the Northmen
Ragnvald Hrolfsson
Brothers in Blood
Lord of Rouen
Drekar in the Seine
Duke of Normandy
The Duke and the King

Danelaw
(England and Denmark in the 11th Century)
Dragon Sword
Oathsword
Bloodsword
Danish Sword

New World Series
Blood on the Blade
Across the Seas
The Savage Wilderness
The Bear and the Wolf
Erik The Navigator
Erik's Clan

The Vengeance Trail

The Reconquista Chronicles
Castilian Knight
El Campeador
The Lord of Valencia

The Aelfraed Series
(Britain and Byzantium 1050 A.D. - 1085 A.D.)
Housecarl
Outlaw
Varangian

**The Anarchy Series England
1120-1180**
English Knight
Knight of the Empress
Northern Knight
Baron of the North
Earl
King Henry's Champion
The King is Dead
Warlord of the North

Enemy at the Gate
The Fallen Crown
Warlord's War
Kingmaker
Henry II
Crusader
The Welsh Marches
Irish War
Poisonous Plots
The Princes' Revolt
Earl Marshal
The Perfect Knight

Border Knight
1182-1300
Sword for Hire
Return of the Knight
Baron's War
Magna Carta
Welsh Wars
Henry III
The Bloody Border
Baron's Crusade
Sentinel of the North
War in the West
Debt of Honour
The Blood of the Warlord
The Fettered King

Sir John Hawkwood Series
France and Italy 1339- 1387
Crécy: The Age of the Archer
Man At Arms
The White Company
Leader of Men
Tuscan Warlord

Lord Edward's Archer
Lord Edward's Archer

King in Waiting
An Archer's Crusade
Targets of Treachery
The Great Cause
Wallace's War

**Struggle for a Crown
1360- 1485**
Blood on the Crown
To Murder a King
The Throne
King Henry IV
The Road to Agincourt
St Crispin's Day
The Battle for France
The Last Knight
Queen's Knight

Tales from the Sword I
(Short stories from the Medieval period)

**Tudor Warrior series
England and Scotland in the late 14th and early 15th century**
Tudor Warrior
Tudor Spy

**Conquistador
England and America in the 16th Century**
Conquistador
The English Adventurer

Modern History

The Napoleonic Horseman Series
Chasseur à Cheval
Napoleon's Guard
British Light Dragoon
Soldier Spy
1808: The Road to Coruña

Talavera
The Lines of Torres Vedras
Bloody Badajoz
The Road to France
Waterloo

The Lucky Jack American Civil War series
Rebel Raiders
Confederate Rangers
The Road to Gettysburg

Soldier of the Queen series
Soldier of the Queen
Redcoat's Rifle

The British Ace Series
1914
1915 Fokker Scourge
1916 Angels over the Somme
1917 Eagles Fall
1918 We will remember them
From Arctic Snow to Desert Sand
Wings over Persia

Combined Operations series
1940-1945
Commando
Raider
Behind Enemy Lines
Dieppe
Toehold in Europe
Sword Beach
Breakout
The Battle for Antwerp
King Tiger
Beyond the Rhine
Korea
Korean Winter

Tales from the Sword II
(Short stories from the Modern period)

Other Books
Great Granny's Ghost (Aimed at 9-14-year-old young people)

For more information on all of the books then please visit the author's website at www.griffhosker.com where there is a link to contact him or visit his Facebook page: GriffHosker at Sword Books

Printed in Great Britain
by Amazon